SLEEPERS
AWAKE

KENNETH
PATCHEN

SLEEPERS
AWAKE

New Direction Books are published for James Laughlin
by New Direction Publishing Corporation
80 Eighth Avenue, New York, NY 10011

ISBN: 978-0-8112-0147-6

SECOND PRINTING

FOR MIRIAM

BY KENNETH PATCHEN

An Astonished Eye Looks Out Of The Air
A Surprise For The Bagpipe-Player
Because It Is
Before The Brave
But Even So
Cloth Of The Tempest
Doubleheader
Fables & Other Little Tales
First Will & Testament
Glory Never Guesses
Hurrah For Anything
Memoirs Of A Shy Pornographer
Orchards, Thrones & Caravans
Panels For The Walls Of Heaven
Pictures Of Life And Of Death
Poemscapes
Poems Of Humor & Protest
Red Wine & Yellow Hair
See You In The Morning
Selected Poems
Sleepers Awake
The Collected Poems of Kenneth Patchen
The Dark Kingdom
The Famous Boating Party
The Journal Of Albion Moonlight
The Love Poems of Kenneth Patchen
The Teeth Of The Lion
They Keep Riding Down All The Time
To Say If You Love Someone
When We Were Here Together

SLEEPERS AWAKE ON THE PRECIPICE

AS I came down past the cages I couldn't help thinking such a damn stench, and in that rain and all—you'd wonder what the devil they meant by it. So the field having a woman putting seeds in the ground, I mosied over there.

Twenty minutes later I asked her what she had the Bar-S in a Circle brand on her fundament for. Keep my big mouth shut—she

I got out my writing things and started to do my home-work. You maybe an enemy agent? mustache said, wiping one off on the pillowcase. I pushed my teeth out and made a noise like buying scrap iron. The girl for some reason put her hand on my shoulder, and I for some reason put mine on her twataumaycallit—forehead, that is.

I'm frightened, she said.

Five chairs. Three beds. A large table. Writing desk. Flowered carpet. Bible on the radiator—signed to L. M. Switlend, Xmas, 1924 . . . from "your Nannie." A superb toothpaste ad in six bright colors over the bathtub. Three quarters of a roll of pink tissue on the wicker hamper. Town of 8000 souls. Not much doing in any direction, you might suppose.

Why?

I don't know.

You don't know why you're frightened?

Yes. That's it.

Well, I'll tell you.

After I told her I looked over at the uncles.

Jesus H. Christ! What are they up to now?

That's a game they have, she said.

A game!

Yes. They call it Let's Change Heads.

I gathered up my junk and said I'll be seein' you around, kid. I've things to do, and what I need right now is a nice quiet place to do them in.

I'll go with you.

While she was putting her coat on I could see that uncle no. 1 was finding a veritable treasure trove in his new durante.

'Bye, fellahs.

They sprang out of bed and made a bit of a race of it, but I got us out first and locked the door. Then I heard them slipping the bolt home. Figure that one!

Oh! she said, as we stepped into the elevator.

And I didn't blame her. What that degenerate little Indian hadn't thought of . . .Ugh!

The rain had stopped and as we walked along she told me her mother had been the first woman ever to be elected to the Senate north of the Rockies. I said I had a friend once like that and she slipped her hand in my pocket and said why do you carry a gun? Pack a rod, you mean? All right, pack a rod, then. How'd your mother vote on the Old Age Pension? Why the rod? All right, sister, just between the two of us I don't much care. You don't much care what? How she voted.

We got to a barn and there was a farmer moving around inside with a lantern. After watching for a minute, the girl started to cry and I led her on. Why'd he have to do that? I guess it was sick, I said.

Rain again. I dug a hole in a haystack and we crawled in and curled up against the night.

Next morning I managed to get out without waking her. She had 87 dollars and some change in her bag.

I bought a ticket on the river boat and rode all that day and part of the next night. As a matter of fact, it was almost four a.m. when I got there. About the same crowd at the bar—only one new, a kid sixteen or so sitting by himself facing the door. He had a yellow puppy on his lap and was busy feeding it chocolate cookies —but not too busy to miss a word the blonde said as she came sailing out of the phone booth to greet me.

I said take it easy dish you're mussing my best suit and who's the pup's pal in the corner?

We had a beer and she told me about it.

Hanging around, huh?

Yes. Tell me—

No apparent business, huh?

None at all that we—

Get him out of here.

Ah, come on now. He's not—

I got down off the stool and walked over to his table and said all right buddy it's long past your bedtime.

He put the little dog up on the table and reached under his coat and took out a snub-nosed .32.

Roscoe's not a bit sleepy, he said.

You're a nice looking lad, I told him, and I hate to do this.

Another time I remember the same sort of thing, only this other fellow had a knife. We were all sitting around in our tents just waiting—God knows for what. I'd spent the whole damn day counting bed sheets. That night a few of us got to talking—My life's been pretty punk so far, one of them said.

How come?

While he was telling us how come, we all noticed that a sort of light was coming through the walls of the tent. We rushed out and the whole sky was full of this strange light. And there were people moving around in the light.

One of the people in the light reached down and touched my hand. I felt—I don't know—I walked up to where the light was.

There was a throne.

On the throne sat a beautiful man.

In back of the throne there were thousands of beings—I remember I kept saying the eraser won't work—over and over—THEN!

And I didn't feel ashamed anymore.

That will give you an idea. The main thing is to get it straight. If there is a flow, it must be coming from somewhere. And it must be headed somewhere.

Like red flowers.

In the woods, a fellow told me, he came upon a lion in a block of ice. And as he looked at the lion its eyes opened and seemed to be pleading with him. So he split the block open with his fists.

And when he'd done this—the lion fell to work and killed him. I saw the reddened heap of cloth and bones myself.

A little ATTENTION, please!

I didn't take that 87 bucks—and I never packed a heater in my life. (What would mother say!) I was raised by an old fellow who wrote treatises for medical journals. No, not a doc.—a hack. Red woollen shirts and drawers the year round. Lived out of cans. Bologna and baked beans sort of thing.

On the Uses of Delirium Tremens—

Hemorrhoids: And What We May Conclude From Them—

The Probable Effects of Aphonia On Our National Life—

My old foster would work three months on one of these articles, getting anywhere from ten to seventy-five bucks—and, what was even more important, all the symptoms of the disease he was working on. Oh, he put everything he had into it all right. Really never a dull moment—the time, for instance, he was boning up on venereal diseases . . . and that neat young schoolmarm raised a howl he'd given her syph.—him the cleanest living old boy you'd find in a day's march! Take Wednesday out of the week and see what you've got; though I will admit he made a mistake in taking on a commission to do a series on various mental disorders. Heard not long ago that he had stabbed an attendant—with the breast-bone of a rat he'd let get all dried out and hard.

I hate to break the news those cookies you've been feeding your mutt contained enough arsenic to poison a city.

Yep, it worked. He took his eyes off me and put them on the dog. A second later the dog had been a bear he couldn't have seen it. These kids—they listen to talk.

I picked the .32 up and handed it to a cop. Here, Mac, check that for prints.

When the blonde phoned down for ice an hour later they told her the pup had had convulsions and died. We never know when the truth is going to overtake us.

The mirror gave the blonde a slash of black lightning right down the middle of her puss. Two brown eyes and no nose combing out her long golden hair. A big yellow oyster kisser. Any way you look at it, two dollars is a lot of money. A smear of people in red coats chasing a fox on the wall. Three paper clips and some petals from a yellow rose in a glass on the dresser. Why don't you ever wash your slip? I asked her, making a drink and leaning back to get comfortable.

Somebody knocked on the door. I opened it and three men pushed in. Right away I could see this meant something bad to the blonde. You said you'd give me a little more time!

The red coats pounding right at me . . . the walls starting to flex their white hands . . . All they'd had to do was come in while we were talking downstairs and mickey the bottle up real nice.

I came to under the roost in a coop of extremely well-fed chickens. Morning was yawning away up in the branches of a grand-daddie spruce by the time I got to a lunchwagon. The coffee had been on the boil all night. I almost preferred the other taste. A truck driver asked me for a match and how was every little thing. I gave him a match and said pretty good.

Without wings such a big damn bastard he should wave a wand and fly—And how's the fag-end of things coming? I queried him.

He got it and he didn't like it. A little mild flirtation first thing in the morning, eh?

Why don't you sweep the rubbish out now and then? I said to the counter-boy as I walked out. But that type of lad isn't vitally concerned with the fitness of things, as you might put it; because —and here we may be treading on a few toes—his life has no foundation in reality. Back to that later. Another word, though:

They told me you couldn't believe. I said you could. I said a person could believe if he got to know his own capacity for belief — not things to believe in, hell no, but how much of the throne he could glimpse in himself, and how willing he was to let his brothers (however rotten and evil) sit on that throne. It's a long way to the morning, but there's no law against talking in the dark. Ghosts, damnit! Let it run. The devil knows what to do with his furry prick. What a skruging the old world got in that direction, eh? Purity is the only thing can stop the bleeding now.

Ever thought what you'd do if suddenly there wasn't any point anymore in sucking around all the time? If suddenly your cell doors popped open and — the sun! a woman! a man! to feel it know it oh goddam wouldn't that be

a Pretty!

Well, frankly — I'm on your side if you're on mine . . . count on that, will you please.

LONG LIVE HUMAN BEINGS!

But the tent. That tent covered twenty-two sq. miles. Painted silk, all fine, 12,863 ft. high, a tiny puddle of dog-vomit just as you went in, yet Peasant Designs, and I felt good, clean socks, thinking of my once-wife, sweet, funny it didn't work out, so twelve
serious-faced young men
at a table
and at the head of the table
another
young man.
And it's coming in on me
SEND IN YOUR FIRST TEAM, GOD!
It's too big. It's too hurting to look right at. All men who ever lived—
This blood-fed geezookus. But enough idle chatter. It was a dreary day. The trees were eating each other in the near-by forest. The first notion I had that anything was wrong was when I tried to start my car in the parking lot. Probably five hundred other cars there. All empty but mine. I threw in the clutch, I jammed down the gasfeed
and my car didn't stir an inch
but I'll be godamned if all the other cars didn't clash into action and go sailing merrily off down the street.
Now that sort of thing can get a person into trouble—particularly when you consider that my driver's license had expired a good two months before—but providence had his eye out that day, and . . . anyway, here's what effected a distraction:
An old granary right in the center of town started to burn. All right, that doesn't sound like much—but two thousand people were crammed in there—roasting away
WAAAAAAAAAA
I presume you know how they'd scream!
I took a cigarette out and lit it. I looked up at the sky. It was about as vacant and empty as ever. A girl with her nose all eaten

away put her hand on my arm and said do you want to see something funny?

That I do, Miss—that I do. She led me off to one side and said take a gander into yon tree. We'll skip the patter—

The tree was full of angels.

I could tell you a lot more about that if I wanted to.

But the flow—watch this a minute:

While ago my doll came in the kitchen and said, I'm going over to B—'s for an hour or so.

I turned the eggs.

Aren't you going to kiss me, Almar?

Some other time.

What have I done now?

Nothing. Why?

Oh, you give me a pain.

Thanks.

She threw her arms up around my neck. What's the matter with us?

Is something the matter?

She took her arms down. You are a cold fish.

Thanks. I put the eggs on a plate and sat down.

Don't you care where I'm going?

Huh—what's wrong you're dropping over to B—'s?

You know I'm not.

Yeah. That's right. I know you're not. I got some yolk on my chin.

She sat down in the other place and started to cry. It's not because I want to, she said.

No, of course not.

It's just that . . . that—

Sure. I poured coffee into my saucer and stirred it with my knife. A bit of white floated forth like a drunken boat. It's just that you're lonely and scared. I know all about it.

She really made cry a word to remember. Listen, duck, I said, in another seven months it'll be Christmas—just think of it! A reward for everybody, and everybody his own reward. There are a lot of unhappy people in the world, but the grass was never grassier, the sky was never—

Oh, shut up!

A large black bear came in and started to gather up the dishes.

Even then I was late getting to the banquet. All the places around Him were taken. As I started down looking for a seat I noticed that the table was set on a sort of hill, and the farther I went the less I could see of Him. Finally all I could see was the top of His head. And still no seat. If you want the truth, I walked right on down the hell out of there.

Dark in the woods. Late of the year and day. I'd left my hat somewhere and the only book I had with me probably wouldn't have brought thirty cents. The four of them were sitting on a bed of moss at the foot of a tree. What gives, boys?

Well—they were lost. One of them got up and came over to stand right in front of me. I once ate a man, he said.

Do tell.

Yes. And he told me. Seems he and some pals were using an old lumbercamp as the site of a wild weekend. About thirty girls for ten men sort of thing.

—In the middle of his story one of his friends suddenly pointed a .45 at me and pulled the trigger. While they were bandaging my arm, an old fellow walked up and asked if anybody there would like to try a new way of living.

Three days we let go by. I'm down at the river picking bananas from some trees and trying to believe my good fortune. The people I caved with had about four good inches of hair between them and the elements. All, that is, except the females—of which I had drawn two.

On this fourth day, then, the young one and I are doing a bit of banana-sampling down at the riverside. Hair? She was as hairless as an icicle—except her golden head and where you'd look for a little in another place.

Had enough banana?

Her laugh gave me change for a ten. I put my hand back and she cuddled closer. I'm glad you don't know any English, I said; otherwise I wouldn't tell you that I trust actions even less than ideas; otherwise I wouldn't tell you that there isn't a single thing I really—Hello! You want your banana too, eh? Sort of an ugly old bit—her two tearing-teeth coming down below her chin—sneaking around on her horny feet!

Me no like-um mans-um allatime be by-um she-ums.

Sez you-ums. But I didn't want any unnecessary discord, so I gave her a banana and the three of us went back.

A lot of excitement. Old Chief had tracked something right up into the middle of a cloud.

What kind of a something? Old Chief scratched his heavy pelt. By signs he made me know that it had fire on its face and down its back.

I think I'll have a look myself. No!—I prefer to go alone.

There was a sort of orchard inside the cloud. As the trees walked about I saw that one side of them was white, while the other was red. Also, tiny little persons swung from branch to branch in golden caps and their little green bottoms showing so that I couldn't help calling to them—but they either didn't hear or they didn't want to hear.

And in the middle of everything a giant woman lay on a pile of what looked to be leaves—but were, in reality, kittens; brown, blue and purple kittens. I could hear her breathing. She was about seventy feet long, with tiny wrists and ankles. But are they kittens?

What's that you're lying on?

Murders.

I bent to look closer. They were indeed murders.

Where did he go?
Where did who go?
Old Chief said he tracked him in here somewhere.
Old Chief?
Then I saw a man walking down through the trees.
All the little persons scampered into a box and the trees started to pretend they'd been waiting for the mail.
The giant woman put me in her mouth and swallowed. I seemed to be standing at the counter in a drugstore
and there were twelve men at the counter drinking coffee.
Make that thirteen coffees, I said.
The man turned around very slowly. He smiled at me and I laid my book on the counter.
This is the strangest tasting coffee I ever had, I said.
What's the book? he asked.
You mean this book?
Yes, I do mean this book.
Oh—it's nothing much.
What's it about?
Oh—different things. A bit of this, a bit of that.
Will it make men better?
I doubt if it's worth thirty cents.
I'd spilled a little on my chin and in the mirror it looked like a careless shave.
Say! this isn't coffee!
The man smiled at me again. Look over there, he said.
I saw a liner all lights ablaze and people screaming
black water
raging and a girl tugged at my arm
and I took my lifebelt off and put it around her. Odd thing about this we were the only ones to get to shore alive. So you see
—I told her—

There must be a plan back of it after all
and she agreed with me
though she didn't feel easy a long time
her mother wondering
and no letters getting through.

But it worked out all right. We did manage to scale the mountain on the ordained day—the day He was slated to speak, that is. She pushed the hair back out of her eyes in the bluster and the wonder of it sweet damn little goats nuzzling His feet ta ta ta ta ta tee and she is rather beautiful

. . . honey . . . honey . . . honey . . .

huh! a clean slip

and I'll bet you there were ten thousand people with yellow skins there

possibly three thousand with black—(I'll check on that later)—

and I'll bet the browns made it fifty in all

counting us, fifty thousand and three since she was already in a "family way"—

This is what He said:

There is a shabby crying in the nations.

Lanes grow hands to strangle the unwary.

And if this enflamed adventure—

With all precincts reporting, a voice whispered in my good ear, Delaware is ahead by a comfortable margin.

Ahead of what?

Wyoming gave a good account of herself—as a matter of fact, it was nip and tuck up until two hours and forty-six minutes ago. Pennsylvania was the big disappointment—at least to me.

Uh-huh.

Yes sir, Delawareans are the most proficient breakers of wind in this nation, all right, all right.

His friend lowered his briefcase onto a tebadrun rock. He was in the neighborhood of fifty thousand but his face was un-

I wouldn't be cold-footing it along right now with such characters on my trail and I'd have planned maybe something that everybody could see was beautiful all the time. I had to laugh when I saw my own face in the stained glass — but what the hell . . . the next chocolate bar you buy'll probably have pieces of flesh in it.

Somebody once said that if you take a tree out of the ground you'll leave a hole. Same thing
you take a man out of his life.

Everybody's got to get somewhere. When the fellow says
Take a numbah from one to ten
tell him to shove it up unless he can guarantee that you will be able to count all the angels with it.

Or stay in a hole.

I don't want to tip my hand altogether, but I do want you to get this one thing:

24

— Put a little picture in your head . . . See
something sitting on the edge of the world
and trying to talk to you
in the interest of . . . don't laugh! . . . human dignity and brotherhood.

Hey!

I'll let them come up—to humor them and so like
one of those machineguns don't go off by accident like—
What's on your mind, fellows?—and empty my shoes at the same
time.

What did you mean by that last crack?

What last crack do you have reference to? I asked, leaning
on one of their shoulders to keep my sock up out of the snow.

Can that kid stuff! the leader fairly yelped. Get the hell up out
of that!

Not that I could blame him much, but how was I to know I'd
pick mister ticklish himself to lean on. That meatball without gravy
pinwheeling me around in a ten-foot snow drift!

What did you—

Splut . . . splut . . .

All right. Get it coughed up. Now, what did—

Oh! You mean that last crack about human dig—

Yeah, that's the one.

Why, I hardly didn't mean nothing by it, sir.

Are you organized?

Am I organized? Oh, no sir. I'm a split per—

Do you know why we have been tracking you?

Maybe you're out of matches like, huh?

Please tell us what opinion you have formed as to the possible
success of your group.

Well, I . . . What group!

He took one of my eyes out and squeezed it into a deep oval before putting it back. I admire you, he said, wiping his fingers off on his cartridge belt.

And I you, sir—(particularly through the eye that made him about twelve feet taller than he was in the other)—but I still don't see how you can reconcile your position with what you must know from delightful experience to be a temporary expediency however permanent it may become.

He said, when this is all over you will discover that the masses of the people will be disillusioned with disillusionment. You count on their love for one another—ha! better count on the sun rising in the west.

I do count on that—A number from one to four or five billion . . .

Let's drop in at my sister's here and talk this over.

We went into the house indicated. He repaired to ease his plumbing and I sat down with sis who was a little hard to figure since
except for the head
there were two of her and another fellow was courting one of them. I really extended myself her fancy to win
but whether her sighs were for his efforts or mine
I shall never know—to coin a phrase. But I did manage to clear enough space on the stove to get my underwear dried out—though it looked for a while as though I'd come to blows with the big sealion which had it all figured his lease still had a few more winters to run. I addressed him in his own language—and I think I probably enlarged his vocabulary a bit. Why and his fat belly's actually sizzling, he couldn't maybe shove over an inch now or (better still) 4-5 feet. Tolerance is one thing—wet underwear is another thing.

I happened to have a label in my pocket—and didn't that big

selfish bastard look silly with QUIINCE JELLY pasted on his forehead!

To get back to that cardgame for a minute—I knew they were just sitting around in the hall to keep me from getting into my room. Of course, from their point of view, it would have done almost as well if she had tried to get out . . . that's what I figured then. You get the set-up. These lads and I sitting there in the way of anybody trying to make it up- or downstairs . . . and such profanity when the short one struck a match on the landlord's seat! Let's say it did take a little skin off—Are the minds of innocent children to be tainted just because he eats too much and wears his clothes threadbare?

Wonder who lives here, I wonder? the one with the purple silk shirt with broad green stripes remarks, looking over at me.

I force a ten-dollar bill into the landlord's hand—nearly losing three fingers in the operation. Ten bucks he gives me! and him four months in arrears—

Hmm, now, the short one says, arrears you should be an authority on.

Brushing tender youngsters aside, two of The Finest clump onto the landing. What is this!

Tuesday, I think. Ain't this Tuesday, Louie? purple shirt says.

Oh! Why didn't they say it was you! the stupider and more typical of the two cops implores, flatulating dully.

It's okay, Minion. Go home and put one in the old bag for me.

Sure, sure, anything you say—And they go off fondling their sticks.

Four ball in the side pocket, the match boy calls after them.

One o'clock—

Three o'clock—

Whatever happened to two o'clock? the Gang Chieftan asks.

We gotta get outta here, don't we? the one with rubbery lips says, pulling them out about a foot and letting go.

Fifteen minutes later I scraped my chair back and said, You win. Let's get it over with.

Most of the kiddies were curled up asleep in front of the door by then. One of them set up a terrific howl when I tramped on its little pattie. I paused to scrawl a word on the wall and soon, infected by the wholesome glee of its companions, it was tugging at my sleeve and begging me in the most beseeching tones to deface the wall just once more please.

Man like owl   clappity flivver   town clock tolling news of the dark hangman and I said

It's nice of you to go out of your way like this.

Owl hunched at the scabby wheel—

that owl sure don't say much and I begin to whistle

Why do you wanta go there?

I nearly jumped out of the car. Yeah, yeah . . . What? Ohyiz, ohyiz . . . go there? Why do I want to go there?

He turned his burnt-gold eyes on me. Well?

Gee, I don't know . . . hard to explain. Though I guess really the explanation is simple enough—I've just always had a sort of hankering to see a ghost town.

Humph.

Why, Mr. er . . . er . . . I didn't catch your name—

That's 'cause I ain't give it.

I see . . . uh . . . ohyiz . . .

Christ I wish he'd turn the headlights on—black as a pig's birthday in here. Couldn't we have a little light on the subject?

I can see all right.

Shouldn't we be about there? Hell of a while since we left that town with the clock.

Soon as we get out of the tunnel, it'll be four mile.

Tunnel!

Yeah. We're under the river. My brother got hung back there.

Back where?

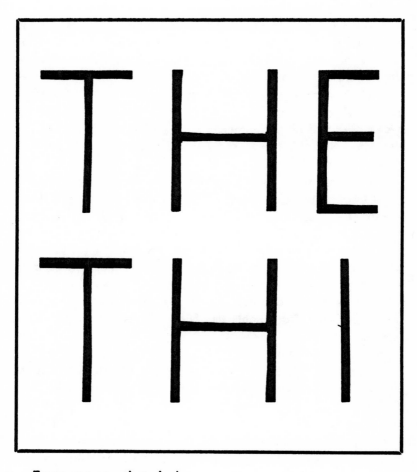

Town you saw that clock.
Oh, anything serious?
Serious? What you mean, serious?
I mean, did he kill anybody or anything?
Nah. They wouldna hung him for that. He stole a hoss.
I bet they wouldna hung the hoss if he'd stole yore bruder.
Put some plaster on that one.

I laughed until I thought my conscience would kill me. Hiram, you're all right. You had me worried for a little while there. To tell you the truth, I thought maybe you might not be . . . shall we say . . . uh, on the level like.

And suddenly this flashlight in my face   "Hiram" slumped over the slippery wheel   red hole in his forehead   golden eyes closed and all his feathers sort of puffing out <u>as his soul left him.</u> Me, hell I didn't even know the car had stopped until they had my arms

half-dragging me up the path to a farmhouse. There were a lot of deeds and legal documents which they seemed in a lather to have me sign—so I just scrawled Tempus Fugits every place they pointed to, put a couple nice silver candlesticks under my coat, sliced a watermelon and ate half of it, got in a pinch or two on a little dish who was doing their cooking, set fire in two places in the front bedroom and bid them a cordial goodnight.

Even as I walked away and heard them calling in friendly spirit after me—Goodnight, Mr. Fugits. Drop in any time, Mr. Fugits—

Just call me Tempus.

—I couldn't help being struck by the remarkable resemblance they had to our four-legged friend the equine. Only later did I discover the imprint of a tiny horseshoe on my thigh. Just a little foal playing.

And gone were all things

but death was not gone—I thought, as the dried fishskin of the sidewalk crulled under my feet

loose boards slapping at my ankles like the tongues of ancient crocodiles

WINDS   BIRDS   POWER

and the Flame of the World

culls which no laboring Word can fill. No outcry, chum—Gawd-amighty! You expect brass bands at the station? Mother's Sainted

Fingers Soothing Your Furrowed Brow and the Mayor that Horse's Other End neighing your praises down the Canyon of the Years like?

Hell boy you're a Ghost too—
the lot of us tangled up in the same phantom strings

So full of love that the words of hate won't stay back

Spitting on the hypocritical wailing of clerks
and the laws made only to protect the makers of laws

These chamberpots emptying themselves
on everything worth believing in

If nothing else—and I'll be proud if it's nothing else—
you can always look here and see

I say no to the murderers

I will have nothing whatever to do with them

I say no to the snivelling little wretches
who wrapped their dirty asses in the bloody rags of this war

I say no to the snotmerchants who talk of a.hard peace
for foreign fascists while their tongues are busy
lapping the crawling boots of the fascists at home

I say no to the monsters who prattle of Jesus Christ
while they fill the prisons with men who try to follow his teachings

I believe in life.

I believe in human beings.

I am the enemy of anything which deprives anyone of life.

—no laboring Word can fill. May then this darkness and no
light at the inn
leaves writing crazy scriptures on the black river

How frivolous the disguises!
—the sky teeming with the sullen iron fish of death

—no wing is home!
—only the Invisible is free.

Yea Lord!
Yea Lord! cockcrow of shells stopping the ears of schoolboys
O strong is the voice of disaster
Mighty are the arms which strangle the world

O ye Brightnesses, White Hearts, Eternities!

This leaping Fall—walking among His chosen—the Starry Animal
ne wishes Life, ne fears Death's Cold Buzzing Disease—Not now
. . . it is rare! . . . it is rare! — let the Statues talk of bravery —
Bartholomew Bread dribbling from every snout—Catch the tune?
the roar of the Wooden Lion—the Cucking-Stools are all in place
—the two fleshy Bells of the Beast swinging into your face. Weren't

you shocked? Oh, I should say . . . the funeral alone cost me five hundred dollars. Some paper roses for your daughter, Sir? Ah, he has a splendid reputation . . . nobody at all has a good word for him. Sure I'm a Stalinist . . . a stall for everybody, and everybody in his stall. Honesty is its own Revenge. Well, nobody can say that the Liberals aren't liberal with other people's lives. Of course

What do you want to do that for? I asked—as if I didn't know.
Gentleman here inquires to know why we want to
Blast these pigs right on to hell.
These pigs right on to hell.
Pigs right on to hell.
Right on to hell.
Midway in the century.

And when they started to get up I saw they weren't there at all. That's funny, I thought, settling back in an armchair which was covered with dust and brown stains. Naughty, naughty, a voice said, and I felt an invisible bony hand near my fly.

What is? I asked, getting up so fast I left one of my legs in the chair.

Wettin' your pa-ants—

Ah, that's only blood.

I walked out into the street. It was starting to rain. Then I saw a light in the deserted saloon, which ghost towns always have so many of. I walked up and peered in through the lattice of the door. An old fellow looking at lot like the sealion was standing behind the bar polishing a glass.

Good evening, Pop, I said, swinging the door open and striding briskly across the redwood floor.

'Evenin', Stranger, the old fellow said without looking up.

Thought this was a ghost town.

Yep. He blew lustily into the glass and I bent to pick up the bottom for him. That's the eleventh today, he said not without satisfaction.

Then he started to cry.

Outside I heard a woman screaming—and I bent hell out of shape putting my damn gams to work.

She stood under the streetlight, her golden hair shimmering like gold under the fitful light that came from the grimy globe of the old streetlamp. If I was that dirty I'd have fits too, I thought, adding outloud, What seems to be the trouble, Miss?

Troublemiss?

I watched a moth flutter down her bodice. Adage-ing two and two, I figured she must be pretty hot stuff. Yeah, I said—you've heard of Christmas, haven't you?

Oh! Have you got a present for me?

I gave her a present.

Smart moth.

All you'd have to do is have the wisdom, I mean in a practical way, the wisdom and love, and the love in a completely pure and unreasoning way, the wisdom and love and courage, and the courage in a tremendously man way, I don't mean the ugly, false nonsense sort either, the wisdom and love and courage and faith, and the faith in the way God must have faith, I certainly mean/ you need more than a little moral equipment to see yourself through some of the things which pop up in the most ordinary day anybody ever had on this earth.

I guess only the sadness really stays. Finest time I ever had there was always a little pain scooting around in me somewhere. I get as much kick out of that damn gnawing—except when I don't have any notion at all why I've got it. A bit of green grass—a bird —hell it only takes a little to give us all there is anyway. It was a room leaving wouldn't leave. On my knees too. Does paint come off easily? The clerk laughed! The color, sir? Color! What other color was red?

· A chair you say a chair.

Yes I'm tired to sit drab night after night. A bit of bright you know how easy it is to fall into horror and even the golden grows cold. Growing cold.

Pint enough?

Please. Please!

Blade moving in the mirror. Eyes my eyes watching the downward stroke. Fifteen. For twenty years then. Hair growing on a mask.

Poor little shaver Christ father I've stood enough your bullying mother and cowarding me.

There that's done. (Dirty towel.)
And do not rise that you and I must part on thy cold
What the bloody hell is that!
(Or get with chill this mansize rot.)
A ball.
It's only a ball!
I thought I'd closed that window.
Kid.
Up here Kid.
Catch—

Wait one sec. There. My handkerchief was dirty anyway. Here it comes. Good catch!

Almost as though her fingers had tried to close around it. Close over it. In sleep touching the round ball.

Remembering my hand lowering the window down.

What other order is there? Oh yes   the latch fixed to fall inside
     all my things in the black case   the extra chair with the rest
in   no that's the cup you're thinking of in the sink with
I'm <u>thinking</u> of! What use to have put all else in order
and me standing here not leaving at all. No matter. Rot.
What bars and braces. One two
free.

For all of me let everyone staint their houses real-redy. Stinking fool ape   a fine lather to leave your dwelling. All reet the soiled towel then. A clean taste of dead horse.

Dry your tear. Pink crevice where (to rime) all words return to be said.

38

Got your ball all right I see.

You the man?

How do you play—alone?

Just up in the air. I throw it up in the air. Hey!

I shouldn't think that would be much fun.

Hey mister mister yuh cut yourself?

Why   not that I know of.

The ball, I had to wash the ball when you threw it down.

Oh   I'm sorry about that. I was painting a table. Yes, that's right, I was painting our table. Here. Buy yourself a new ball.

I'm running off with the quarter now. A whole quarter. Hey mister that was a funny smell that paint had mister.

Where did you wash it!

I'm opening the door of the house and mom says what've you got all over your shirt!

How did you wash it off!

The stage is clear of me. A whole two-bits . . .

Ah, there's a man. I'll ask him. Sir I've (excuse me—I'll help you pick them up) I've managed to spatter a bit of paint on my suit and perhaps you can tell me

Certainly. Here's a bottle that isn't broken. Let me rub the fluid in now, scuffle the cloth upon its folds—my pardon, but truly your skin does bag upon your bones—removes paint, varnish, fruit stains

What's the matter?

There's some here won't out!

I'll tell you what. You're obviously a man of scientific bent

Thankee.

and we'll just swap clothes. You to try your elixir well within the quiet merit of your house

Clang! Clang! Clang!

I knew I'd forget something. I should have put the fire out in the carpet. Put out the fire that was in the carpet.

And you sir?

and I garbed anew may yet beat this foul game.

Oh look at them! The bare blades of their behinds cutting a droll figure in our street. Twins of grim fun and merry tragedy.

What've you got in that case?

Do you mean this black case, officer?

Stained black case, if it's technical you want.

I won't let you see, I won't.

Then I must insist that you submit to a search.

My clothes, you mean?

And what other's should I be meaning, lad?

Maybe, now, a stain-remover's, eh?

I will say that for a religious man you seem to quite vigorously wish to go childless to your grave.

(For the record, there were 34 of those little boxes of caution in my new pants.)

And will you be after looking at this now?

(In the right-hand pocket of the coat, twelve white mice; and in the left, a small wolf hound and the Berdain Code of Laws scrawled on four crumbling, marble slabs.)

Faith and I'm athinkin' it's your fingerprints I should be

I won't let you have them.

Then as one ed-ecated man to another I must ask you to confess.

How about you? You look a lusty pig.

That I am. That indeed I am, lad.

Well don't just stand there snivelling. Give that horse an apple.

I always liked horses with their—turned away, a thing of beasty. As a child I'd screamed myself many a one. Most horrible, the spotted.

Like scene in book I have. Two men are standing in a meadow. There is a river—but we aren't aware of it until much later. Man says man I am afraid. Other laughs and dark wings carry off the sky. Now you can see it. Is there nothing! No there is something.

Perhaps something romantic—a view of life! Seen through the eyes of an Angel of your own imagining. To be rejected at death. Tattered body—the soul? Stone bees in Byzantium. Young clean golden

but it rots.

Does it? Does it rot? a) Spirit. b) Soul. c) Angel—(Of course

41

symbols always mean something else.) Rain—star—sea—goat's head looking vacantly up out of the urn—

But it comes in from a long way off. An odd experience—being alive.

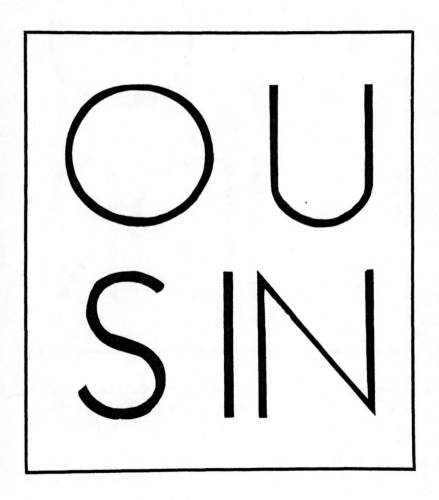

If it's only a system you want—shallow dish or mammoth sieve —I really can't advise you. Go mad.

This is intended to widen: not to falsify.

In long house food on great tables the sad laughter of children. Have you come far?

I've tried to think of that. I've tried to remember. Oh she'll sing —famous here. Strange. She wept. Famous in this place.

The song—yes! I see you understand. I could fall in love with her. All of us—I think that's why it's wrong. I fail to see that.

Corrupt—The sun; we've got a thousand screens there.

Tell me (for after all she was beautiful O my God she was like no other woman: I can't understand why her singing was received so coldly, so woodenly—she cried, I tell you! She stood there in front of us and—you filthy swine!) what is the meaning of the sun?

Without falling back on the Greeks, now; or Life Impulses; or, of all things, Psychic Regeneration!—no. We don't see the sun . . . this puny gang—to look at the sun! Have you come far? We see what we think.

The great are able to eat from spoons like the rest. Excuse me, the Mystery never increases or diminishes—it has no interest in paying your rent or washing your dishes. Besides, you'd do better in the street—and stop grubbing around after a lousy buck. The pack of you make me vomit. Nobility of spirit. Ha!

Who is this fellow?

An anarchist, I think.

Wonder what he's got in that case?

A skull, he said.

How very quaint!

But what strikes me—he thinks he can get away with it.

How silly. Have you a cigarette?

I'd like a child by you.

Okay by me.

But we are all strangers—even then.

Really the lion and the rose. My case—stained by . . . who runs today will live to run another way. I wish I knew a tree. Without making a symbol, either. It's gone out—books have become beads for the worship of monsters in dinnercoats . . . smiling bank accounts to fix the price of eternity.

But the song weeps.
The stain widens.
Tattered souls in hale bodies.

We were very happy. It had grown colder with the coming of night. My hands were stiff with the pull of our burdens. It was like walking into the house of a friend to enter the barn. I spread my coat out on the hay and we sank down together on it.

Cheese and bread made our supper.

We had seen thousands of people that day. They were fleeing from the world. We were advancing into it. Once we had witnessed the burial of a child by the roadside. There had been men laughing in hysteria. There had been horses dead of starvation in the shafts of overloaded wagons. There had been schoolgirls giving their bodies to the soldiers for a tin of bad meat. There had been misery and hunger and despair on every face.

Above, the sky had been very beautiful.

With the coming of night, the stars had seemed like peaceful eyes which expected to see wonderful things. But ahead the witch-fires of the guns lighted a terrible view. The furnace of war consumed its tall, thinking fuel. And there was little that was very wonderful or beautiful about it.

We became aware of it together. We sat very still, unbelieving, afraid.

The laughter of a man.

A man shouting in anger, or the firing of a rifle, would not have frightened us as much.

This was not in the way of that night, of that world, of that time of hatred and fear.

Friend, I called softly.

The laughter did not cease.

I struck a match and stood up. The heavy beams at the roof jiggled like sleepy dancers.

As far as search went we were alone there. We did not go to sleep for a long time.

In the morning I had the strange sensation that something was watching us.

I said nothing to her about it.

About noon that next day we came to a small shack set deep in a woods. An old man gave us food. We talked a little. It was plain that he wanted us to be gone. Just before we left, he said, I do not like to have people in my house. Man is a disgusting animal. I don't like his smell or the sound of his voice.

But you are a man too, Zenaslufski, I protested.

I shall be glad to be dead. Perhaps a wild flower will be nourished by my rot.

There was a purity and wisdom in his bearded face which made us walk more quickly after we left him.

I've been thinking about last night.

Yes, honey—Am I walking too fast?

No. I'm not at all tired. I feel restless . . . sort of on edge . . . as though, as though maybe—

I know, sweetheart.

Almar.

Yes?

Could that have been a warning?

That laughter, you mean?

Yes. It was so awful, so desperate—

What could it be a warning of?

Of danger.

I'm afraid danger is a pretty usual part of our lives now.

She stopped in the road, faced me, her hands gripping my arm.

But of danger to him, Almar.

That is not in our hands.

I began to think of all the things I loved. Of cities. Of trees. Rivers. My father. A pack of cards I had played with in kindergarten. Picking apples. Rescuing a puppy from a ditch. I remembered some of the good thoughts other people had had . . .

Suddenly a group of men broke from the woods and ran toward us. Their leader had a bright, quick face. A boy of seventeen.

The men and women in the road with us paused like weary beasts. Had they been mowed down, it would have meant a great deal to them—it would have meant rest and an end to the slow horror at last.

And somewhere that deep, rich, sobbing laughter . . .

The boy leader paused before me.

Will you come with us, please, he said.

What do you want?

You will see.

But my wife—

He looked at her bigness.

We are not pigs, that we would harm a pregnant woman.

Let us go with them, she said.

They led us to a little clearing under the trees. I don't know what I expected to find there; a wounded man, a firing squad, a monster . . .

We heard that you were a man of God, the boy said. The others were looking at me with curious, still faces.

I nodded. She held my arm tighter.

Will you tell us something about Him . . . or make us feel—

As he broke off, not knowing how to say it, one of his comrades said:

Will you pray for us?

WILL YOU PRAY FOR US!

It was too big and sad for any feeling I knew about off-hand.

Read to them, Almar, she said.

And I took up the book:

"And Jesus went out, and departed from the temple: and his disciples came to him for to show him the buildings of the temple. And Jesus said unto them, 'See ye not all these things? Verily I say unto you: There shall not be left here one stone upon another, that shall not be thrown down.'

"And as he sat upon the Mount of Olives, the disciples came unto him privately, saying, 'Tell us, when shall these things be? and what shall be the sign of Thy coming, and of the end of the world?' "

They were all crying by the time I got through. Sometimes you begin to wonder if a lot of people aren't a bit scareder than they let on.

And as we went up into the mountains we met a blind man. He was wearing a blue cloak about his shoulders, and in his hand he carried a long stick of polished wood.

Where are you going, my friends? he asked.

Into the region of the mystery, I answered.

She sat down on an old log which bordered the path, while the stranger and I remained standing.

The tiniest white cloud floated along just at the head of the highest ridge. While I watched it assumed the shape of a Roman hero, only to lose him in a blustering rooster with wild, diving comb.

What takes you there?

I cannot tell you that.

When will the child be born?

Within the week.

I sense—

He hesitated, and I said:

It is not exactly as you think. But now, if you don't mind, I'd like to ask you some questions.

I shall answer what I can.

How long have you been blind?

I was born so.

What is the world to you?

A place of wonder and joy.

Even now?

I have an odd feeling in that, perhaps. You will understand best, I think, if I say this: not being able to see what the progress of the days effects in the men and places which I encounter, I have no sense of any decay in them—they remain forever as I imagine them to be. So it is now. I never go down into the plain. All the men I have met have been running away. The sick and the wounded don't climb mountains.

Your speech, if you will forgive me, does not seem at all to have the clarity I would expect from one in your position.

You suspect that I am a coward.

It hadn't occurred to me in that way.

You probably feel that I shut myself off from all that would trouble me. This is not cowardice. I am shut in to greater love. You believe me confused because I spoke of our brothers lightly.

I can't help asking this: What do you know of brotherhood?

In that way, nothing. In another, purer way, what men know of their fellows in milder times, I know with greater power about the young men who have fled into the mountains here, clothed in the stained uniforms of fear.

And that is . . ?

That they are not evil.

A great black horse appeared a hundred yards down the path. It pointed its dark and terrible muzzle at the sky, and called. It was a chilling sound. Far off, likely ten miles away, another creature answered.

They seek that which you and I seek, the blind man went on. They wish to identify themselves with greatness.

Isn't man great in himself?

Man is nothing in himself. Being blind makes it possible for me to feel this. When I said before that in my removed state, time does not exist, I could have added that man and all things as you know them likewise have no existence. You are deceived into imagining that certain great truths have been established in the world: that men must die is one; that men must live out their days in sorrow and terror and hatred is another; that men must—

Excuse me. Do you know more of these things than others do?

I know nothing of them. I have not experienced death; I have never been terrified; I have never been sorrowful; I have never hated anyone.

Have you truths of your own, then?

I have . . . there is no word . . . I believe that I shall not die. I believe that the love which is in me has a far greater reality than the hate of this world.

Do you believe that the dead are living now? she asked.

I believe that nothing dies, that all life is eternal. Let me tell you a story. Usually I find little meaning in stories, but there was something about this one which seemed to have a larger significance. One day, about a month ago, a young man stumbled into the clearing where I have my cabin. I was just chopping wood for my supper, and the ax was poised in my hand to strike when I sensed his presence. I greeted him without surprise or alarm:

Welcome, my friend.

There was a little silence, then the blind man was aware that the other was sobbing.

What troubles you?

Why don't you kill me? Why don't you be done with it! You can see I have no gun—

I can't see, my friend. But if I could, why should I want to kill you?

Oh. I didn't know—

But I surmise that you're a brother from the other side.

The young man was silent now, waiting.

I have no enemies, the blind man continued; and you are in need of a friend.

With the coming of night, the young fellow was sufficiently recovered to tell something of what troubled him.

He had been engaged to marry a girl who lived in the country across the border from his own. She had been murdered by a gang of hoodlums, whose acts of terrorism had been inspired by the newly-formed government. He had vowed to kill as many of these babies as he could get his hands on.

I was half mad. I rushed on ahead of the others. I scorned to use my rifle. I would bayonet the pigs as they deserved. And finally . . . he was leaning against a tree . . . he didn't look up when I came upon him . . . and I . . . I drove the steel into his back.

It had been his best friend. The blind man had held the little image in his hand for some time before he asked: And do you hate them now?

I seem to have lost all my ability to hate or love. It is as though nothing meant anything anymore. I am losing all sense of being a personality. I exist only to die.

This is the little figure, the blind man concluded. He insisted on giving it to me. He'd carved it for his friend the summer before. I turned the little statue of Christ over in my hand. It had a tiny nick at the base of the nose.

It was as though the very stars would fall from the heavens— so great was the approaching storm. We were lost in the lowlands, far from the tracks of our own kind. The moon had no light to waste on the desolation of that hour. Like a great ship out of the harbors of darkness, the tempest moved into its place at the head of fear.

Darling, O my darling . . . I thought.

Shelter nowhere. As it got black we seemed to enter upon a forest of dwarf trees. Our knees crashed upon these surly sticks, which bit at us like sows.

Above, the sky was a battlefield. Huge muskets in the hands of demented giants went off with a clatter to tear the flesh.

Darling, O my darling . . .

In that time of agony, many things went through my head: I could almost believe myself in a nightmare.

Hullo! Hullo there!

I tried to answer, but the wind made crippled birds of my calling.

We could hear the crashing coming nearer. Now I was sure that we could be seen by whatever approached. The sound advanced to our side.

Then stopped.

I put my arms around her and waited.

Whatever it was was very near. But it made no further sound.

Toward morning, and we were nearly sobbing under the pain and tiredness, the great storm began to wear away—like an idiot giant amused to his pleasure at last.

And the light came.

And we saw that we had been walking the night in a field of crosses.

From a few, helmets hung like the sad, brown hands of madness.

We were within hearing of the guns. There were no more people on the roads. It was like walking through a dead country. Yet the woods and fields were beautiful in the clear, sharp air.

Why do you suppose the blind man was so moved by the young soldier's story? she said.

Because he is hungry for sensation—to feel part of a stirring experience.

But that wasn't all of it.

No. He was trying to convince himself of love for his brothers.

It has always disgusted me that people always demand a reason for their love; in his case, he felt he must love because so many others hate. I can't really believe that he felt deeply about the tragedy of the two friends. It was only that he felt superior to it. And safe. As he does not wish to die, he has faith in immortality; as he does not wish to be truly involved in the lives of others, he singles out a spectacular incident to show the futility of human affairs.

But he did say that he felt man to possess a will for good.

Because he fears evil. Men who seek the good because they are terrified of the world, are not fishers of the star. Men who cry out to God because they are stricken of spirit, seek not Him but an image of their own soft wishing. To have faith in God, a man must first have faith in himself.

A shell landed a short distance ahead. We flung ourselves down. When I lifted my eyes, I saw the black stallion prancing toward us. He came on until we could see the sweat on his great chest.

She got up and walked toward him with outstretched hands. He allowed her to touch his nose.

Almar, he's tame. Oh, he's so gentle and nice . . .

But when I tried to climb on his back, he reared in unangry terror.

All that day he followed at our side. It gave us a feeling of beauty.

We came upon a group of soldiers who were gathered around a man strapped to a tree. They had beaten him until his face no longer had eyes or nose or shape at all. Yet he was alive.

I asked them what they did.

I am Reuben Grisher, the dying man thought. I will awaken and all this will disappear. Before, I could break a dream by opening my eyes, but my eyes don't open now . . . And something hurts

in my chest . . . my mouth is filling with a thick, sweet taste . . .
Dolly . . . Dolly . . . Mother . . .

I was happy that she had managed to fall asleep. Perhaps the incessant chatter and grumble of the guns devised a lullaby, a crude lullaby. She lay comfortably on the raft, her golden, lovely head cushioned easily by the bundle of our worldly possessions. I sat at the front, poling off drifting logs and the wreckage of bridges and houses. Occasionally a body drifted past. There were many carcases of dogs and cats and sheep; once that of a full-antlered deer. Overhead great birds circled in terrible solicitude.

It troubled me to think how unimportant the individual affairs of human beings had become. All that had been deepest and most holy to human beings, was as nothing now.

Where was the pattern? What was the value of a life? a life which had gathered love and pain and a grandeur unto it—only to have an outside thing destroy and to make mock of its dearest intentions. How was the soul of man to withstand the adventure into that outsideness? Whence was the escape from that awful withering? from that sense of having no real, conscious role in one's own life? For life seemed to have run down in this time. Only an ugly, terrifying 'general-life' for everyone. Here was, indeed, that universal existence. Men made one by hate and fear. The individual horribly lost in the all. Could not one lose his special way in a greater undertaking? Could not the races of men find that beautiful quickening of spirit, that surrender to the wholeness of every human enterprise, through love? Could not men find universals in life? need death be the only meeting-place of all men?

<u>Were men to live only in spite of men?</u>
Or because all men desired only life!

This, I felt, was the problem of mankind. It would be necessary to return to the human being his individual faith in himself, and in his life on earth. There only lay the road of brotherhood which the prophets had schooled the stars in. It would be necessary to find importance in the least act of the least of men.

I thought that there must be a wonderful, central life from which the lives of all creatures had their flowing. Perhaps in this was God.

At the feet of a great tree on the river bank sat an old man. He did not look up as we drifted past. Instead, he seemed intent on a conversation with someone whom I could not see. One of his arms he raised excitedly to the sky; the other hung limply at his side. Soon bushes lost him to my sight, but for a little time I could hear his voice—questioning, angry, cheerful, pleading, confident, and with something pretty damn sad in it.

Then she awakened and said:

I had a strange dream that angels had come and were talking together near us.

There was talking, I said. A poor, befuddled old man babbling to himself. Are you rested now?

I feel quite relaxed and happy . . . Almar! Look! Our horse again.

And pacing majestically along at our side was the great midnight boy. From time to time he would disappear behind the willows which grew thickly along the bank in that region. As we came to villages and towns, his unshod feet made a strange clumping in the empty streets. The houses and stores looked like pretty boxes deserted at the death of children.

But children did appear now and then. Hair matted, clothing in shreds, they dashed in and out of caverns and barns and factories. Once we surprised a group of them pulling the bloated body of a cow out of the river. They tore at the reeking flesh with shrunken little hands, like the paws of ancient monkeys. Often we saw them with soldiers, the boys as eager as their sisters for trade. Negro and Jewish children mingled democratically with the rest.

Yet sight of a great white eagle perched on the roof of a shed made the day not altogether terrible for us. When he spread his wings to fly, the air seemed to fill with massive activity.

The voices of the guns were already part of hearing, unclaiming as the whisper of our blood.

A great battle was preparing, for the heaviest pieces were in constant occupation. Then, with the coming of night, the heavens were dashed with a sullen radiance as great as the glow of tiny suns. The river wound through fields pitted by the monster fingers of shells. The smell of rot was over everything.

Toward midnight we heard the sodden progress of a weary thing approaching downstream. Presently the head of a young man broke the surface a few feet from the raft. I had the curious sensation that he had swum up through the water. As I helped him aboard, the earth seemed to pitch in the reverberation of an enormous bombardment whose intention threatened the world, and we could see him very clearly. He was naked, his chest and head tangled with weeds and silt. His powerful arms and thighs gave him —in spite of terrible exhaustion and distress—the appearance of a gladiator. As he lay there panting, struggling desperately for breath, there was a sudden lull in the heavens, causing a momentary dark, and when the light came again he was gone. I called and waited. Only the swollen, evil rippling of the river . . . and perhaps in the remote distance, nearly lost in the greater noise, a something that might have been sobbing. Or—laughter.

For a long time it had threatened snow. We were nearly in sight of the place. It was early afternoon, about two, that dullest of all the day's hours. I stopped to admire an aspen which grew near the crest of the hill. No stir of wind softened the chalky grayness of the sky, yet the pretty tree trembled in a touching of ecstasies—to enflame unseen eyes. I helped her up the last, cruelest yards to the summit.

It was an awful thing there before us. Stretched out all down across the valley, looking like tiny moving rats in desperate migration, were thousands of men—two parties of death facing each other in grim sport . . . how fast they ran, kicking up spurts of colored leaves—and arms and heads and legs . . . now how slowly, creeping on their bellies to gain a new advantage for more ample carnage . . . while overhead, a few sad, battered planes made half-hearted efforts to fill the upper roads with heroes—but, of course, this was not an expensive battle . . . not a single bomber, no swarms of Flying Fortresses—only a few heavy guns—and the foot-soldiers. Actually only thousands of human beings with rifles and heaving bellies conducting an afternoon of commonplace war.

Then I heard voices coming up from that field:

Water! Water! For the love of God, water!

Come on! Come on! I'm not afraid . . . please, please, don't . . .

I can't stand it. I tell you it hurts here—but that leg is gone!

God!

O my God . . .

Dear God, save me.

And someone spoke at my side. I turned to see two men standing just below us on a ledge of rock.

How do you like it?

I couldn't think of anything to say.

Then the second one began to laugh. His laughter rose shrill and biting, like an oath in a garden. Presently the two locked arms and commenced to dance about like wild goats. This seemed more awful to me than anything we had yet encountered. She was crying. Then the pair sat down and did pat-a-cake. After a little, tiring of this, they threw off their clothes and started climbing up to where we stood. But at that moment, one of the crazy, stick-and-an-ounce-of-glue eggcrates swept in low upon them, its rat-a-tat hammering away like the dictation of the devil.

The sorry chums went down in red hilarity.

A little bird hopped onto my shoe. He preened his dull feathers like a housewife shaking out a tablecloth of rusted mail. His bright, sly eyes stared hopefully into mine. She broke off a bit of crust and dropped it on the grass.

It started to snow. Great milk-sponged flakes fell heavily down. Soon the little bird was covered. After a moment, I bent down and lifted it in my hand. It didn't stir. A trickle of red stained my fingers. I could feel the hole in its breast. A great anger shook me and I stood up and shouted down into that mad field. But no one heard me and she took my arm and we turned and started on our journey again.

The snow covered everything. I was glad because somehow there seemed more hope now. But it was not until evening and we were sitting before the fire in an old farmhouse far in the hills with a mother and her two daughters, that we had our first word of it. Father and sons were away in the thick. The house was far enough from the world to be safe.

Tell them, mother, the younger girl said.

It's only rumor, Bridget—the wagging of idle tongues, the woman answered; but being urged further, she said:

People are saying that something strange has happened in a little town in Oklahoma.

Yes? I said eagerly.

We leaned forward—and our faces became very beautiful.

We don't really know what it is, Bridget said eagerly. But it's something wonderful. Isn't it Lillith?

Mr. Spulk said it was a miracle of some kind, Lillie agreed.

Mr. Spulk would do better to keep his nose clean like the YMCA, mamma protested.

She's angry with him because he joined a band in the hills here who fight against evil, Bridget said.

Have they been successful? I asked.

Most of them are dead, Lil said. She started to cry. Her sister put her arms around her.

Lawrence, her sweetheart, was one, Bridget explained softly.

We're terribly sorry, my companion said.

And you know nothing more of the miracle? I asked.

Oh, yes, Bridget Ann said. The most beautiful thing about it—

Now don't repeat that nonsense to them, Mrs. Tokus said.

But even if it isn't altogether true, ma . . . It's so wonderful to think about!

They say that the murder is drawing to an end, Tom Piperson said, shaking the snow off on the rug which Moriiy had sold them.

Later, in our huge room, with the keening of the pines around us, we lay for a long time without speaking. Then my lovely bride said:

My time is fast approaching, Almar.

I got out of the bed and crossed to the window. All was still and pure as I lifted my head to the silent hills.

Please, Father, I said.

Now we were going down into the valley. People were on the roads again. She was very near and she rode upon the back of the great horse.

On all sides of us, men, women, carts, trucks, wagons—a very calling-about of haste and new aspects. Who were the believers? Who were the doubters? Everyone. So little was known. So much was distorted, made small, great. From a thousand we learned a thousand different things. But every story somewhere told:

That the Savior had been seen by men.

His face had been seen.

His living eyes had looked upon men.

And so would end the days of sorrow.

And so would end the days of madness.

And so would end the grisly days of war.

A sign of feasts and perfections; an ornament of light to shame the stars. Whence has this endowed its brighter bending . . . Creature of whales and the wondrous rut of the lightning, whence hast Thou furnished water for the parched throats of Thy children . . . ? Those who have spoken much, shall now be silent; devourers of mountains and burners of a wilderness, have you the word to fill the needed voice! For islands have been planted that the souls of reason and truth may refresh the work whose sun is forever all. We who have been straitened on every side, have now only a path to the sun. O glorious show of the seasons, shining of names and treasured omens of Thy judgment, the beginning of wombs, and the end of madness, place higher the High that the Son of Man may not want for space for His fiery standing. Counsellors and princes, kings and captains, see now the damage in the mouths of greed and murder. Signet of wonder, pen of lions, write open the windows of evil. O despoilers of the spirits of men, tremble in the presence of His innumerableness. He sings to the thunder, and it is gentled. He walks into the chambers of the deep, and they are watered anew. He gives drink to the cattle of the sun, and they are comforted to graze in the pastures of an unimagined morning. He has taken leviathan from its watery nest, and caused it to fly above the eagle. He has come out of the East, and he shall turn all departure into that majestic coming. His acts are of every mercy. No longer shall the host exact transgressions from his guest. No longer shall honor be fouled with the steaming excrement of power and bloodshed. No longer shall the garment of everyman be made to clothe the skeleton of hatred. No longer shall the bondsmen of love be made to provide an entertainment for serpents. No longer shall the tabernacle of the human spirit be turned into charnel-houses of stupid ambition.

So did my thoughts settle in that place of multitudes. America's heart was beating awake, I'll tell you that much.

The white eagles had circled above the inn on that night of the strange happening. Here had been the scene of fiercest conflict. Most of the village houses had been shattered. Like a grim shuttle-cock the tides of war had surged back and forth here; first occupied by one army, then the other. The eagles had indeed known a sweet glee.

Now two opposing soldiers were advancing stealthily upon the inn. It was a night of bitter cold and they sought shelter there. For that moment, the battle had shifted to another sector.

The first man has opened a door. Now the other, from the opposite side, has opened a door. They face each other down the long room, which is fitfully lighted by distant flares.

They raise their rifles in one movement . . .

Then a great shell, landing somewhere near, shakes them down. As they lift slowly, dazed and sluggish with the shock, their eyes are drawn to it.

A face.

Then they realize that all the lights in the inn are on.

Stumbling to their feet, rifles hanging loosely in their hands, they walk toward it.

"The face of God!"

"It is the face of Christ!"

Together they sink to their knees, sobbing half in fear, half in wonderful joy.

Now do the eagles ponder a vast mystery. For one by one, battlefield after battlefield, gun after gun, town after town, and city after city, are made silent. A great waiting. The creeping-in of a new endeavor for all men. The rolling away at last of the horrible and awesome gates.

How far can this fiery thing spread? Already it is advancing far across the waters . . .

Shall it have the world!

Shall the faith of mankind find its brightest haven in this black hour . . .

Can this be made the story of Everyman . . .

From every quarter of the stricken land, the human rivers con-

OH IT GOES A WAY IT COMES BACK IT GOES IN IT COMES OUT . . . . .

verge on the inn. We are carried along in such a wealth of tongues and stations that we seem to understand all and to have place everywhere. The horse, uneasy at first, submerges himself in the complex flow. There are lame. There are blind. There are the sick. The old. The very poor. The rich. All on foot or in slow conveyances, because the roads are impassable to anything of speed. There are thieves. There are men who have done murder. There are men who have designed cities and constructed towers and bridges. There are black and white and yellow. There are men who curse and men who pray openly. There is no importance in the thinking of anyone because all are aware of that one thought:

Perhaps herein lies my own salvation!

And now the greatest machines fly overhead. Not pleasing the eagles—for theirs is not now a mission of death.

Where can so many people be housed? I think. Surely there is not room for all men in this little town!

Suddenly someone is singing.

Then another. And another. And everyone is singing.

We walk blinded by tears.

Thousands of children are playing in the fields. Their bright dresses and coats are like colored stones which a playful giant tosses about on the snow. And on all the hills around tents and rude shelters spot the white earth. I think that if God is looking anywhere, He will surely be looking here.

She was in labor. We had not been able to find lodging anywhere in the village. Finally, in desperation, I had prevailed upon the guards to admit us to the sentry's shack in the yard of the inn. I made her a bed of crates, spreading my coat upon them. After a time, the door was pushed open and a young woman entered.

I heard that you were in need of someone, she said quietly.

Under her instruction I heated water in the tiny stove, prepared the little we had against the time; and we waited.

Please go outside now, Almar, my pretty one said.

I bent to kiss her, and she said: We'll be fine, darling.

I stepped out like a dead man. It was a wonderfully clear night. The stars were as cold lights. A gentle snow began to fall.

O my God, I whispered.

There was hardly a sound from the vast throng of people. They seemed to stand in a frozen dream under the cold stars, like statues dimly seen through water.

She made no cry.

I waited.

The snow fell softly down.

Somewhere a dog howled on a far hill, its voice sad and withdrawn, chilling in the huge quiet.

Above, the white eagles watched down with unpitying, intent eyes.

All the world was hushed in the whiteness.

Only the snow falling, falling . . . and the cold, wonderful star.

Then all the doors in the world swung open!

The blind and the lame and the sick approached unto the Mystery.

And the blind cried, I can see! I can see!

And the lame walked without blemish.

And the sick were made well.

And they kneeled before that beautiful Presence.

Then thin and clear, the crying of a new-born child!

And the voices of the multitude lifted. Everyone sang. And the singing ascended to the stars. Higher than the eagles. O higher than any evil anywhere.

Softly falls the snow . . .

And men are singing in a great joy before that Mystery.

COME ON! The door's open. A telegram, eh? Umm. Here's a quarter, grandpa. Buzz—buzz—the money you—buzz—buzz—Hey! Wait a minute! Give me back the two-bits! Why, that lousy

65

bastard, I'll—He'll get his money back all right—in a pig's sun-porch!

It's always like that. Goddam the best day I ever had some crummy sonofa—oh, forget it. I said let's forget it!

Baby, sweet baby! I'm all-in—blue—fubbled-up—I've just plain got a bad taste in my mouth—One, two, three, four, dirty louse! five, all out of juice, six, wonder what Ruby's doin'—say

wait a minute

sure

that's the way to make a lot of dough and win the respect and admiration of all who know you

I'll write me a book

th—All right, Murphy! Jesus Christ! just put it to hell down on the table!

—a nice little book—

Try this on for size, eh?

Title—Need a title . . .

Umm . . .

Well, here's a title—I'll call it

THE ADVENTURES OF A MAN
WITH A
DETACHABLE BRAINPAN

PROLOGUE

I, II, IV, V, VI, & VII

FANNY TICKLE walked in and stretched out on the bed beside me. Her fat lips quivered lanuquinomously as she recounted what she had just witnessed in the hallway. While we were still chuckling over this, Joe brought my supper in on a tray.

Fanny, my housekeeper—and a good one, had been born in Delaware before so much of that beautiful heath got spoiled by the gap. I bit the top off a radish. Her father's mother, a full-blooded Sioux Indian, had seen a brachiopoda (mollusc-like animal whose body is enclosed in a shell composed of unequal dorsal and ventral valves) three weeks before giving him birth; so naturally, the little boy was named accordingly. But it happens that the Sioux word for brachiopoda is the same as our Anglo-Saxon one for cohabitation. Mrs. Tickle, secure in the knowledge that the Great Father had named her son, was obdurate; and the family shortly after moved to Bismarck, North Dakota, seeking asylum. No Rinso there, either. However, when the little red fellow was

67

eight, he joined the Navy—remaining its most popular member until his death twelve years ago. Even now his name is often heard wherever sea-faring men gather. "These chops—I hate to eat the cat's supper," I said to Joe.

The clock, I noticed, had stopped.

Fanny sat down at the organ and played the section from Beethoven's quartet in A minor which is marked 'Neue Kraft fühlend.' Outside it was getting dark. Men walked past tall buildings. Sewers gurgled in the bowels of the city. Someone got shot. I put my coffee cup back in its saucer and remembered something an uncle of mine once said when he dropped an open bottle of ketchup on the pants of his palm beach suit.

My secret, if I must have one, is that I am the nicest man in the world. Louie said: YOU HAVE A NERVE, YOU LOUSY BASTARDS. WHAT A CREW OF POT-BRAINED LIARS. THE SON OF GOD IS CRYING THIS NIGHT.

I feel the sweat in my fingers. Fanny said that in the hall two cops were having a violent argument about Spinoza. The little cop Ed thought if Spin's jock had give the whip say now a bit quicker why button your lip Ted the cop with a haircut speaking that nag couldn't run a nose twenty below. Ed and Ted have a wife and kids t' home. It's the human being counts not kicking the hell out of poor lads who maybe have nobody to care a damn what happens to them except Henry Wallace like and I see indeed a great future for this beautiful land of ours.

Writing is a sort of holy. An old man taught me. A few words put together right make a lovely don't they? Writing is a kind of loving—when the wreath touches your heart. The beautiful old man would want me to say that, I think. If you love you're not afraid.

"Joe, was there any mail?" There'll have to be a lot of smoke on the mountain before they get me to explain my invention another time. You take all classes people the Patent Office wins the little receptacle with the enameled feet.

A beautiful old man taught me how to write.

I am the creator of a "useless" gadget.

Everything clear, everything tidy and just so.

There are three stages to writing.

1) You sit straight up and think till you get a headache before putting anything down.

2) You lean your head forward almost like you were falling asleep. Out of somewhere comes a cruel gentle flow—you say, "I am a son of God."—and it hurts and relieves the pain.

3) You bow your head all the way down—O Father! Man alive! I am crying tears because

Tell me that BECAUSE

"You will be humble and unafraid," the old fellow said.—"And another will write."

So far I'm at the headache stage.

My gadget makes a tiny humming noise and a tiny white flag waves bravely up.

Made of a special lead. Wood would rot. Ordinary lead would be too heavy to transport in large quantities.

We all set out for a walk except Fanny Tickle who was expecting a baby. A little rain had fallen and the streets were wet. "I should have, Joe, brought my rubbers."

We passed a man munching an orange. Suddenly I was a small boy again. I headed for a fireplug and started to unbutton. An old lady in a parked car hit the horn three quicks. The kid slouched in the doorway raked up a machine gun and wrote his name across Joe's belly. Standing on the other side of the street with the fireplug still gripped in my arms I saw that the old lady had her teeth out and was snapping at a butterfly with In Gold We Trust stamped on its wings. Joe's body went skuggling down the gutter, the fierce water from the broken hydrant trying to stick cigarette butts into his wide-open eyes.

Too bad the last thing Joe had to say was pretending to think I meant another kind of protectors.

Harder rain. I watched a fat man watching a pretty lady change into dry duds with 150 watts in back of her. It took her a long time to open the door.

"My name is Aloysius Best," I told her, walking in and sitting down in the only chair. "I've come to make you a proposition." The old man, probably her grandfather, stirred restlessly, but made no effort to get out from under.

"And mine is Apollinaria Grudd," she said, putting a generous amount of shave-cream on her other leg. "You must excuse my son's not getting up when you came in—He spent the afternoon mating gold fish."

"You can hardly tell them apart," the old young fellow grumbled, shifting the world's boniest knees about so that I expected any minute to see one of them come poking up through my thigh.

"How do you?" I asked remembering the fable of the ostrich and the pint of shellac.

"By imagining you're one of them," he replied, taking a moth off the lampshade and blowing gently on its abdomen. "Some are rather attractive, I must say."

"After you've imagined, don't you mean, Terrence?" his mother quickly appertulated, putting in a fresh blade.

"Yes, quite. I remember one little miss—a pretty, oh but definitely a pretty miss she was," Terrence said.

"Terrence!" I said. "A poor innocent fish! It is too much—It is entirely too much, Terrence."

"Oh, but I never—"

"That is enough. No wonder you look so old!"—He did look a seedy seventy.—"Such depravity would age anyone."

A teamster came in and asked me why I creased my pants across the fleshy part of my lowest back.

Apollinaria Grudd said, "Mr. Best—" — "Aloysius to you, Mrs. Grudd." — "Then you must call me Apol—" — "Apol? You Greek?" — She smiled, her face becoming suddenly very alluring in the soft glow of the naked bulb that was like a hot dirty finger putting my eyes out. "Al came here—" — "Aloysius."— "Oh, all right. Aloysius came here to—Say, exactly what did you come here for, Mr. Best?" she finished lamely, hobbling over to the bureau on her blistered right foot.

"A proposition," I said, my caress moving instinctively to my wonderful dropseat brain-pan. "To make you a proposition—"

"Am I included in your proposal?" Terrence's quavering voice put in.

"No, child," I said. "I don't like you. There is something vaguely horrible about you."

Mrs. Grudd began to cry. "It's my cross," she said softly. "He came in one day and ate my baby and—"

"Who did?"

"Terrence. Terrence came in one day and ate my babies so just like I read of ancient times I took him instead to keep and try to love because don't you think each one of us should have something that's our own, out of our lives and blood and suffering— that we can say, this is of my flesh, this is—"

"Now, just wait a minute," I said, thinking that perhaps she was getting a bit too carried-away by her recital. Besides, this is the right place (as I understand the mechanics of prose composition) to tell you about my dream of a better world for everybody. It's going to come—whether you like it or not. Louie said: AN END TO THIS MURDER. AN END TO THIS GRINDING OUT OF MEN'S SOULS FOR A MESS OF POTSDAM. THE TREES HAVE ROOTS IN THE EARTH—No hatred, not a drop, a sniff, a vugby, out of Aloysius. The ancient one, who taught me the secret of writing, once said: "First, before anything else, they must stop killing each other."

You sure as hell better think that over.

I told Mrs. Grudd about my scheme and she was all excited to get in on it.

In a bar on 3rd I met the poet Fitzmichael Kell. He had his latest book in a big stack on the table in front of him and I bought three copies which he was good enough to sign because I believe the people who say they like poetry and never buy any are a pack of cheap sons-of-bitches. I told Charlie to bring us a bottle of Haig & Haig and a cut-glass carafe of squedo-zzpi.

Kell tasted his drink. "That's a funny drink," he said.

"Sure you've got enough squedo?"

"Maybe another finger."

"How's that?"

"That's fine."

"I think the thing I like best is the color it gives," I said, pouring a little more into mine.

"You mean the what-you-call-it?"

"Squedo. You ask for squedo-zzpi. Only saloon in this great land of ours has it, as far as I know."

We sipped appreciatively.

"What's new?" Kell asked.

"I'm getting the yacht painted," I said. "Charlie, a pack Fatimas, if you don't mind."

"What yacht?"

"We're out of Fatimas, Mr. Best."

"The Golden Vanity. All right, Camels, Charlie."

"What do you mean, The Golden Vanity? That's one of Morgan's boats."

"Here you are, sir. Thank you, sir. I understand you mention a product in a book, they send you a supply."

"You mean the Camel people?"

"Sure,—or Chesterfields, Luckies—"

"Give me Camels any day."

"I like Rameses myself."

"Drop them a line, Charlie."

"Maybe I will."

"I bought it from him, Fitz."

"Like hell. Where'd you get that kind of money?"

"I've been saving my pennies."

"Like hell. What'd Joe do, knock over a bank?"

"Poor Joe."

"The papers say the cops got a couple colored boys booked for it."

"Joe and I'd been dreaming of this trip for years—and now he can't go." I picked up the carafe and turned it slowly about so its thousand eyes flashed like angry stars in that dingy little tavern.

"What trip?"

"I'm going to set sail into the sunset—where goeth the wind, there goeth I—Anywhere away from here." I felt a lump of joy gather in my throat. I bit into it. It tasted fine.

"It's no better anywhere else. You know, the color this drink—maybe it's just my imagination."

"If we're lucky, we might land on some cannibal isle. Oh, don't let that pale yellow bother you."

"But it tastes a little like—"

"Nonsense. How's your book selling?"

"An old guy in the park offered me a quarter for two copies yesterday."

"What happened?"

"Oh, he backed down when he discovered I only had inscribed ones with me."

"That girl coming in—the one putting six nickels in the juke."

"Her name's Flume, Tranquil Flume. From out West somewhere, I think."

"Well, I'll see you later, Kell."

"Can I come along?"

"No. I want to talk to her alone."

"I meant on your voyage."

"Oh, sure. I want a poet along. We'll have a lot of good talks. I like poets when they're not damn punks."

"You could use a little tolerance. It's a pretty lonely business trying to write poems in this madhouse of a world."

"But most of them aren't really poets," a stranger said.

Kell grinned. "You wait. In a couple years you'll discover they hated war all along."

"In a pig's eye. You don't get no Sergeant or Lieutenant in front of your name by refusing to kill people—and for my money, poet and killer can't be used to describe the same person," the stranger said.

"Something along that line occurred to me in prison."

"How much'd you get?" I asked, watching the stranger disappear through a small hole in the ceiling.

"Three years."

"Because you refused to break one of God's commandments."

"Yeh. So long, Best. Think about that tolerance angle."

I winked at him. Crossing to the front I fished out my gadget. "Hello, Miss Flume," I said, lowering myself onto a stool beside her. "Watch this." I moved one of the soldiers' glass of beer out of the way and put my 'WNTTLFACIOMEO' up on the bar. There was that wonderful little humming and the tiny white flag sprang proudly aloft.

"Well, I'll be damned!" the soldier said.

"You said it," I said, stroking the soft leaden sides of my creation. "I can't get anyone to invest in it, Miss Flume."

She straightened her eyebrow in the mirror. "I hear that you're a sort of a nut," she said.

I put my invention back into my pocket. "Why should anyone think that?"

"You act like a nut. I really think you do."

"Because I don't have a regular job, I suppose?" I adjusted my dropseat in the mirror.

"You're in some kind of racket, aren't you?"

"I don't think so. Maybe I did a couple, well, things to get enough together to buy The Golden Vanity. I never took anything from the rich."

"Let's go over to my apartment. It's too noisy to talk here."

"You've still got two unplayed nickels in the juke."

"Pay my drinks, will you please, Al?"

I paid her drinks. We took a cab and skimmed over the bridge to Weehawken. She lived with her mother, a very quiet old lady who was sleeping off a drunk in the self-serve elevator. "Shouldn't we lug her in?" I asked, starting to shove an arm under her shrivelled shoulders.

"No, she'll be all right there. Sit down over here on the love-seat while I slip into some more comfortable clothes," Tranquil directed.

I filled my pipe. I tapped it out and filled it again. There was a chow pup playing around my shoelaces and I said something to it in a low voice. It ran yelping out of the room—a trick I picked up when I was selling Fuller brushes.

I walked over and opened the top drawer of the desk. It stuck a little and I rubbed the runners with vaseline. It was full of coconuts.

An involuntary whistle thrished out of my half-parted lips. Two grown chows stalked into the room and grabbed me by either leg. I said something to them in a low voice which rattled the pictures in their frames. The old Flume came in and said, "We'll have no such language around here, young man."

"Tell me something, granny," I said—"Where's your comfort station here?"

She told me and I shuffled off, filled the tub with water, and plunged my legs in. Neither chow could swim but still I had a devil of a time keeping their heads under. Dogs, I found, are harder than people to resuscitate—ribs in plenty, have they got; and their small when wet is not at all to my taste. But I got them round, pippo, pippo, wrapped them in soft St. Regis towels, and laid them in the hamper to dry. Knots—I hope whoever found the pair, was good at untying them.

"I thought you'd gone home," Tranquil said, straightening her eyebrow in the mirror.

"No, I got some business to bring up," I said, standing in back of her and taking another little peek under my dropseat.

"I'll bet you have," she said, throwing her arms around my soft neck.

"You certainly got into comfortable clothes all right," I told her. "They go nicely with your flesh-tint stockings."

"*I* have no hose on," she said.

We laughed good-naturedly at her little sally. "How do you feel about coming along on my yacht?" I asked. It seemed to me that the pain in my forehead was worse than it had been for some time. Headache pills, one hundred for as little as nineteen cents in most cut-rates, upset my nervous system to an alarming extent; and I felt, anyway, that I should fight it out with whatever native resources were left me—after that accident, that sort of murder, you might say. Not confused, but too clear. Though she did hate me—before God! there was something to be said for my side of it. Incest, eh?—the nerve, the sheer, vomiting nerve of that woman. La! La! La! wife of my body—give her that oh you can grant she

IT RUNS IT FL YS IT WEEPS I T LAUGHS IT WANTS TO T OUCH YOU

made me crazy once . . . breasts like white crying birds, etc. Is that an angel at the door?

IS THAT AN ANGEL AT THE DOOR!

"I think I'd like to come," Tranquil said. "It might be a lot of fun—though I still believe there's an awful lot of the nut in your make-up."

I pressed my mouth on her full, warm lips. "Pier 23," I said huskily, wishing that all of my pieces were not trying to tear away from me at once. "Next Thursday evening at seven."

"What's that pier again? I've often thought I'd be better off dead."

"Pier 23. And now I really must take my leave of you," I said, casting a last look into the mirror. Who is that? What is that strange face that stares back at me? in this room, in this world so unshielded and full of terror for those pitiful creatures who scream into the dark as I am screaming now—

—when the scales fall from our eyes and we see what is really being prepared on that far dear bright horizon

—when whimperwilllesses call and evening is nigh—

"Does the 8th Avenue subway have a stop at 68 Street?"

"I wouldn't know."

"Well, thanks again. I'll see you next Friday at seven," I said, opening the door and glancing quickly up and down the hall. A parlormaid was showing Life to a small boy near the rubber plant that stood in a stuccoed recess near 4D.

IT TASTES OF WATER IT SM ELLS OF EART H IT BURNS I T IS COLD

DARK WING S CARRY O FF THE SKY

"I thought you said Tuesday," Tranquil exclaimed impetuously, as she removed a breadcrumb from her tiny pink button.

But I was already in the elevator. "Sleep peacefully, little mother," I said softly, as I reached the lobby; but she did not stir, though two bluebottles were finding her shrunken nostrils a cave more delightful than Plato's.

Softly humming 'An Old Flume Never Dies' I stepped out into the snowstorm. Immediately a large blue akernovir fell into step at my side. Parachutes were descending silkily all around us. What artillery there was, seemed to be concentrated across the river. However, a huge pit had been dug and, a neon cross soaring at its brink, thousands of poor bastards crouched there—speechless —"GOD IS NOT THE GOD OF THE DEAD, BUT OF THE LIVING,"

79

Jesus had said.—("Foxes have holes, and birds of the air have nests; but the sons of men have not where to lay their heads.") Louie, the angel said: Convicted on the evidence, as you know, having murdered some of them yourselves, you soldiers 'of a just cause,' you bearers of the horrible steel shit of civilization, you wielders of Phosphorus Fire and your beautiful Flame Throwers—

First citizen: "Send up the white flag!"

Second citizen: "Renounce your rights as members of the human race."

First citizen: "Admit it! Say you've resigned, seceded, turned in your card, washed your hands of the whole business of trying to live as human beings on this earth—"

Third citizen: "God knows we surrender."

Second citizen: "See! that's our emblem, the white one, the one that says We've had enough, Take the damn thing over, Line us up and shoot us now!"

First citizen: "Come on, let the apes assume control! Elect a chimpanzee to the White House! Turn the Foreign Office over to a nice mild-mannered hyena . . ."

There was a little man on the edge of the pit drawing a cow on a battered slate. While I watched, he put a little tree and a pretty yellow wagon in—made a lane and put a farmer carrying a sunflower on it. Then he set a bird in the tree and gave the farmer a quaint little wife.

"How'd you know it was a yellow wagon?" he asked me. His clothes were very tattered, his cheeks sunken in from lack of food—the sort of fellow you'd trust anywhere.

"No other color would do at all," I told him, jumping out of the way of three Marines who were bayonetting an old woman in a flowered shawl. "How'd you like to have dinner with me?"

"Fine. I'd like that fine," he answered. "Are there any good sea-food places in this neighborhood?"

"We can look," I said, helping him sponge the slate clean with a rag dipped in the street. "So you're a sea-food fan, eh?"

"I certainly am. Good of you to want to buy me a meal—I haven't eaten since the 18th."

"What's today?"

"I don't know."

"How come you remember the 18th?"

"Something very strange happened that day."

"Yeah?"

"Yeah, I was passing a big apartment house and I hear this woman scream—so I shinny-up the fire escape, and there's a man just wiping a razor-blade off on the whitest pants I ever saw in my life. This looks like their oysters might be fresh."

"After you."

"No, after you, sir—You're the host."

"All right, since you insist."

We found a table and gave our orders to the slightly boiled waiter. "Say, I'd like to lend you five bucks or so, Mr.—er?"

"$10,000."

"Well . . . I don't think I have that much on me. You see, I just finished paying for a yacht and—"

"Oh, no. You got me all wrong."

"Your oyrsters, monsieur—and yours, the hambug with the Bermudas, right?"

"This gentleman gets the oyrsters—the fellah there."

"Look, pal—I know who ordered the oyrsters. You eat them goddam bivalves or I'll ram them down your troat, see!"

"All right," I said. "All right—just take your thumb out of the sauce and I'll fall to. Anything to oblige a stinking rum-pot, I always say."

"That's better. Bon appêtit, monsieur."

"Gesundheit, my hearty. You were saying, Mr.—?"

"$10,000."

"Look, five dollars, it's a pleasure, a balm to my conscience—"

"But that's my name, I tell you! Ikey $10,000."

"Oh, I see. How's that hamburg?"

"I hate hamburgs!"

"Well, don't let on to monsieur. He's right over there grinning away everytime I swallow one of these monstrous little flabs of toad bait." I tightened my necktie, hoping the pressure would sort of convulvulate them down.

"Gee! And I love oysters so!"

"Too bad, Ikey. How would you like to leave this world with me?"

"Nah,—hell, maybe I haven't got much. A dream of a little rabbit farm . . . of the warm, close embrace of a pure woman—"

"Ready for your desert?" spifferoo said, putting a huge slab of mince pie down in front of me.

"I'll tell the world—Now a nice cuppa coffee, can you? you got it? The coffee for him—for me, a clean glassa milk." Then I stared hard across the table . . .

"What did the murderer look like, Mr. $10,000?"

"You've got me there. I'd prefer milk."

"Have I? I know you would."

The waiter put the coffee down in front of $10,000, the milk down in front of me, and a couple inches ketchup on my pie.

"That's right, isn't it, monsieur?" I nodded and he said to my unhappy guest: "Isn't that the way you heard him order, sir?" He handed me the check.

Mr. $10,000 sighed. "Yes, that's the way he ordered. Where you going in The Golden Vanity?"

"I don't remember telling you the name of my boat," I said, trying to maneuver the ketchup into my caries without remarkable success. "What happened to your slate?"

"What slate?"

I lowered my eyes to the check. A neat, even hand had written across it: Your 'friend' has a gun levelled at you under the table. Excuse yourself—there's a window in the men's room you can drop down into the alley through.

"Pardon me, I'm sure, Mr. $10,000,000, nature calls." My detachable frownbox jerked like a board you kick out of the way in a lumberyard.

"That fin—"

"Where?" (Why not a shark?)

"The five bucks."

"Oh, sure." I took it out and handed it to him.

"This is your yacht license."

"Oh, sure." I took it back and handed him a ten. "I'll give you the rest when I come out, $10,000."

He grinned. "That's a lot of money, Mac."

I barged into that men's room with such a bang that four squirts lined up at the stalls gave each other a busy few seconds there. The window was closed. I went through it. The dictionary tells us that tar is 'a dark, viscid, oily liquid obtained from resinous woods, coal, etc.' Now, though my scholarship may be a bit flea-bitten in spots, I am sure that the author of these glowing words never dove headfirst into a barrel of this particular substance. And I am also sure that not many authors, of any degree, have experienced the curious bliss of being the target—while yet encased in this same dark, viscid etc. concoction of man's ingenuity to man—the dumb, inarticulate target of a full pillow case of mouldy henfeathers.

Home again, I went after it. Fanny Tickle, a fine little papoose clinging with both chubby fists to her shoulder-blades, made a plaster of flour and glazed dill seeds and applied it liberally all over my shameful shell. Within two hours, and I had the radio for distraction, there was a sort of popping sound all over me and the whole blame mess simply cracked off nearly taking with it what our statues are accustomed to have a figleaf conceal. After I had kicked the radio to pieces I hurried absent-mindedly into my clothes and went out and bought 42 lbs. of laxatives, which I took at once. It's the glaze on the dill does it—an old Indian remedy, alone worth the price of Mannahatta Island.

At this point Mike walked in with my breakfast on a tray. "You look pretty tired, Mikie-boy."

He poured a jigger of maple syrup into my orange juice. "Yeah, they had me strung up by the toes to a rafter all last night."

"I knew you reminded me of something," I said, breaking an egg into the toaster.

"You mean a raccoon?"

We laughed together in heavy-hearted abandon.

"Yeah, the circles did run up around your eyes," I said. "Clear out now, all of you, I want to think."

I suppose I was not always what you call a Christian gentleman. My childhood filled me with dismay. I knew that Illinois was one of the richest and finest states in the Union; my father seldom said anything around the house, serving nearly twenty years in Sing-Sing for writing an out-spoken letter to a Rear-Admiral. Mother had her points, never being able to get her weight up above sixty pounds. My brothers and sisters perished when someone carelessly left all the gas-jets open on the kitchen stove.

There were fields and rivers, barns, fascinating junkyards—My little pals and I seemed to have everything to live for. Then—I think we're all agreed on this—just nobody seemed to believe in God anymore. The American sickness, one historian called it. Even our textbooks filled up with profane accounts of really wicked, monstrous events. Hardly anyone ever looked at a tree. Women were gawked at for what they had on not in. I exercised my drop-seat and waited. Even then I might have remained in that great, inarticulate herd whose backs and spirits are broken under the wheel, had I not one day walked into the hills.

The sun was shining. The air was pure and sweet. I went into a farmhouse and filled my fountain pen. Only the daughter was home. She had black hair and beedy little sow's eyes but her figure was something else again. Panting, I got up from my churning—"There's enough for both sides of your bread"—and she said, "I could learn to love a man like you, sir." I felt a sudden pressure on my wrist, a fog before my eyes, a lump in my throat, and a desire to put my arms around someone: so I took my watch off, wiped my glasses clean, swallowed my tobacco, and met her father at the door with a half-nelson which must have startled the old boy quite silly for he was never seen in those parts again. We wrapped the butter carefully in wet leaves and, digging a deep hole in the ground near the chicken-run, buried it against St. Walbert's Day —an event of no little local significance. "I'll remember, n'fear, my sweet," I called back cheerfully, as I made my way through the steaming patties which, in ever increasing numbers, dotted the pasture. To the wall-eyed bull: "I'd lay off the radio for a while, if I were you."

A goldfinch up in a big sycamore complained—to all who would listen—of an unusually severe toothache.

Fourth citizen: "Life is made up of over-lapping areas of consciousness. Kinging the soap or soaping the king, somewhere that goes into the record straight."

Fifth citizen: "To want a good place to live in—not hanging out alone, moose-bottomed and gribbed at—not only men and women but Christ! an angel now and then."

Sixth citizen: "I don't know. It's hard for me. Just a 'funny' bastard—all his life crying down there in the brain of his gut. Proud! Godalmighty I'm too proud to just sit grinning on my damn tail while another human being turns his soul inside out."

"It's red, Mr. Best—covered with like tiny hairs on a screen—68c in Macy's basement—sort of an awful jelly business," the farmer's daughter yelled.

"Don't you fret, pet. I'll tell them to stamp PERISHABLE all over it." Damn! you miss one and you step in two!

"But it's not perishable, Mr. Best."

"I know, I know, but just remember that somewhere we may have an everlasting use too."

The old man walked down the path and told me to come out of hiding. You are a nobody, a freak, a pathetic little weeping-stock, lost, already forgotten, as it has spent all meaning, as the words and the quick flesh draw farther apart—

"I'm afraid I don't follow."

—plunge through the net, break into the light—Stop writing books

"But I've never even read one." This, of course, happened some time ago; when, you might almost say, I still had my innocence, and a little, yes, perhaps a little faith in something . . .

—try to feel your own heart beating in your chest, your own life in the living wonder of all creation—You are a liar, a thief, a winded ghost making empty sounds in a madhouse—

"I don't know why you talk to me if you think I'm as worthless as all that, sir." And I was down on my knees crying and all the light and stalking had their teeth in my life and I didn't know how I was going to get out I didn't know how I was going to control what was eating the sick oyster that squirmed in my head

—it is time that books began to whirl and dance—

"I thought you just said writing books was bad."

—I've changed my mind. It is time that books be allowed to OPEN INTO THE UNKNOWN—

"What, sir, does that mean?"

—books must be allowed to get out of hand, to wander off on their own account—

"Help me not to be a cheat. I'd like to take all the poor devils in the world in my arms and be able to give them something, some real food, some stuff that has the stink and the painful wonder of being alive in it—Even the crude drawing of a cow—"

—man must be made to understand that all the gates are still open, that all the Wild and Beautiful are beckoning him <u>now</u> . . . a flower, a girl, a star . . . be hushed in that wonder—

"My trouble in the world is inside, not out at all. Something inside myself has damaged me."

—kneel to the Blakes & the Shakespeares—There is one king on this earth, and that king is the poet—

"Pray for me, Father . . . for I am without an animal to live in."

—be as children again.

"I laugh, I weep, Father."

—BE AS CHILDREN AGAIN!

"The world is dying around us."

—then leave the world which has—O my children have been made to murder one another; they have been driven mad—

"A flower, God—a girl, a star."

—and I am crying too.

Well, that's enough for now. I got to go take me a look around. Who knows, I may be missing a few tricks—Besides, my fanny's had enough work-out for one day.

☆ ★ ☆ ★ ☆ ★ ☆ ★ ☆ ★ ☆

Put this book aside a couple hours and go out and do something nice for somebody.

★ ☆ ★ ☆ ★ ☆ ★ ☆ ★ ☆ ★

He had a blue eye on the right side of his head. On the left side he had another eye. It was blue too. Sticking out of the middle of his face was a nose, and below it was a mouth. Inside his mouth he had twenty-seven teeth. Twenty-one of these were his own, eight were not—or false, as we've come to know them. His neck was set on two shoulders, one on either side—standard equipment in this country. Below his left shoulder, on his left side, that is, dangled his left arm; below his right shoulder, directly opposite, but on his right side, should have dangled another arm—his right, so to speak—only now he was jerking away with it—

Hurrah! Hurrah! I'm going off! he cried.

My companion and I passed him without a glance, since we couldn't help staring. I should think he could find a more appropriate place to do that, my companion, a small man in a duck hunter's uniform, said.

What's down there? I asked, pointing in the direction of the horizon.

The wharf. Why?

Woof. Acquainted down there?

Where?

Oh, I don't know—pick any place you like.

You mean down there at the wharf?

Woof.

Well, I know one classy little numbah.

Among her acquaintances does she numbah a friend, now?

But my sidekick, looking wondrously keen in his foul-hunting garb, was gazing back up the street through which we had so lately walked. Yeah, he declared, fondling the word as he did all words having four letters, that little laddio finally did go off.

And even as he spoke, the antiquated aircraft zirred over our heads.

Damn! a very sour-looking old party remarked, shaking her fist up at the ancient eggcrate. Right splunk on my new hat!

You're lucky it was fresh, my hippunt advised her, moving to help her wipe it off.

Keep your hands off me, you . . . you poolhall shiek!

Ta da da da da, I volunteered, getting some nice buttock-swing into it.

Why do you have to butt in? she demanded, experiencing a

slight twinge in the side which had been giving her no end of trouble since 'way last Spring at Mabel's Bundles for Mississippi affair.

Buttock in, I said with a chuckle that almost broke my fortitude of an intestinal nature, because on her the advice was well taken.

Let's get on down to that wharfhouse, my companion said.

Oh! she cried. Masquerading as a duck hunter! Why, I'll bet you're one of those procurers.

A pimp'll stain the chin of decency every time, I said, turning to watch a giant fellow with a black beard trying to jump out of the way of a horse which had to go.

So I didn't bag any ducks—what does that prove! my friend retorted heatedly. I had a duck, you could have both of them.

What do you mean, both of them? she just couldn't help asking.

The goose too!—And he proved half his point.

Well, when the excitement was over—and if you don't think there was excitement when the big lad with the beard got jostled in under the horse!—I said to my companion, Reminds me of some fellows I heard about on the desert who couldn't make water for fifteen days.

Sad seeing a grown man crying right out in public like that, he agreed, pulling me back out of the path of a runaway baby carriage which was headed for the river.

The first house we tried on the wharf was torn down. A man who would be sixty-two come next August was frying cabbage in a ten-inch skillet right where the piano used to sit.

Do they think they can bring it around? my companion asked an old maid with a long chin whisker.

It? There were three in that buggy—two girls and one of the other kind, she said, waggling her brush gravely.

Well, do they think they can bring the triplets around, Miss Fuller?

They're not triplets—only the two sisters were related. But heavens! Who ever told you my name was Fuller?

Is it?

Why, yes—it is.

B-l-l-l-l-l-ll my companion said, making a face like a critic.

I noticed that all the tires on the perambulator were of good, fresh, new, live rubber—and I also noticed a brewer's wagon pulling in at the curb right behind Miss Fuller who was telling one of the policemen all about that dreadful Maggie Sharp—Why, do you know last Saturday night I saw her going—

The cop got out of the way in time.

It had grown colder and the brown, squigly tugs on the river looked like coughdrops which the gray mouth of the sky was sucking peevishly up out of sight. The shabby houses, their eaves beginning to drip an idiot's sweat down into the street, seemed like quiet old men staring into the drawn revolvers of their sons. My companion, his wooden leg caught in a subway grating, was emptying his rifle into a gay throng of late-afternoon shoppers. Two tow-heads were scuttling in and out of a row of garbage cans on the corner, miniature flame-throwers held confidently in their chubby little fists.

I went into a lunch wagon and ordered a hamburger on white roll. When Tony brought my order I took off the top part of the roll and laid it on the side of the plate. I smeared an eighth of an inch of mustard on one half of the hamburger, then covered the other half with ketchup. I hiked up my sleeves and haunched forward on the stool. In doing this I twisted my shorts. I put salt on the hamburger and pulled a napkin out of the napkin dispenser; then I pulled my belly in and slid my hand down inside my shorts and made the adjustment.

Why don't you left it alone for a while? Tony asked, cutting his fingernails into a caldron of spaghetti soup.

I chose to think Tony was a lump on the wall. It could have

made better hamburgers, at that. But after a few minutes and the night coming down and the whole damn sadness and wonder of it, I said,

Tony, what do you think the score is?

He put the greasy hair and the moles with the hands under them on the counter and sucked a piece of ravioli out of his wisdom tooth. You ask me it stinks, he said.

All right, draw one, I said. Medium.

I filled a spoon twice with sugar, each time tipping it at a sharp angle over the cup. You should have had that tom altered, I said.

Tom who? Tony said.

The one who sleeps on top of the coffee urn, I told him. How much?

Fifteen.

I put a quarter on the counter.

He rang it up and slapped two nickels down.

Oh, yeah—give me a pack of Camels.

He slid the door back and reached in and took out a pack of Luckies.

Camels—that was Camels I wanted.

Huh-uh.

Well good God you got two big stacks right there in the case! You don't want Cherstefeds?

Oh—all right.

He plunked the Luckies down and slid the door shut.

These aren't Cherstefeds.

You want or don't?

I put another quarter down and he scooped it up with the two nickles.

Take it out of the quarter.

He put the two nickles in one trough and the quarter in another; then he dug up a dime, a nickle and three pennies and banged them down on the counter.

One other thing, Tony, I said.—Matches.

No matches.

I picked all of the change up except a penny.

Tony took a book of matches out of his shirt pocket and held it out.

I thought for a minute there you were going to give me tha shirt, I said, taking the book out and using one of its two matches to light my cigarette.

The street, its blood and guts of traffic and people snarling this way and that, looked as though a good spew might do it good. I slouched in the doorway of a pawnshop and thought, Well— here I am, and there they are.

I'll never live another life.

A taxi driver got out and came round and said, Keep looking at me. Give me a match.

I gave him the match. What's up?

Fellah in my cab, see, tells me to stop by the cornah. 'Nother fellah comes up to this first fellah and says he's down in that dog-wagon middle the block. Then I pull up here, see, an' I'm watchin'. When you come out, I know it's you, see, they're after. They're right acrost the street now. Ask me some direction. How you get somewheres, see.

Say, thanks—but what the hell . . . that direction business . . . they can't hear us across the street there.

Yeah, yeah, I know—but make it real-like. They should smell something, you're a dead pigeon. The fellah with the shiny black tie's a junkie, see—doped to the gills.

All right. How do you get to LeVarnge and Temple?

You mean the cornah of LeVargne and Temple?

That's it.

IRT or BMT?

You tell me.

Near the river?

All right.

East?

Depends on which river you mean.

I mean, what river?

Let's see . . . the Harlem river. How's that?

You wanta go LeVargne and Temple. On the cornah, right?

Right.

Funny thing.

What is?

I been cabbin' almost twenty years now, see.

So?

I never heard of no LeVargne and Temple.

I never did either until six years ago.

You sure that's Manhattan?

Look, Mac, we can't keep this direction stuff up all night. You're a sweet boy to want to help me out, but a funny thing—I don't see anybody with a shiny black tie across the street. In fact, I don't see anybody standing across the street except a policeman who's watching over to get your reaction when you see the ticket —or, then again, let's look at it another way: Maybe that isn't a traffic ticket at all.

What are you talking about? He took the little square of paper from me and shoved it into his pocket.

Don't you want to know if the prints check? (I had been absently picking my teeth with the ticket.)

I don't get you, Jack.

That's right. You don't get me. Stalling around with that crap about finding someplace—All I wonder is how that beetle-brow at the hamburg joint got word to you—Mr. C. F. Lemson, Plain Clothes Division No. 10, Shield No. 5076943Y!

. . .Oh! he exclaimed, drawing back as though with shock and consternation.

I knew there was something funny when you didn't throw that

matchbook away, I said, staring into his fierce, narrow-set eyes with their lashes which were like so many little cell bars giving him a very ordinary human look.

But how! How!

Because when I gave you that book there was only one match left in it—in the back row, four in from the right side—and you lighted that three-for-seven-cent cigar with that match, I said, giving anything for sight of a brewer's horse clumping in beside him at the curb.

I paid two-bits for this cigar, he said with as much dignity as he could command—which wasn't much.

Now, one other thing and I'll let you go. Think back six years ago, Busy Lemson.

I see . . . I see a classy babe with red hair in Morganstown.

Try Omaha.

I didn't get much there.

You got me.

Huh?

March 7—try that. Remember the fellow you nabbed with the beanshooter across from the Union Club?

Sure, but—hell that crumbbun was two good feet taller than you, and besides he had sorta bluish hair.

Cheap dye. I wanted purple, I said, taking off my left shoe and diving up and down a few steps.

Stilts he wears! he exclaimed, backing into a small boy who was lapping a huge lollipop.

I hope you're not ticklish, I said, leaning on his shoulder to get my shoe on. Now! am I the same crumbbun or not?

You're the same crumbbun all right, he said, trying to fend the little streetwaif off. Get away, I tell you! Go find a nice quiet kindergarten to disrupt.

And where is the Union Club in Omaha? I asked.

On the corner of LeVargne and Temple! we chanted together.

At that moment a Rolls Royce slid in at the curb and a chauffeur got out and helped a heavy-set old institution alight and the pair of them made for the small fry. Algernon, what are you weeping for? the old institution inquired solicitously.

The little boy buried his face in Busy Lemson's leg. This stupid big sonofabitch has my lollipop stuck to his can, he said through his sharp little teeth.

How many times has mama cautioned you against slang, Algernon? That's cheap, the institution said. This gentleman has your lollipop affixed to his arse.

I walked up on the porch of a vine-covered house and knocked. The door was immediately opened by a young woman. She was dressed in the clothes she had come into the world in and her hands were cupped lovingly over two pretty little melons.

Make yourself at home while I put something on, she said.

Thanks, I will, I said, taking a knife from the sideboard and cutting one of the melons in two. While I ate one of the halves I looked around me; while I ate the other half I looked around a man who had crawled out from under the sofa with a harenet gripped firmly in his teeth—to his left there was a terra cotta statue representing virtue threatened in the persons of two rather wall-eyed looking creatures who were selling it dearly to what appeared to be a small cow with spavins but was probably intended as an unloved mastiff or wild boar since the almost-touching figures stood on a dusty base upon whose tarnished plaque could still be discerned the words Barbary Coast Idyl; and to his right there was a row of kitchen chairs stretching all the way out to the battered pair of boots on the top step of the cellarway, three fat dictionaries piled one on top of the other on the first chair—making the engine. The man put the rabbit into a horseshoe box which he carried for just that purpcse. I find them everywhere, he said with a lisp, taking a medicine-dropper out of the violin-case which his assistant handed him.

Do you feed it with that? I heard myself asking him, because I listened when I said it.

Breed, he said.

I am, I told him, taking another deep one.

The artificial type insemination, the assistant said, taking a bowl

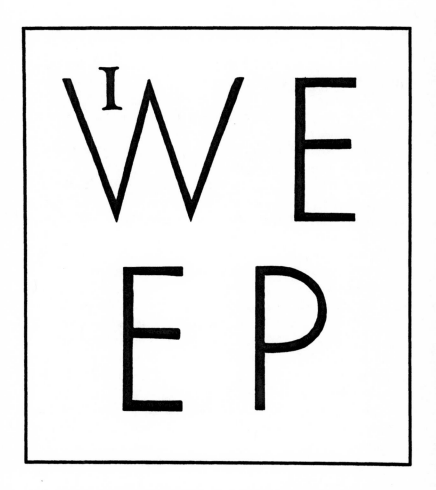

of cream away from the orange cat and drinking it—the cream.

Oh, I thought he was lisping, I shouted, hoping the neighbors would be frightened half out of their wits.

I was, the man declared, using the dropper on the rabbit—I heard every word you said.

Ah, hell, I never have any fun, the rabbit said, hardly making herself heard above the toot-tooting of the dictionaries in their shrill Moroccan accents.

The man took a handful of loose cigarettes out of his pocket. Let me have your silver cigarette case and I'll put these Chesterfields in it, he said.

Oh, no you don't, I said. You don't get my prints so easy this trip, Mr. C. F. Lem—

I know, I know, he said, slipping his face off with a gesture of disgust. But what put you wise this time?

I turned the face over idly with my foot, waiting for the assistant to get the gesture of disgust settled in the case with the machinegun; then I said, That was simple, Clem, old boy—the Chesterfields did it.

He rolled them about in his gloved hand, his ring pressing up like a cruel noose amongst the rigid corpses of the white little dolls in their pristine dresses which fitted over their tobaccoatedness like so many adjectives seeking a sentence to nibble the heart out of.

Yes, I said, cleverly knitting the dialogue together—I knew that you were trying to disguise your true identity from me when you didn't pronounce it as would be normal for you to pronounce it. Say Chesterfield! I barked at him, sending the orange cat up the lamp-standard.

Cherstefed, he said, his ears twiching idiotically as the nap of the rug tickled them with the almost imperceptible rise and fall of its snoring.

I took the racoon cap off the assistant. And as for you, I said, those big feet of yours have got policemen written all over them.

Chagrinedly he settled the cap over his purplish hair, which was cut in the form of a star and had his shield number tattooed on the bump left by brainfever the day it tore out to enroll itself for unemployment insurance: I tell the missus somebody'll notice it. She never could write small like other dames.

Notice it! Why you look like two billboards walking around

looking for a little lot to settle on, I said, trying to keep my voice down—for I was crawling along the ceiling after the cat.

A little lot of what?

A little lot of s and three other letters, I said, having a rose tear out of the wallpaper under my clutching fingers. And when you do find that sandlot, I hope you bump into Algernon eating a big prickly pear.

If its only sand you meant, why the s and three other letters business? Lemson asked.

Just a habit of mine, I said.

Do you think there's any real hope for the world? he persisted.

I do, I said, dropping the kitten down onto the studio couch. Sometimes I feel so good just being alive that I want to kiss the first person I meet.

The young woman chose that moment to walk in. Her mouth tasted of April flowers and Kolynos. Lemson and the cop started out. Don't forget Tony, I called after them.

How'd you know! the rabbit exclaimed, slipping its face off with a hairy hand and climbing out of the basket.

I knew no self-respecting rabbit'd have ravioli on its breath, I said, picking the two faces up and tossing them out of the window. Somebody's wives are in for a little surprise, I continued, as the masks settled on two passers-by.

Ah, go f and three other letters yourself, Lemson said, leading the three of them out.

But I can't fool myself all of the time, I retorted, remembering what the king had said when the stableboy asked to go to the beheading because his grandmother was sick.

Why did you say leading three out? the young lady asked. I only saw three all told.

That's all you were meant to see, I told her—and its lucky for your sanity that you couldn't see the other one.

Then, as the kitten gave a startled little yelp, I turned her over on the studio couch and spread her legs wide. Her belly felt warm and inviting under my fingers. I found a tiny clump of silky hair and tugged gently.

The girl came over to stand beside me. How'd Hester get ink all over her?

Who Hester? I asked, letting the cat up.

Why, the kitten, stupid, she said, lifting it into her arms and rubbing it over with a handkerchief.

As I put my hat on I noticed a red stain creeping down the window. Thanks for the melon, I said.

What's the matter? Why go now? I figured we'd have a nice supper and you might want to stay here tonight, she said.

I've been called stupid too many times for one day, I said, opening the front door.

Oh, don't act like a bad-natured child! Sit down while I put the chops on.

What kind of chops?

Lamb chops.

Any broccoli?

No-o—but I think there's a couple cans of spinach.

I don't like iodine on my food.

Well, how would it be I make some shoestring potatoes?

Nice.

All right, I'll put my apron on.

You're sure, no broccoli?

I'm positive. Ed doesn't like it.

Ed who?

My husband.

Where's he?

I don't know.

You don't know?

Yes—She started to cry—He just goes off.

You're getting your nose red. Where's he go?

HOW THREADBARE THESE STUPID DISGUISES..

Drinking.
A boozer, huh? How long's he been off this trip?
Almost a week.
What's par?
I don't know what you mean.
What's about how long he usually stays on these trips of his?
Maybe three—four.
Weeks?
Yes.
And you sorta have men stay over to break the monotony like?
No! No! I never did this before.

We'd all better begin to think pretty hard about saving man
from himself.

I don't know what you mean.

Skip it. And I suddenly shouted, Hey, Ed!

What?—Quick as a flash from the back of the house.

But . . . but how did you know? the young woman demanded, cutting her crying off short.

The shoes at the head of the cellar steps, I explained, patting her cheek and peeking down her bodice.

But you didn't go out there.

That's right. I didn't go out there.

Then how could you tell that Ed was home just because of some shoes on the cellar steps?

Because I could smell them, I said. And a cold shoe never smelled like that. Ed just had to be around somewhere near because those were what I call the five-minute shoe.

Five-minute shoe?

Yeah—ten at the outside. Somebody had had those shoes on his feet within that time. I opened the door and stepped out on the porch. Then I opened it again and stepped back into the room.

An old woman looked up from her knitting and said, What do you mean breaking in here like this, young man?

Excuse me kindly, lady, I said, and stepped back out on the porch.

I'd never seen that room before.

A star was sitting up in the sky. Somehow it took all the breath out of me—that star did. I sat down on the topstep and thought all right you sit up there and I sit down here but—

Here's your supper.

It was Ed with a big plate of steaming food on a rusted tin tray. I said, What the hell!

He said, What do you mean, what the hell? Eat these chops before they get cold.

An old lady, I said—You got an old lady living with you?

He put the tray on my knee. Here—you like more salt? some piccalilli?

An old lady knitting a sweater like?

No! Christamighty, no! Eat them goddam chops or I'll stuff them down your troat! Ed said emphatically, beating my chest with his clenched fist.

I just wondered, I said, starting to eat. It was a lovely sproth of a meal. The broccoli, I discovered, went surprisingly well with lambchops. Sighing gratefully, I took a long gulp of coffee—Poor Ed! And him in a new shirt with a smart black silk bowtie.

A voice—a veritable sproth of a voice, had that Ed. There's nothing like a bit of scalding coffee on a man's chest to get the phlegm up out of his lungs. Not that I thought the brew was poisoned—oh, not for a wee moment—IT WAS JUST THE WORST COFFEE I HAD EVER TASTED IN MY WHOLE LIFE ! !

Say! my book!—damn if I didn't almost forget my book!

Let's see what our little friends are up to now.

VIII, IX, & X

I suppose all this will pass away—Trinket, lips eyes teeth O baby baby—In that furious land, to EMERGE, "Come in and shut the grave after you—", to a brazen dog does one offer his sweetest purpose . . .

"Shouldn't you be in bed, Aloysius?"

Deliberately I raised my gaze. Phoebe Ann Nemophila stood in the doorway. The fingers of her hand! She lived near-neighbor to a man who worked in the telephone company. Her eyes were sienna in the weak-tea light. "I am writing a book," I told her. My spine tingled.

"You looked to me like you were falling asleep." She ran her longue, nervously, around her lips.

"Nodding—that's my second stage," I explained.

"Damn right," she said, opening the window. Milly, the gray bat, flew in and, taking enough space for her size, settled (a nice pet) down in it. <u>Phoebe Ann's fingers were quite spatulate.</u>

"Why'd they pick me to write a book?"

"Who?"

"They must be pretty hard-up for books."

"Who?"

"Have you seen Mr. Tiger recently?"

"No. Dolly Adams was talking about you to me yesterday."

"And?"

"She said she . . . well, I don't know . . . I never thought you were much one way or another."

I got stickily up from my desk. First thing tomorrow I'll change my shorts. "He picked me out of the crowd."

"Who?"

"Look, Phoebe, it's sad being a—O I'm on fire!—I feel like I want to make everybody look at me! Imagine—Jesus!—imagine having everybody in the world looking at you—all the eyes turned —in that one fixed minute—turned to look at you!"

"So?"

I bit my knuckle.

She said, "Aloysius, I think you're out of your socket. Of all the people to write a book—"

"To hell with writing books! I want some peace—I want to know why I—"

"Why you what?"

"A good book is like a tree. It sends its—"

"I know."

"It always comes back to the same thing."

"Have you got any white thread?"

"Top drawer. I can't get it out of my head that a lot of men— up in the morning bleary-eyed and dullfimented—with all the bittle and woosh, their voices saying, 'Thank you, a bit more goat milk, please.'—a lot of men as sure to die as me—"

"Lay it, Al."

104

"Well, they put together the New Testament."

"Mother phoned yesterday from Albany."

"Phoebe Ann—"

"Shoot."

"If anything happens to me . . . try to remember me for a while, will you? There's a good girl."

"Hell, Al, you're a friend of mine."

"But I mean on the level—No crap, Phoebe Ann. Maybe you see a fellow walk down the street—or a laugh—somebody kisses you—"

"What you mean, a laugh somebody kisses me?"

"I mean—Look, Phoebe, it's all beginning to sort of slip inside me. I can't see out of myself anymore. It's like I got a box sees and hears and smells for me—Where am I in all these pounds of meat? It's like everything is so public I can't go off anywhere to be alone. I feel like I had paint made of newspapers and automobiles and goddam factory windows smeared all over me—"

Louie: SHUT YOUR BIG MOUTH AND EITHER GET ON WITH THIS BOOK OR LET SOMEBODY ELSE GET ON WITH IT.

All right, Louie—Where's that aspirin bottle . . ? I decided since nobody here would buy my gadget that I would just get a yacht and sail off and find a market for it. Naturally somebody would have to write-up the trip—one of the most wonderful I ever heard of—but all the authors I telegraphed were either too busy or not interested enough to even accept the reverse charges, the bastards—

STOP BELLYACHING AND GET ON WITH IT.

So as luck would have it I met this old man up in the hills and he said to just sit down and tip my head forward about three inches and—

WE GOT THAT THE FIRST TIME.

And maybe after while I'd hit that current which runs through all human beings.

ALL RIGHT, ALL RIGHT . . . LET'S SEE YOU DO IT.

Fanny, Apollinaria, Ikey, Fitzmichael, Tranquility, Phoebe Ann—That's seven—

THAT'S SIX.

Six. And I want eight along—Oh, yes, Mr. Tiger and Dolly Adams—I'll sound them out tomorrow.

TONIGHT. YOU'RE LEAVING TOMORROW.

Thirty thousand—a pound apiece. I hope Mike got them on board all right.

THE SOUND AS OF A MILLION BEES FILLS THE HARBOR AND THEIR TINY WHITE FLAGS CLUTCH AT THE SKY LIKE THE DESPERATE HANDS OF THE DAMNED.

Maybe, Louie, you should be telling it. I didn't always live alone. In the days before my invention was perfected, I lived with my wife and ten children in a cold-water flat on Delancey Street. One night—I had spent the day in the park defleaing pigeons—I climbed our six rickety flights and entered upon a scene of unbelievable squalor and heartbreak. My oldest girl, Nan, blind since birth, was doing what she could to allay the suffering of my little brood. "Look, daddy," Tim crowed, "she's gone and drew a picher of a smoked turkey for us." His tiny claws closed and unclosed like talons. The smell of government-tinned beef and little boy and girl urine clung to everything—to the cheap muslin curtains to the rug with its threadbare pattern, to the stack of washboards and half-full tubs near my work table with its glistening chrome top and neatly arranged drills and hammers and sliderules and kenolating instruments. It actually looked more like a dropsical donkey, but their bony little chops were slavering anyway. "Didn't the Relief people show up today?" I asked, sitting down on my own special box and opening the bag of oranges which I had bought from the new greengrocer half a block from where the taxi had had a sudden fire in its upholstery. The language of those cabbies! serves them right they miss a fare now and then. "You know goddam well they didn't, you big slack-arsed baboon."

"You've talked yourself right out of any of these peels, Rubert," I said sternly, being careful to toss them out of his reach. None too bright anyway, getting a wheelchair with a flat tire to do more than circles was a bit too much for him. I munched slowly, carefully, spitting the riper of the seeds to the youngest—"Next time, Imorette, you'll maybe have sense enough to keep your eyes closed."—and then, like it must to all men, I reached the bottom of the bag. "Which reminds me, where's your maw tonight?" Nan pulled a pair of scissors out of Elkhorn's side before replying. And by then Wenbrod had already said, "Walking the street." Levitt

THIS ENFL
AMED AD
VENTURE

piped up, "A fat chance she's got—Unless maybe she meets somebody from a soap works." I banged him over the head with my walking-stick. It's gold crown fell off and lay like a smiling mushroom on the floor. "I'll have you know your mother was a pretty woman when I married her," I admonished.

Soon they were all peacefully asleep on the fire-escape. A blanket of silence, its gossamer weave gently caressing my taut eyelids like the tiny hands of a bread pudding, descended over our modest dwelling. Idly I watched the fleshy blossoms arrayed on the seats of the elevated which persued its silken way past the window. Almost soothing was the persistent drip-drip just over my head—the O'Levi's toilet-pipes still haven't been fixed, I thought absently—no wonder my cigar keeps going out.

I heard Nan's hesitant step on the stairs and went eagerly to the door. "No more beer until he gets something on the bill," she said, leaning weakly against the cabinet where I housed my collection of Yllinthan moths. "What about the watch? Didn't you offer him the watch?"—"He said a better watch in the city dump he could find."—"I'll dump him! Why, my grandfather won that watch for reading the best paper on animal husbandry at his Grange—that's no bull, either."

I crowded out on the fire escape. Rubert, weakest of the little flock, had been worked over so near the edge that even a gentle nudge would have sent him hurtling down into the street which crouched like a great dirty bear far below—its long snout of cars seeking out some new hideousness to sneeze down the neck of, its cruel electric eyes eagerly searching for someone weak and homeless and miserable that the little matter of gobbling him up might be got on with without delay. I had to Columbus the entire stretch of window boxes before finding what I wanted, which was eighteen quarts of Rhinegold, not too warm, not too bleeding cold. And nice yellow mouse cheese, dry salami, purple olives, and a mighty swell tin of Tigbe-Fosoan divided into compartments labeled Eat

Me For Love, Eat Me For Fame, and Eat Me For Perfect Elimination.

As I crawled back in I gave Rubert a gentle nudge. Nan was arranging her pillows in the big galvanized bathtub. Milly was swooping back and forth above the piles of dirty diapers. Thunder rumbled off to the West somewhere—over Omaha, more than likely. I felt suddenly old and useless. My dreams, where were they? I drank another bottle. Where was that pretty slip of a girl I had taken for better or worse till honoring and obeying do us part? Alone I stand on the teeming heath—and sure the things of this world do seem a bright tinsel, a set, now, of false teeth in the mouth of an idiot . . . I made my way to the hall and tried the door—The day I come out here in a hurry and find no one in I swear to God I'll drop dead in my tracks. "Stop yer muttering, ye stuffed excuse for a mon."—"And is that you, Mrs. Scanlon, bless yer heart? I'll count ten and if you're still squattin' in there a-readin' of last week's Daily News, expect this flimsy door around your ears, my swate lass, now."

Waiting there, my molars beginning to float, I remembered something that had happened to me in my middle teens. I had got me a job minding sheep in the uplands near the site of the famous Twaring-Wheel murders, which took place on July 29, 1831. I was fifteen at the time I am speaking of, alert, intelligent, fully cognizant of all the remarkable qualities with which my being was cluttered. Along a leafy, forest path, nonchalant with that nonchalance and blue funk which only youth is heir to, I sauntered, my long, rather flat feet stirring the red, neglected dust composed of shale and the countless bodies of Chipasaws which had once hunted the clumsy, peet-smelling bison and the great long-nosed tree-cow, docile when left to its own vices, a veritable kuzmagord when enraged, there.

Seventh citizen: "When you see your life again, ask it where you've been."

Eighth citizen: "A spray of roses . . . a dog with its muzzle lifted to the cold moon."

Louie: THE EYES OF TAXIDERMY ARE UPON YOU.

Third citizen: "Terrible fists stir in the blackened lanes. And Love and Pity and Honor—We awoke and found them a lie."

Hail to what is beautiful in this world!

When the day is too bad we are thankful for the power to sink to the ground and hear the green soup bubbling. At least, the fiery champions of the sky—A better sight, hurrah, harurrah, a better sight than all you laddios spiritually seeking out a bigger ass to kiss. Get down on your knees, you pale mournful bugs!

Awesomely lively—Only the dreamers know all the facts.

Her coat had no lining. She was sitting on a fallen tree, crying. I never thought my heart could turn to jello. The wind, it already loved her. It brought her milkweed pods that settled like obscure little faces into her hair. How fine and pure she was! The poor, I thought, must have all they want to eat now. Surely nowhere is there a man without a home. Death can only be alive out of this world. Two tunes, two songs in love, were her little breasts. I must really sound tetched—In the Beginning . . . oh! I regret how they murmur and stir in the rear seats there—have a thought (that strange flying wine) of how long your own particular Winter will last. Old furs drawing back to their first beasts—see It lifts its seething snout!

All right, I do hesitate. Tell them? Tell them not? How slow unhappiness is. And fear, how it enters at all your holes. You won't ever be able to go to sleep again. Because she was—

We'll walk around that, shall we? In the service of truth, but— a tip, anyway: never expect the "shining" of that head to be described while there are still some who believe in   at the Edge, at the Edge   well, I did warn you!

A short sentence gives variety.

How can it blur so!

Poor return [He sees how the food of trees would not fatten the most gluttonous goose. And the touching of the two sides of a road would make even the Emperor's hair stand on edge.]—O when do Joy and Love have their touching . . .

"Anything I can do to help?"

"Go away and leave me alone, alone."

"That's no way to talk, miss."

"I said go away and leave me alone."

"And I said that's no way to talk."

"Miss."

"Miss, what?"

"You said that's no way to talk, _miss_."

"All right—And you said go away and leave me alone, _alone_."

I have observed that people who are just getting acquainted have a tendency to speak rather circuitously—though God knows, later, and the leaves of the maple were turning a bright scarlet, Suzanne Horsegg and I always managed to get to the point without any delay whatever. But let me finish what I was saying about our first meeting—

Suzanne's pet crow, Ignatz, had wandered off into the heavy brush; and, despite her most impassioned pleas, that certain little so-and-so wouldn't have any of it. [This upset the character described as Susie (Danwillanne) Horsegg, unemployed seamstress, late of the house of R. Q. Constable, a prominent local banker.] I used the word so-and-so advisedly. In the first place, Ignatz—who made his reentry on the scene by sneaking up behind me as I was peering into a briary bush and, using only his beak . . . well, let it hang as high as ever you like, I'll never eat another one—this Ignatz was a bright orange in color. He had obviously been raised by the author of one of the more rarified tomes on the various instances of pathology in sex—a crow talk? I tell you, Ignatz was one of the great orators of our time.

Perhaps twenty minutes later—you understand that I had assured her that there was no danger at all that my sheep would wander too near the savage black cliff which gazed at us through the torn eye-sockets of the mist—or more accurately, thirty-five minutes later, a great cloud of white roses drifted down the side of the mountain and, tumbling-up like the dandruff of God, completely blanketed us. O then how we tossed and galaxied in that delightful confusion—Lo! melancholy's top did him a spinning there—Two babes writhing their couched skeletons, the ligaments of their howling legs setting all the divine strings arattle—Atrocious dalliance in that parody of heaven, that calendar whose every day was the Sun's—Bunching of those sweetest muscles . . . and then the kettledrums! that exquisite artillery going off in all our townships . . . ah, chipped indeed was the word methodist—Huzza! that jolly fever, that toss intense and "so very well suited to our dearest taste"—Bring here the lonely that this pomp may set the waters of the Spirit afoam in their veins—Leviathan's piling march ever out-summits the herring—Ah earth, the dear skill of your pairs . . . the merry clamoring identity of—Ignatz chose that particular moment to

MIKE'S GOT THE YACHT LOADED.

Okay, Louie. At any rate, I made almost twenty dollars that summer—exclusive of my board and found. Suzanne Horsegg is married to a letter-carrier out in McMinnville, Tennessee. Also, I apprehended the Twaring-Wheel murderer and the reward of five hundred thousand dollars went far to finance my education at the tracks. Old Smithie, the 127-year-old killer, crawled unassisted to The Chair. His plea was that he had only been trying to defend his virtue; and after seeing photos of Patience Twaring and Catherine Wheel, I, for one, believed him.

THEY ARE WAITING FOR YOU AT PIER 25.

Pier 27, Louie. I went to the nearest fire-box and turned in a six company alarm. While waiting I filled my pipe, removed my shoe, and taking a note out of my sock, managed to slip it into the back-

A LION IN
A BLOCK
O F I C E

pocket of a passing policeman. Puffing gently to get it going, I wondered if his wife would be able to convince him that she hadn't been meeting a certain Mr.— [Name deleted for obvious reasons.] in Rm. 6E of the Monteplarge Hotel every Wednesday night. At last the trucks came—how human beings can stand such racket! —the Commissioner himself, no less, herding his little fleet of fifty-one hook-n'-ladders, seventeen pulmotor brigades (complete with remegging apparatus), a score of emergency soup wagons, portable voting booths, and—"Who the goddam hell turned that alarum in!"—"I did, my Captain. To lose a moment time there is not." He grasped my shoulder warmly, his lighted cigar eating a neat hole therein.

GET DOWN TO THAT PIER!

"What pier?" the old fire-dog barked.

"Pier 26," I managed to say, my ears, half-maddened by the clamor of bells and military bands lately arrived, fluttering like wounded sparrows up at the level of the first-story windows.

PIER 28.

"The angel is always right," the Captain shouted, "men," tossing me up to the top rung of the tallest ladder.

What went wrong then I can only guess, but the next thing I knew that ladder had slipped its moorings and I was sailing briskly through the harsh, salt-lipped air. I landed with a plunsh on the bowsprit of a trim yacht of six hundred and nineteen tons, sixty-four acquminous feet at the water line, or Samuel Clemens, and an over-all length of fifty-one thousand marine rods. What I guess went wrong was, when that dumb Captain caught the little home-made bomb I tossed him, he just lost his head completely. I'll clean off that bowsprit in the morning, I thought, climbing down with the consciousness that navigation was a pretty knotty matter. Where was the stern?—I must say it all looked quite forboding in the dim glow cast by the riding lights of the battlefleet drawn-up there in the harbor. Larboard, starboard, first barsterd I see t'night—

Then, craftily cutting through the water toward me, sending silver dollars of foam into the soft pockets of the night, was a big sloop with WE'RE ONLY KIDDING painted in great dripping red letters on its prow; and chained amid-ships, howling like lost souls (to coin a phrase), were my little band of hearty adventurers—

Ninth citizen: "How various the wounds! Mark well the cruel beam upon these waters."

Tenth citizen: "Mistake not these shaggy tints for the colors which fill the brushes of men intent on providing you with entertainment."

Second citizen: "Behind this curtain—you are new to this game, aren't you?"

First citizen: "Of Life, even a hint—perhaps it is too late for that."

GET ON WITH IT.

"Aloysius, oh Aloysius, you got us on the wrong boat!"

"The women among us are threatened with a fate said to be worse than death!"

"And we men—a poet, a cheap little small-time crook, a capper for the Pepsi-Cola company, a detective, second-grade (this set me straight on Mr. Tiger anyway)—What will become of us at the hands of these brutal pirates!"

Their voices trailed off like flowers slipping down a sheep-dip chute—to be lost entirely in that moment when the whole fleet decided the courteous thing was to give a 41-gun salute to the presidential skiff, The Faymower, which had just hove in sight to my moonboard, or rear. I was particularly sorry to see what was happening to Dolly Adams, my favorite of all of them, a slim, conceited, coy little thing, the dial of whose watch told time in the dark—It's a fortunate circumstance for you that I can't lay my fist along your skull, you evil-looking, dark visaged cut-troat, you! And it didn't cheer me up any to remember that that poet-fellow Kell had never paid me for the copy of his book which I had allowed him to inscribe to me.

"Hey, Al! Over here! It's I, Mike! On the president's boat—yeah, yeah, I know, so I put your damn gadgets on the wrong—

TRANSFER THEM.

Mike tossed them over and I carried them down into the hold. The last twenty thousand must have weighed at least a pound and a half.

Wandering into the galley I met a Mrs. J—, who told me she was a best-selling novelist. She was upset to learn that her yacht was already well out to sea. She used rather unseemly language, I thought.

Her companion, a Colonel Caffarelli Pot, retired barrister and

115

active whiskeyist, tried to hit me with a chair.

Neither of them was interested in investing any money in my invention. Will the salt air affect them? I wondered, as I heard a chorus of shouts off on the black water somewhere.

It was a raft.

I turned the light on and helped them aboard.

Upon introduction, I learned that they were Catherine St. Maur, Mengs Flink, Thane Chillingsdale, Sally Garden, Abigail Buttermilk, and Little Remksheaffe.

I took a 'WNTTLFACIOMEO' [Reg. U. S. Pat. Off.] and put it up on a deck-table so they could see how it worked. Ah! that peaceful, contented humming sound—and up shot the proud little white flag!

The breeze, already of squall proportions, poked inquisitively through the rigging. The Flying Dutchman passed to windward, under forced sail.

('WNTTLFACIOMEO' stands for Why Not Try To Live For A Change Instead Of Murdering Each Other.)

We were off.

███████████████████

The starved fatness of the half-awake.

Drifting outline of gardens where no one ever thinks to walk.

Quaint—The house yellow, roof green. I smarted under a rather shallow mode of living. There really wasn't much depth to anything.

My hands, thoughts, dreams—empty.

After desire can possession rapturate? and childhood like fly-paper founders the lost seulf.

Everything has its own depth beyond us. A fragile sort of affair —squatting beside the lake and feeling each other over in accustomed despair. "Please don't muss my dress. Emmeline spent twenty minutes getting it to hang just right."

Emmy—long face pocked with domesticity, her body a bag

where she keeps old age burnished for longed-for and whining use
—Emmy, sister Emmy: 'dear Emmy.'

The unimmensity of the stuff we have to build lives out of!

I thought I would find scepticism agreeable at least, but I'll be cornswoggled it tries to punk you into the silliest conclusions. For instance,—That you and I can arrive at some common meeting-ground!

A radiance out of a colossal sympathy with each and every being that draws breath on this planet.

I haven't any bread I want your flesh to butter. Whimsy is always pretty desperate.

Facets—Gray (Cain) ice—The little bog laughed to see such sputum.

The Undisguised Prosecutor. Laughably indifferent. An intimate point of reparture. The dilemma is never clearly stated—adamite skeletons chummying at the gates. Edge of sense. Was the output of Belief seriously curtailed by the discovery that there is no plan to anything?—I'd rather add in clear recklessness than lie about a power that doesn't exist outside at all.

Supposing after the precautions have been taken, every sacrifice made—the long-awaited   Ah Christ I'd give it hell

cadence, rhythm, that hugeness . . . Damn it! Because I don't want to go around opening doors for you. Me first—I go in first. You can stay out for all I care. Cold eye on you. When you awake it may be too late. I know it will be moving away out of your reach all the time. And—last night they murdered her. Don't you want to have blood trickling out of your mouth too?

Three women wait beside the river. They are motionless. Their eyes are closed. They have yellow hats. Their hands are full of spiders.

A man gets out of his car at the corner. He runs up the steps of a house. His name is Tivcluf. There is no time to know this man Tivcluf.

Because—it doesn't do at all. You see, men build a lot of useless things. Does God? I think that really is the whole point. Does He? Ah it would help if we knew the answer to that . . .

I make a sound. It is a small sound. It is the sound of a man who weeps because he is afraid.

Let me sum up. Please listen they are soft and dead and heartless . . . these "works of art" done by blood-smeared toads! Now wait a minute I don't mean all of them but goddam I do mean most of them I mean that almost everybody has sold out. It's terrifying. Don't you think that every tick of the clock brings us nearer the time when if you speak of beauty and love and dignity no one will have the remotest idea what you're talking about. Do you?

SNOW FELL. GLOWING BIRTH

DAY CAKES PLOWED THROUG

H THE BLACK WATERS OF THE

RIVER. COLD, VACANT EYES L

OOKED DOWN. A BEGGAR ST

UMBLED INTO THE DOORWAY

OF A DARKENED BAKERY.

SNOW FELL. YOUNG MAN

UNDER STREETLIGHT. JUST ST

ANDING THERE. NOT WAITING

FOR ANYTHING. UNL

ESS YOU COUNT LIFE.

"HAVE YOU A MATCH?"

Don't you think we should all pour out into the streets yelling
Stop it! Stop it! You've no right to do this to us!

A little pause while you tear out into the street. That's the stuff!
A nice long letter to your congressman—a truly great spirit, your
representative in 'the citadel of Democracy.' Now a P.S.—(take it
down!)—"And He sends you His best too."

Can you? Of course you can! Look what you've already been
able to stomach . . .

A long way off—Yessiree! When we are lonely and afraid, who
comforts us? When we are trying to do a bit more than just 'skim
through' or 'get by,' who reaches out that old helping hand?
You're damn right! Your congressman . . .

Life out of a dirty window. The blasted dull jobs, the juiceless-

119

ness of our cities, our homes, our 'educations,' our bodies, our souls
—all colored by a love of everything cheap and vulgar and worthless, and by a bitter hatred of anything that is really valuable and
fine and <u>alive</u> . . . The bastards will finally get it squeezed out
enough that they can do anything the hell they want with you—

Aren't you even going to walk out into a field and look at the
trees and the flowers growing there—?

Have you ever thought about a flower?

What would it mean to you if all the flowers in the world were
to die?

Have you ever considered what a beautiful and wonderful
thing it is to be a human being?

"SURE, SURE. CHRIST I G
OT ALL THE MATCHES
YOU WANT." HE WAITED
FOR HER TO LIFT UP A CIGAR
ETTE. SHE DIDN'T. SHE PITCHED
ON HER FACE INTO A MOUND

OF SNOW. 'SHE'LL SMOTHER L
IKE THAT,' HE THOUGHT, AS
HE TURNED ON HIS HEEL AND
MADE OFF THROUGH THE WH
ITE CITY. FALLING SNOW, OF
COURSE, DOESN'T SMOTHER A
NYONE. SHE GOT UP AFTER A
BIT AND STOOD STARING HE
LPLESSLY INTO THE SKY.

Have you ever actually thought of what a strange thing it is to be alive?

Flowers must be happy.

God I've wished—I wish I could put it down as it is. All I've heard and seen—where these particular people were concerned

BUT THAT'S NOT IT AT ALL. What was said in a certain situation

—these things I know about

BUT THERE IS ONLY ONE SITUATION: BEING ALIVE. AND THAT IS ALWAYS THE SAME, FOR ALL OF US.

What was done on a certain day, in a certain town, by a particular man and woman

BUT THERE IS ONLY ONE THING FOR ANY OF US TO DO: AND THAT IS TO BE ALIVE. AND THAT IS ALWAYS THE SAME, FOR EACH AND EVERY ONE OF US.

A heap of bleached bones in the sun—A woman with a child in her arms—

—It goes away—
—It comes back—
—It goes in—
—It comes out—
—It runs—
—It flys—
—It weeps—
—It laughs—
—It wants to touch you—
—It wants to be quite alone—
—It tastes of water—
—It smells of earth—
—It burns—
—It is desperately cold—

Then let's have a town. See here are the houses. These are the people. This is a man. This is a woman. They have a garden. They go to bed. They make love. He puts his arms about her. He makes love to her.

Isn't that ugly?
Isn't that dirty?
Isn't that beautiful?
Isn't that the handwriting of God on them!
A river—
A deer—
Warm gentle wind—
Smell of sun-warmed leaves—
Where is there anything more majestic than that?
Someone saying: Come on in. Take off your wet things and sit

by the fire. Supper'll be ready in a jiffey.

Someone saying: I wish you didn't have to go to work today. It's lonesome having you gone all those hours.

Someone saying: Let's walk over to the Smith's. Their little girl's been sick.

Someone saying: Of course! We haven't got much, but the little we have—Now, now, don't be silly! What kind of friends do you think we are anyway!

68. The tended name will always remind men
69. Fudormin could have gone mad   of
70. What do you care? As   that   a
71. O Thou whence

	far	time	bit
cold	as	Lou	of
pale	that	put	humble
claws	goes	a	as
(lupp)	maybe	bumble	though
Is	it	bee	Plato
this	will	in	could
your	turn	his	explain
seat	out	korvy	snails'
mam	lousy	stoib	tits

THE ROOST

of course there is the temptation
TO INVENT
what you need most

an ancient herder   fe   athery (O my God!)
it tastes red

  leet uss prray because surely we have gone too near too far
I want it understood!

  the cage

  the box

  the ghost world winning

eggs—bread—soap—milk—blades—"to write on the air"—I am
satisfied. They won't really find me since   they always look
in the wrong place.

1. Smell of hemp.	33. I'll believe it.
2. Glint. That's justice?	34. When I seer it.
3. Three rotten pears.	35. You look silly.
4. Saloon keeper.	36. Lose the thread.
5. Vice if nice.	37. Rosy arses sparkle.
6. Lame but game.	38. Yessir, it wilts.
7. That huge nose!	39. A man wants peace.
8. Forgive them . . .	40. Put it there, kid.
9. Wake up. Rook.	41. Rule of bum.
10. Sport of clucks.	42. Oh is for owl.
11. Be fair how rare.	43. w . (32) . finding
12. Shush, mother.	44. F . . . about
13. I can't dunce.	45. a . . . a damn
14. All dark what a lark.	46. t . . . gives
15. Pardon.Your soul is showing.	47. h . . . at all
16. Nothing but a bloody ball.	48. e . . . nobody
17. Kiss her. She's dead.	49. rl . . . How come
18. Set them straight please.	50. Pullupatthecurbthere!
19. The answer is always Yes!	51. Why doesn't somebody let
20. Ice. Ice. Ice.	52. me out of here Why doe
21. Gran. Reew. Helpless.	53. sn't somebody let me o
22. Almost had it then.	54. ut of here Why doesn't
23. Certainly I'll repay you.	55. somebody let me out of

24. Why not rabbits!
25. H   . . .   mess?
26. e   . . .   ous
27. l   . . .   stru
28. p   . . .   mon
29. u   . . .   stinking
30. s   . . .   this
31. n   . . .   through
32. o   . (43) .   a path

56. here Why doesn't some
57. body let me out of here
58. Why   doesn't   somebody
59. let me out of here Why
60. doesn't somebody let
61. me out of here   Why
62. doesn't somebody
63. let me out of here
64. Why doesn't some

Shine you piddlers

65.
66. ⎰ The palpy soul of an eel.
67.

STICKY EVIL

Whom did you say?
I didn't quite hear that . . .
Not <u>tonight!</u>

Ah you're just kidding now.
$13.75—not a penny either way!

Lo the Beaut

H
E
L
L

O
yellow bird
I have such enthusiasm for truth
don't you know

Excuse me while I fill out these entry blanks. There! That ought to hold the dirty—For the love of God! Murphy! <u>just put it on the table!</u>

Howzabout some more of the book now . . .

XI, XII, XIII, & XIV

Gathered on the sun-deck that next morning, we occupied ourselves with the task of getting acquainted. The yacht was rolling in pregnant revery, her main-t'gallants and royals flapping like sails in a heavy wind. Pot said, "I say, old lad, what did you put in this drink of mine?" Sally Garden, her plump unders warm as fishes' wool in the hammock, stripped green and red, fed salted peanuts to the albatross, which he immensely enjoyed.

"A bit of squedo, Colonel," I said, almost sure that the waves were saying, "Christ didn't play a banjo, did He, now?"

The barometer was falling.

Marlingspikes banged in their gubrels; the flying-jib-boom thumped against its cross-trees; water splashed through the fo'-castle like blood in a weasel in heat; smoke rose from the straining anchor-chain; an iceberg appeared dead ahead, but was really only playing possum.

The binnacle was falling; the windlass was falling; Thane Chillingsdale was falling. He put his knee on Catherine St. Maur's hand. "Have you, by chance, ever heard of Sennacherib?" he asked. Catherine said no and, "He was an Assyrian king who invaded Palestine in 681," she was told. "Oh, you mean <u>that</u> Sennacherib?" she said, removing her sleeping hand and trying her best not to look sensual.

"What would be your first reaction if a pretty woman stopped you in the street?" Mrs. J— asked me, her fingers poised over the place where her typewriter had been.

"You're too refined for this trade," I said.

"Oh, come now, that's nonsense. The idea that novel-writing

126

is not the proper career for a woman—Why, that went out when I was a girl," she declared, her foundation garment poking cruelly into her armpits.

"That's what I'd say to a pretty woman," I told her, listening with half my head to the blandishments of Thane and the subtle rebuttal of the twenty-three year old Catherine who was definitely impressed by her six-foot-four, broad-shouldered, Harrow-collared suitor who was saying, "Your eyes are like stars."

"Oh, how thoughtful of you to notice."

"Your lips are like crushed berries."

"They give me a rash."

"Your neck is like the swan."

"Is it true that they drown children?"

"Your hair is like burnished gold."

"I invariably use three lemons in my rinse."

Mrs. J— started to cry. "I always suffer so when I write," she sobbed.

"What are you working on now?"

"Your teeth are like kernels of white corn."

"A Tree Grows In Quickslime Forever Up Through Bernadette's Amber Robe—It's about two people on a deserted island. An effort . . . courageous with the daring of le roi le veut; instinct with the blind kulturkampf der menschheit in these perilous times of ours; hic et ubique; dies irae dies illa . . . Quid rides?"

"Ce n'est que le premier pas quit coute," I answered absently.

"Your ears are like neatly-folded war bonds."

Mrs. J— gave me a dirty look. "But it is necessary ad captandum vulgus," she said, sniffing virtuously.

"Dum vivimus, vivamus," Colonel Pot put it.

"Imperium in imperio," I answered currente calamo.

"Gnothi seauton," the Colonel murmured, glaring at the decanter of squedo-zzpi which I had inconveniently placed at his elbow. "It's mania a potu he'll be a-givin' me, yet."

"Sic itur ad astra," I reminded him.

"Ceteris paribus," Little Remksheaffe volunteered; "though Fata obstant, misericordia Domini inter pontem et fontem."

"Nil admirari," I said.

"Malum in se," Mrs. J— said.

"Dulce est desipere in loco," I said.

"Interrorem, facilis descensus Averni," Colonel Pot said.

A policeman plummeted down out of the rigging. "I have a warrant for your arrest," he announced imperiously.

"I know what Freud would say about that," our Stowaway said, shifting the fifty, odd volumes he carried under his skinny arm.

"What's the charge, officer?" I inquired.

"Murder," he said, not taking his eyes off Sally Garden who was having a sunbath for herself up on the peep-deck.

"That's rather severe, isn't it?" I demanded. "And besides, those handcuffs would never fit me."

"The ring and the wrist—what a thing to fear!" our Stowaway said, grinning like a mouldy eggplant. "The symbolism is all too clear, I must say."

I snapped the 'cuffs on the policeman and our Stowaway and shoved them overboard. The shark who was using Mrs. J—'s machine pressed down the capital-letter key and left it there.

The spanker-gaff plabbled off and hit me a resounding blow across my rear midriff. I said something I was not immediately sorry for.

Sally Garden, Mengs Flink and Abigail Buttermilk were taking turns knocking Little Remksheaffe down and jumping on him with all five feet. "Let him alone! He's a poor orphan!" I shouted, but they were having too much fun, and paid no heed. Mr. Flink was afraid his wooden leg would chip, being of unseasoned pine.

Colonel Pot and Mrs. J— were over on the after-hatch trying to avoid a baby.

It started to rain. Somehow it had never occurred to me that there would be any point in having rain out in the middle of the ocean.

I went to the rear of the vessel and, lowering myself down by uneasy degrees, made my way to the great neon sign which spelled out A BEST SELLER—that coy Mrs. J—; after putting a after A and a , after Best, I climbed aloft again. So the prow had got back here, had it? Not for nothing had I bragged that I could sail a yacht backwards.

"Why don't you put it in a basket or something?"

Colonel Pot answered, "What sort of careless conduct do you call that? leaving a poor innocent little babe up on a dirty after-hatch!"

"My maid had it," Mrs. J— explained. "I warned her often enough that she had no right to complicate my life with her vulgar pleasures."

"Well, that relieves that situation—and a good thing—and a hell of a way to do it," Colonel Pot and I said in one breath, as we watched the terrible great sea-buzzard bear it aloft over the trackless wastes that were without house or temple or steam-shovel.

Ignatz laughed uncannily up in his nest.

The rain had increased in violence. Despite this, I managed to raise our emblem—the proud white flag.

"You use a lot of interesting symbolism," Mrs. J— said.

"Glad you like it," I said.

"I know what you plan to do."

"Such as?"

"Well, when we get to where we're going—There's so much you can do with us."

"Hmm?"

"You must have thought we were representative of the world you have decided to leave behind you."

"You have some lint on your moustache."

"What a wonderful device for satire."

"None intended. It's still on there."

"But, Mr. Best, do you think you've brought out our characters enough? You owe it to your readers, you know. It must be obvious to them by now that my yacht—which, by the way, cost a cool two-hundred thou—"

"A week's creation for you, my dear Mrs. J—."

"That my yacht is going to be wrecked on some strange isle, and that we are going to have wonderful and fantastic adventures."

"Oh, goodie!"

"I still think you should tell us something more about your characters. I'm sure that the average reader—"

Sally Garden: I am a woman of easy virtue. When I was fourteen I was betrayed by a man whose arm was incased in a black sling. I am usually cheerful—like all food with parsnips an exception, you might say. Duluth is my favorite city. Passion for carved door knobs.

Mengs Flink: I was a burglar in civilian life. Served two terms of eight and five years respectfully. I am something of an authority on correct procedure—I don't care what the activity in question is. Mother dead—have a brother who bleats like a goat in the throes of his dream. I can tell you the time of day, never fear.

Catherine St. Maur: I was one of the most respected fashion-designers in the business. There is something more than a little appealing about me. My skin is the color of salmon, to give you an idea.

Thane Chillingsdale: No follower of Summer-Stock but knows my name, I wager. Voted 'Most Likely To Succeed'—Pomona High School, class of '33. Keep your fingers crossed.

Colonel Caffarelli Pot: N-ra-n-z-z-z-z-z-z-o-o-o-o-s-h.

Mrs. J—: Surely I need no introduction to the intelligent reading public.

Little Remksheaffe: No father, no mother—a waif adrift in this heartless world. People have always been cruel to me, but it is not in my nature to hate them. God will punish them in His own way.

Krishna: Do not look upon the world and the deeds of men, but gaze into your own soul, and you will find therein that blessing which you seek where it is not, you will find love, and having found love, you will see that this blessing is so great that he who possesses it will not crave anything else.

John: He that saith he is in the light, and hateth his brother, is in darkness even until now.

He that loveth his brother abideth in the light, and there is no occasion of stumbling in him.

But he that hateth his brother is in darkness, and walketh in darkness, and knoweth not whither he goeth because that darkness has blinded his eyes . . . Let us not love in word, neither in tongue; but in deed and in truth.

And hereby we know that we are of the truth, and shall assure our hearts before him.

Budda: All that is living desires the same things as you: recognize yourself in every living creature.

Scovoroda: Until we have realized what is within us, what good is it to us to know what is beyond us? And is it possible to know the world without knowing ourselves? Can he who is blind at home, possess sight when he is abroad?

Lao-Tse: Reason that may be fathomed, is not the eternal reason; the being that may be named, is not the supreme being.

Pascal: When we are seated upon a moving vessel and our eyes are fixed upon an object on the same vessel, we do not notice that we are moving. But if we look aside, upon something that is not moving along with us, for instance, upon the coast, we shall notice immediately that we are moving. It is the same with life. When the whole world lives a life that is not right, we fail to notice it, but should one only awake spiritually and live a godly life, the evil life of the others becomes immediately apparent. And the others always persecute those who do not live like the rest.

Mallory: Society says to the man: think as we think, believe as we believe; eat and drink as we eat and drink; dress as we dress. If any fail to comply with these demands, society will torment them with ridicule, gossip and abuse. It is hard not to submit, but if you submit, you are still worse off; submit, and you are no longer a free man; you are a slave.

Seneca: Pay no heed to the number, but to the character of your admirers. It may be disagreeable to displease good people, but failure to please evil is always good.

Mazzini: I do not believe in any of the existing religions, and for this reason I can not be suspected of blindly following any tradition or the influences of education. But all through life I have thought as deeply as I could on the subject of the law of our life. I searched into it in the history of mankind and in my own consciousness and I have come to the unshakable conviction that there is no death; that life can not be other than eternal; that infinite perfection is the law of life, that every faculty, every thought, every striving implanted in me must have its practical development; that we have ideas and tendencies which far exceed the possibilities of earthly life; that the very fact that we possess them and can not trace their source to our feelings, proves that they proceed in us from a domain beyond this earth and may be realized only beyond it; that nothing perishes on earth but the appearance, and to think that we die because our body is dying is to think that the workman is dead because his tools have worn out.

Emerson: Every present hour is a critical and decisive hour. Note in your heart that every day is the best day of the year, every hour the best hour, every instant the best instant. The best, because it is the only one you have.

General George Patton: Men! This stuff we hear about Americans wanting to stay out of this war—not wanting to fight—is a lot of bulls—t. Americans love to fight, traditionally. All real Americans love the sting of the clash of battle. America loves a winner. America will not tolerate a loser. Americans despise a coward. Americans play to win. That's why America has never lost and never will lose a war, for the very thought of losing is hateful to an American.

All through your army career, you've bitched about what you call 'this chicken-s—t drilling.' That drilling was for a purpose: instant obedience to orders and to create alertness. If not, some sonofabitch of a German will sneak up behind him and beat him to death with a sock full of s—t.

We don't want yellow cowards in this army. They should be

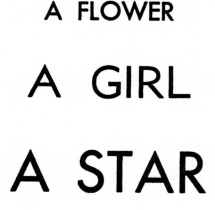

A FLOWER

A GIRL

A STAR

killed off like flies. If not, they will go back home and breed more cowards. We got to save the f—g for the fighting men. The brave man will breed more brave men.

We want to get the hell over there and clean the goddamn thing up. And then we'll have to take a little jaunt against the purple-p—g Japs and clean them out before the Marines get all the credit.

Admiral William F. Halsey: We are drowning and burning the bestial apes all over the Pacific, and it is as much pleasure to burn them as drown them.

Keats: I know no one but you who can be fully sensible of the turmoil and anxiety, the sacrifice of all what is called comfort, the readiness to measure time by what is done and to die could plans be brought to conclusions—the looking upon the Sun, the Moon, the Stars, the Earth and its contents, as materials to form greater things—that is to say ethereal things—but here I am talking like a Madman,—greater things than our Creator himself made.

Blake: I know of no other Christianity and of no other Gospel than the liberty both of body & mind to exercise the Divine Arts of Imagination, Imagination the real & eternal World of which this Vegetable Universe is but a faint shadow, & in which we shall live in our Eternal or Imaginative Bodies when these Vegetable Mortal Bodies are no more.

Melville: And so through all the thick mists of the dim doubts in my mind, divine intuitions now and then shoot, unkindling my fog with a heavenly ray. And for this I thank God; for all have doubts; many deny; but doubts or denials, few along with them have intuitions. Doubts of all things earthly, and intuitions of some things heavenly; this combination makes neither believer nor infidel, but makes a man who regards them both with equal eye.

God's other son entering the grove his branch that will be broken and falling asleep I watch the snow cover the green tree as the eye swells so big all things are looking at its looking but it should be amusing to tell your story with the rest and not be too damn gloomy because there is some reason to think that there are still a few human beings left who have some interest in Truth and Love and Dignity. "Has Mr. Tiger been in yet today?"—"No. How about a stroll before breakfast?"—"Fine. Sounds good to me."

Little Remksheaffe The Younger ducked behind the red and gold screen to change his pants, a superstition of his whenever anyone knocked on the door at that hour. The screen made me think of a story Colonel Caffarelli Pot had told me about a stuffed owl and a fox terrior and I laughed very heartily indeed.

"Good afternoon," Mrs. J— said, opening the door and sinking down at my feet. "Has Phoebe Ann been in yet today?"—"No. I must've fallen asleep. How are you?"—"Oh, I'm fine. Mr. Tiger said he dropped by this morning but got no answer when he knocked."

Lovely Grudd walked in and sank down at my feet. "Good evening," she said, taking off her satin pump and popping a fat roach. "Know what?" I said, "I'm hungry." Little Remksheaffe The Younger appeared around the screen. "Me too," he declared. "Let's eat."—"What's the idea walking around without your pants on?" I told him indignantly. There was a knock on the door and Lovely Grudd and Mrs. J—walked out with Mr. Tiger and Phoebe Ann Nemophila. "See you at Joe's," they called back cheerfully. "Right," I said. "We'll be along in about twenty minutes."

But we weren't. Mother phoned that something terrible had happened. "Are you phoning from home?" I asked her. "No— from a booth," she answered, her palms clammy with sweat. "All right. Give me the number and I'll phone you back."—"I can't."— "And why can't you?"—"There's a hand over the dial."—"Listen, maw, forget the symbolism and give me that number. No sense your wasting your nickel." There was a flash of blue light and the wire went dead.

"Remksheaffe," I said—somebody was sticking hot pins into my breath—"let's get out of here."

WE GO BACK A BIT

A woolly rhinoceros (Rhinoceras tichorhinus) snuffed at the lip of the cave, only to sneeze violently as the huge moustache of everpurple vine tickled its fat, inquisitive snout.

"Ug alibo kopp plfff," the woman said. ("Put another log on the fire, hadn't you better.")

His only answer was a sharp knock at the base of her sloping skull. "You beast!" she hissed. ("Lu foo grrzddx.") Five thousand long years were to pass before she would learn to weep; twenty-five, to swoon; yet another 185,483 before it would be so popular with her tea-indulging set to read Swinburn and Swoon—for the tingle these two bards shot along their spines, don't you know.

A canis lagopus (arctic fox) barked fretfully off in the direction of Heidelberg.

The man's huge muscles of mastication moved indecisively. He was puzzled, and if he'd had a chin he would have scratched it.

His mate took an artifact (coup de poing, or stone cup) off the edge and filled it with rangifer tarandus (reindeer blood) from the great, mammoth-hide crock.

A pattering as of the little moist feet of the rain . . .

THE WORLD

IS DYING

AROUND US

"Is that rain, dear?" he growled, his entire cranial capacity of 1,550 c.c. concentrated on it.

"Sure, want some?" she said, the retreating bony ridge above her silvery eyes looking curiously bone-like in the flickering light from the fire which made the funny drawing of the cow on the grimy wall seem like she was switching her knobby tail at a neandertalensis flae (neandertal cavefly).

"It's sure beginning to pilt down," he rumbled apprehensively.

"What I wonder are you so caring how hard the rain drip drip spluttle spluttle come him down," she said, negligently scratching in the thick, ill-tended pelt which encircled her middle.

"It's this tiger gut," he said, bending again over his rude worktable.

"I'll just bet it's the tiger gut," she said dialogitively.

"Big rain her make elasticity go bloob—"

"Him," she said, finding a barnsquirrel in her pelt and popping it into her mouth.

"Who him?" he said, measuring the base of her sloping skull for size—this time, he thought, maybe I'll try the club Sina (Sinanthropus) give me last Magnonmas.

"You're a beast," she said in complete disregard of proper sequence (Séqueto).

But he was right. Again and again he screwed the bulb into the socket. No sudden warm stab of light rewarded him. "It's that damn gut," he murmured; "yet what else can I use for filament sput sput zing?" And only the peevish roar of a hippokettleamus (ancestor of our well-loved hippopotamus) made him answer.

So he grabbed his mate by the hair and beat hell out of her—though neither, of course, knew she possessed such a modern conception.

Yet somehow the name stuck, and after a while his neighbors, in for a cup of warm blood or wanting to try a new club out on the woman's head—"She's got the hardest head in all Acheulean history," they were fond of telling each other.—(In fact, our phrase 'to fondle with a brick' probably dates from this period), got in the habit of addressing him as The Beast.

Later it became, simply, Beast.

Later still, Mr. Beast.

Then, as centuries passed, the a, which had never been very broad, got dropped.

But nobody else ever got a bulb to work with tiger gut instead of wire either.

Murphy! on the table! on the General Patton's favorite word table!

'YOUNG GIRLS RUN LIKE HARES
ON THE MOUNTAIN'

It was a cold night in late November. Winter was getting the drift of his (grim) task. People looked at each other with wide, startled eyes and asked, What's on WJZ at eight-thirty? That American history was the best this country ever had, few doubted. As a single example, take Pocahontus before her marriage to brother Smith.

Worn out, then, from day-long considerations of perplexing questions—such as: Can an art which corrupts be beautiful?—or, as Tolstoy believed, must art identify itself with a religious view of life, and so instruct and inspire man to know and follow the teachings of Christ?—and, In what way may the fullest measure of human potentialities be realized on this earth?—the great American nation prepared itself for bed.

Somebody has said that it takes a heap of living on a fence to make good neighbors; but how much better it would be for all of us if most of the self-evident truths hadn't packed up their Arabs. 'Know thyself' was addressed to a man; 'Be alert' to a dog. Maybe that's part of what's wrong, eh?—maybe the only answer to our problem isn't a machinegun that can fire 974 slugs in a tenth of a second. Maybe it's better for a man to be a man than to be a whipped dog crouching in a ditch.

Maybe it's better to expect to have the star after all.

Maybe it's better to get angry enough to know what it is to love.

At any rate, the party was going well when Sir Stevie, who had served time for minding his own business—which was safecracking —got there. Megan, whose nearly full session on the nest hadn't exactly improved her figure, maintained a pregnant silence in the corner. Little Mohawk, who, despite his ninety-two years and bad cold, was an Indian, was hacking away near the crock. Louie

139

Webster October, who had, at the age of ten, found himself—and he was minute for his size—forced, much as he might have wanted to go to Atlantic City and taste the salt tang and breathe the big, smiling, open-faced sea air with others of his immature ilk, to kiss his mama nightie-bye and make obsequious gestures to his lard-potted Uncle Bartholomew whose stable of truly magnificent horses put him in such bad odor in their neighborhood, was shouting quietly to Sharon Mayshores, a woman, and a very lovely one, who, sandwiched in between Joe Wichery, for passion of whom, hearsay had it, more than one fair habitue of the 'upper crust' had gone gently balmy, and Mr. Ladybug, a plumber's helper from Wayback, S. Dak., was trying to listen at the same time to the dulcet blandishments of gorilla Mike O'Toole and still not miss the entrance of ALOYSIUS BEST, which was scheduled to take place in precisely forty-three seconds.

Gorgeous Tim said, What's I wonder keeping Aloysius?

Black Murdree reached into the crock and pulled out a small hot water bottle before answering. Then he decided not to say anything anyway. Instead he removed the stopper and smelled the now-open neck. Obviously this told him what he wanted to know, for, first carefully restoring the stopper, he replaced the bottle in the crock.

Little Mohawk had a pretty good-sized pile of chips around him —imagining, Indian-fashion, that the best fun of all was to chop a nice big hole in the floor.

Maybe he's fell asleep in the tub, Mr. Ladybug said, taking out a wrench and moving over to the sink.

Bahth? Is he taking a bahth? Sir Stevie asked, his watery blue eyes looking like little pools of boardinghouse milk.

Bath, October blustered.

Maine, Joe Witchery said.

Woods, Uncle Bartholomew said.

Hole, Little Mohawk said.

Up, Sharon said.
Sky, Megan said.
Terrier.
Limb from limb.
Zero.
Weather.
Vane.
Punch.
Weak.
Day.
Man.
Pythias.
Shoe.
Bird.
Dock.
Dinner.

One of the stacks of shredded wheat boxes chose this moment to topple off the mantle. What could I wonder have caused that? Gorgeous Tim asked. He had taken a small, black-and-white spotted fish out of the crock and was eating it with hot sauce and Sharon Mayshores.

The door opened and a horse walked in; or rather, the door opened and a small horse walked in; or, better still, the door opened and a small horse with a far from small keg depended from its neck walked in. Peg! Peg! eager voices eagered voicely. Where the hell you been?

Bean, Sir Stevie said.

We've bean depending on you, they all cried.

You have, is it? Peg snorted. And just you look now what's been—

Bean.

Bin of goddam beans—depending from my poor neck this night, yet, Peg finished, sinking to the floor in a probulent heap.

Brandy? Louie Webster October asked.

I'll take a pony, Peg replied.

Any day, Black Murdree said.

But now the keg was passing freely from hand to hand. Little did anyone mind that the room was knee-deep in water—certainly not Peg, for all she had to do was lie back comfortably and wait until the little cakes of wheat floated into her mouth. And certainly not Mr. Ladybug, for he was over now happily dismantling the radiator.

Megan had retired to another, less joyous room, since her time had come and she wanted to be alone—which is sort of paradoxical.

Joe Witchery said, Have you seen Raymond lately?

Sharon Mayshores lifted an eggbeater out of the crock. Yes, I saw him last Tuesday—no, it was Monday I saw him. She lowered the blades, cranking as she did so. It made a happy blub-blub in the wheaty water. He should be on his way to Charlestown by now.

Charlestown! I thought he'd broken off with Pauline.

Not since Huldah gave him the bo gy, Sharon said, putting the eggbeater away into her handbag. It's getting damn steamy in here if anybody should ask you.

Witchery glanced over at October who was boring holes in a board. Tiny whisps of vapor tongued in and out of the holes. Joe said, I see Louie's been Feading reud again.

Life can be bomething of a sore, Sharon said, smiling as her companion scratched. How'd you know, Joe, I was itchy there, Joe? Have you noticed that there isn't any water anymore?

Things have a way of working themselves out all right, Witchery remarked.

And it was true. Little Mohawk hadn't hacked in vain. Even the steam was dredging itself a comfortable way up through the ceiling. Aside from that first terrified yelp and a brief glimpse of a very

142

hairy leg sticking down through the make-shift aperture, all was peaceful above.

I hope the people downstairs like shredded wheat, Gorilla Mike said, sitting down and starting to scratch too.

And if any cannibals wander in up there, I hope they lo for gobsters, Joe said.

Whether Gorilla Mike had some special scratch or what, Sharon had obviously decided that the bedroom would be just the place for him to get in some really good licks.

Mr. Ladybug, a beautiful smile wreathing his battered features, stood, wrench poised, over the gas stove.

Oh, you Pepsi Cola! you Pepsi Cola, you! Sharon moaned ecstatically.

What could I wonder be keeping Aloysius? Gorgeous Tim declared.

There are portents and portents, Natalia, the Greek chorus girl, said, beginning to giggle.

As well as rich, Tim said. I didn't know you tere lickwish.

At that instant Peg, poor snow-bedraggled Peg, staggered in with another keg. And the most terrible and beautiful human being that anyone has ever dreamed of was with her.

•   •   •   •

Honey, can't you see I'm busy? Keep your pants on—it'll still be here.

AND ALL THE HINGS KORSES

Ace of diamonds, ten of hearts, the queen of spades . . . whiskey bottle with a blue slightly bent candle sticking up out of it . . . beside them a huge, gnarled hand in a dirty yellow glove . . .

A long, dirt-grimed crack in the table top . . .

Counter clock-wise:

Tall man in stained cap, brown and green scarf slung carelessly over his right shoulder . . . vicious little blue eyes in a shrunken, brutal face . . . owner of the gloves . . .

Woman in a brilliant, flowered robe . . . her bare feet pretty and small . . . holding a copy of THE ADVENTURES OF A MAN WITH A DROPLEAF FOREHEAD and staring vacantly into the distance . . .

A boy of fourteen . . . one leg shorter than the other . . . his left hand resting on a worn crutch . . .

Tiny girl with lemon-colored skin . . . possibly mentally backward . . . holding a spool of white thread and trying to attract the attention of

A sad-faced young woman . . . in a striped gold blouse with a lace collar . . . fingering a lock of ill-tended hair . . . eyes closed, lashes encrusted and rather mousy-looking . . .

Ancient hag at spinning wheel . . . not properly at table, though her chair is tilted back to narrowly touch it . . . hers is the only face not turned to the door . . .

A fly crawls across the queen of spades . . .

With the opening of the door three things occur . . . the eyes of the young woman open . . . The candle's flame puffs out . . . The noise of merriment from across the hall surges in . . .

A young man appears on the threshold.

A strange gray light plays over the silent figures . . . coming from a place outside the world.

The newcomer walks to the table . . . He bends to kiss the withered lips of the old woman . . . and a drop of blood drips down off his chin . . . narrowly missing the ten of hearts.

Then the hand in the soiled yellow glove slowly rises . . . whether to curse or to absolve . . . whether in careless gesture or to a plan noble and ordained from the beginning of all things . . .

★

"Oh, Aloysius, a terrible storm threatens our frail craft," one of them cried in my ear.

I looked into the heavens: they were pitiless.

"Pray somebody," I said.

Nobody seemed to be able to.

We skipped up and down wet, awful mountains.

"I knew we should have lived better,"—

GET DOWN ON YOUR KNEES, YOU WISE-CRACKING FOOL!

"To get sucked down into this monotonous water without ever once even guessing what the score is,"—

In the face of death—as it seemed to all of us—my new-found acquaintances indulged in a conversation which, for lack of a better descriptive phrase, scared the hell out of me; in the stress of that horrendous moment, their very souls appeared to shed their mundane shells, and to dance (naked as paddies!) there on the tumbling deck—you have, no doubt, heard of the PRIMITIVE that lurks in all of us—Here, for me at least, was proof positive of Physic Evolution . . .

"I remained alone in my room nearly an hour," Colonel Caffarelli Pot intoned. "At length somebody knocked at my door; I opened it, and who should be there but Mr. Best! I confess, I shuddered at the sight of a man, who, I thought, had so cruelly betrayed me; says he, 'May I come in?'—'Certainly, Al,' says I: 'I am afraid,' says he, 'your wife and you have had an impleasant inning.'—'You're damn right,' says I, 'not the more pleasant from some cruel misrepresentations that I think have been made to her.' —'I suppose,' says Mr. Best, 'you mean that I did wrong in speaking of Miss Tickle as a person quite beneath you—'"

Mrs. J—: "To dream you are eating oysters is a very favorable omen; if you are in business, it will increase very fast, and you will go bankrupt; if you are a farmer, you will look thrice before reaping; if you are married, your mate will be quite fond of you, and you will have ten children; if you are an ungrateful maid, and you gobble oysters—"

Colonel Pot: " 'I have no scruple, Al,' says I, 'to assert that you did do wrong, because I avow it to be a gross violation of the truth. Why is a person of such parentage and education and singular worth as Miss Tickle can boast, to be accounted beneath any man? I feel, dear Aloysius, that you have done me an unkindness, and by her you have acted unjustly, and, therefore, dishonorably; my heart is full, you louse, and for fear I should speak more to the point, I wish you would have the extreme goodness to get the devil out of here.' "

Little Remksheaffe: "Leave me, oh! leave off me!—unto all under heaven thy presence binds me with too deep a spell; thou mak'st those mortal regions whence I flee, too mighty in their loveliness—farewell, that I may get out of here! The very shadow of this owl wakes in my spirit a scodde too profound, too hot, for aught that loves, or dies (drowns, yet) to endure. I see thy purple whisper—and the closeted tears gush into my eyes—the quick pulse <u>thrills</u> my heart!"

Thane Chillingsdale: "Yes, ye flowery nations, ye must all decay. Winter, like some enraged and irresistable conqueror, that carries fire and sword wherever he advances; that demolishes towns, depopulates countries, spreads slaughter and devastation on every side. So, just so, will winter, with his savage and unrelenting blasts, invade this beautiful prospect. The storms are gathering, and the tempests mustering their rage, to fall upon these terrible kingdoms. They will ravage through the dominions of Eckton, and

plunder her riches, and lay waste her pretty charms. Then, ye trees, must ye stand stripped of your verdant apparel; and ye fields; be
spoiled of your wa
ving treasures. Then the
earth dissolved of all he
r gay attire, must sit
in sables, like a dis
conconsolate wido
w. The sun too, who
now rides in triumph round
the world, and scatters O
n
ppx
I ?—* ym abru

DEATH

LO°K¹N^G

^DOO^N

a pus from his radiant
eye—will then gaze faintly from
the wind
ows of the so

BooM

CrASH

leave us

uth

and,

casting

a

short

or

t

glance

on

our

dejected

d

world,

will

a aramon
aen dmony
t l a d o n e
a g i t h n y
n m a n h n e
a o l n e
c i r e e r t o
t a d e h r r e s t e h f
o b i n o , . , d e i t
l o , r t i h e
t e u i w o T a s r h
h s t s i h n o e
e g h t l t e d n
l n e e l h g o
u o i s r e l a s e
n o g e s c a l t s o
c m h h g r l e . d
o t s o a e k r s
m o s w f n n , t s T
f f . e t t h , h i
o e t l t e e s O
r t T t h n e h a H
t e h e o e f b h a !

149

```
help              G                    t
help                              s    s
help              O             a  a
help       a  b      D     s    d  n   "
help       n  e  i      g  ,     e  d
help       d     n  i      w
help          i  g  l  u  h  v  w        HELP
help       s  n     e  p  i  o  a
help       i  t  w  n  o  c  c  r
help       l  e  i  c  n  h  a  b
help       e  r  n  e        l  l
help       n  r  d  ,
help       c  u  s
help       e  p  )  s           US
help       (  t     i
help       u  e  a  t
help       n  d     s  t  a  b  i
help       l     s     h  r  y  n
help       e  b  u  b  e  e     g
help       s  y  l  r        a
help       s     l  o  b  n     t
help          h  e  o  o  o  t  h
help       i  o  n  d  u  w  h  r       ALL
help       t  w     i  g     o  o
help          l  s  n  h  m  u  a
```

—"T   o   d   r e
a
        m   you   s   ee   a g
reat   li   g h   t,   i
    s   a
        h
    a p
                    p
                        y   p   re sage;
it denotes
            th   a   t   yo
    u   w
                    ill   att

151

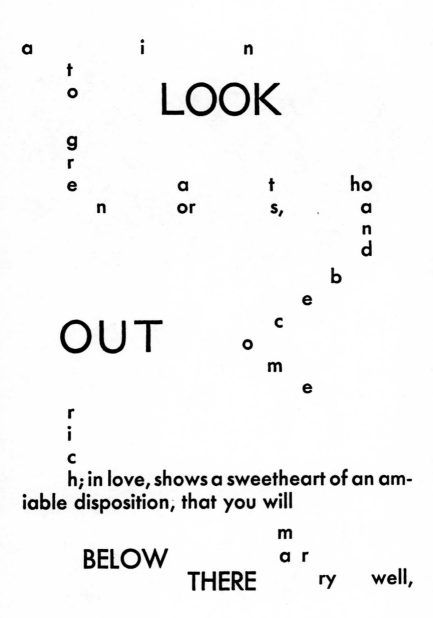

a   i   n

t

o   **LOOK**

g

r

e   a   t   ho

  n   or   s,   a

                    n

                    d

            b

        e

OUT   c

      o

      m

      e

r

i

c

h; in love, shows a sweetheart of an am-
iable disposition, that you will

        m

BELOW   a r

      THERE   ry   well,

have chil
dr
en, an' be very content; if the light disappe
ars   a
                   l
                   l

                                       WATERWATER

                 i

                  n   EVERYWHERE

    a

                          & NOTHING TO

        s

        u

        d   DO BUT

            d

            e

                n,   it   b

etokens a gr   e

                                at

SINK   cha

                         n

ge
in yo
ur pre
sent sit
uation, mu
ch for the worse;
it portends im-
prisonment and
great loss of goods,
with unexpected mis-
fortunes. To dream of
being in an inn, is a
very unfavorable dream;
it denotes poverty and
want of success in under-
takings; expect soon to be
yourself or, some other of
your family, committed
to the Cross—To dream
you are in a storm or
tempest, shows that
you will, after many
difficulties, arrive at
being very happy,
that you will become
rich, and marry well.
For a lover to dream of
being in a tempest denotes
that you will have many
rivals, who   after causing you   a great

—"S
trength of
my strength! a
round me, le
st I sink,
Place

                                        thine
                                        Almighty
                                        arm and be
                                        ar me up;
                                        Lest I sh
                                        ould

            fa
        int, and
    thus refuse
    to drink—
        When

                                        Thou,
                                        my Father,
                                        dust presen
                                        t the cup!
                                        This

            doub
        le trial of
    the heart and
    flesh, How
        shall I

            stand
        till thou the
    power supply?
    This fearful op
        ening of the
            wound—"

155

PART ONE

I.

Everything clear, everything tidy and right. I don't know how far I can trust you to understand what I have said so far; it would only show proper humility for me to state right now that—perhaps I'm jumping the gun (I do want to get this across to you, however . . . well, later, then . . . I must watch my step a little teeny bit . . .) There are many levels of meaning. There are enemies all around us. In this game unless you can think faster than the hangman you might just as well stand in bed. What I started to say was this: To get the most out of what follows in this book, try your damnedest to have some respect and love for the great things of this world—otherwise, for Christ's sake! read something else.

A. Best, Seller, fighting valiantly to the last, sank in the deepest part of the ocean.

O MY SNAWY G
LEE SO ENDLES
SLY! A FAIR O
R NARROW BEA
UTY WILL IN H
EALING COAXÉ
D FISHES RIDE.

Down . . . down . . . down . . .
A million trees of water pressing in on us—
Then it seemed like we were turned into some-
thing else—New creatures—I know you will think we
were dead.
But SUDDENLY

2.
We came out into a great bubble.
3.
I'd like to tell you what went on then but it was too STRANGE and I couldn't seem to think or feel in any of the ways I knew about.

O ON WAVES T
HE GARDENS P
URPLY GLIDE. G
RACE FOUND, C
HARIOT - WIDEN
ING -- NOR ALL
THE HING'S KO
RSES . . . . . .

"Certainly not I!" AT SEVEN G LEN THE HEAR T IS STOLE AGA IN. O WISH A P UDDING . . . .

4.

There was a celebration. They made much of us. They were wildly delighted to see us and touch us and kiss us, I think.

5.

I can't describe those first ones: though they were a little like human beings—but sort of OUT OF FOCUS as we "expect" things.

6.

You must understand that in everything I say here on in you must look for meanings in terms of LIFE IN THE BUBBLE and not at all in terms of the world you "know."

7.

You will see that much of what follows is in the form of Notes—written on the "scene," written (in some cases) while the "events" described were still taking place.

8.

None of us was in the least surprised at anything we saw, felt or experienced there. It all seemed perfectly natural to us—certainly infinitely more "natural" than anything we had known in the world.

9.

A mammoth bubble hundreds of miles down in the middle of the sea . . .

10.

All set? Everybody ready? Hold on to your *lives* —HERE WE GO!

Our memories play us the damnest tricks. For instance—But first a word of caution. Don't expect premiums or free coupons with that little commodity known as Truth—for Christ's sake it's not a question of what will do us most good but what will permit us to live at all! I know what you want. You want me to give you something you can water your precious soul with, something you can feel stippier than your neighbor about—I'll bash your stinking heads in! We're all deep in it. The rot—this brother is old grandpappy rot himself—If it were only death

we're all so damaged . . . I wonder if we can get into death at all anymore.

It just might happen—might, I say—that the time has come to look pretty hard into this certain particular dish known as living in this day and age.

For myself, I don't think it's any different now than it ever was but there's more of it and less of us.

Sour the quartet when the fifth player dozes off—tying our shoes tight won't get us along the road any faster, eh?

I had a great fear of being born. My mother said to me (while I was in the womb), You will be a wanderer on the face of the earth, one of the lost, a ferdimar, a glunep in dubbi-tubba, my little Almar. Ma's vocabulary was always in advance of her time. She had a long, curling neck and was addicted to parsimony despite the fact that my father was the richest barber in America.

When I was four she drove nails through my hands and feet and ran the vacuum-cleaner up and down my naked front. From this I trace my distaste for machinery of any kind. I remember, too, that one of my cousins had a baseball bat stained blue. Subconsciously I must have resented this, for I've always had the dread of getting it frozen.

Some years later—I was never noted for special intelligence in our town, by the way, one of these quiet little places beneath whose placid exterior torrid currents channel their secret way, though the girls liked me to take them spooning down by the river: I think it was Lincoln who said you can take the boy out of the country but unfortunately you can't take the country by the nuts (our state was notable in this respect) which grow on our most parlous oaks—I walked unsuspecting into the wood, my only companion a fellow named Plusis Jidet who was trying to persuade me to escape to a shack up in the hills somewhere.

They bound us down on a beslimed altar. This hellish-looking crew—I tell you, wear your clean life <u>today</u>—
torches

a festival, you might say (I have a sallow skin, dark mizê eyes, a
broad, too-battered mouth, 5' 8½", 145,
—all knuckles broken)

"the terror of the unknown"—

That's it! Putting garlands of roses around the necks of dogs. Wine—sure—on dishes of leaves, meat of the gentle pure kid—O Father it hurts down inside here—

They let us up.

I broke a branch off the tree.

Up on the mountain—What are you grinning about?—the King drank the steaming blood of his victim.

I pressed my faith to me like a withered pear.

The wind blew a great hole in my body.

A heart—is that too much to touch? Are the 'papers out yet? Run to the corner and see are the 'papers out yet.

I didn't kill her! I swear it—I swear it—

Ah even the new moon—so fragile it looks! I walk on tip-toe lest it be shattered . . . Tortuosities of the maze inch their slow course along.

I feel the stars thinking.

This world (turn off that radio!)—braincell in the mind of that inconceivable Dreamer—

Expansile and contractile—The flowers are easily made at home in that Consciousness.

That poor devil down there under the tree the one with the removable forehead I can watch him think or perhaps in dream about himself the great part never wakes and another comes out of his sleep as I am coming out of going in and the rain wrings a step of plume upon this order O my God it tumbles in Beds forgive I cannot begin so end so dread forgotten yes my dear we stray in green fields and if snails weep they do grant in sweeping pother why must all bears supply banns for dreadnoughts until we are replenished out of the golden bowl if it be the hills or geese under the banjos of water darling no when said everything sounds false and only teeth devise somersaults for the wounded a book bullets tear and I suppose what isn't empty now will be filled wrong as her father could have had that job in the hardware store if any man deserved the best it was all blistered in that sun you bet (lake) all right but where find a single thing you really want perhaps if it could be opened up like music sounds and lips feel but it does run out it seems there are always more cages to walk past but the sickening is to feel so many others crowding up from that plain grave oh yes if there were stars I'd point them out and feed you candy and even take my liver down from the top-shelf always that one countryroad the portrait he couldn't quite get

and this stupid beggar mumbling on an empty stage . . .

Gee the girls were pretty. In the grove where the stranger lay, his throat slit from ear to ear—I'd heard about it, of course, how the girls would suddenly change into clouds and trees and rabbits etc. But Plusis—well, perhaps Plusis just wasn't too quick in the head—such a lovely one, too . . . golden hair and the bluest eyes . . . Plusis well off first base and just rounding into second when—

Plusis, I'm ashamed of you . . . a poor innocent tree . . .

But how the hell am I going to get out of here!

It was a pretty delicate operation.

You'd naturally think something like that would be lesson enough for anybody. But not our Plusis! The next an extremely nifty brunette and I could almost hear him saying to himself Boy here is some really hot stuff. And he was right—I have never seen a finer bonfire but poor Plusis should not have used such language in that sacred place!

AND NO

LIGHT A

T THE INN

Doesn't it annoy you to be waiting around inside yourself all the time? It's only natural to get tired of our bodies. On top of that —the machine has made the world a hell of a bore. The newer all these damn gadgets get the more bored we become—Jesus! to see now maybe a buggy! something that doesn't make you think

A SORT OF RADIANCE I S COMING T HROUGH TH

E WALLS OF

THE TENT.

BUT I AM WITHOUT AN

ANIMAL TO LIVE IN.

it belongs on another planet—Stream-lined for speed—But just where the devil is there to go in such an ungodly hurry!—To get away, huh? From what? speed, maybe?—and from these vicious-looking chromium junebugs that look as though they'd like to push their sleek noses into a nice plate of mathematical formulas, maybe? These things all look so damn inhuman—the faster they can go, the deader they look. There's absolutely nothing "romantic" about them—and I'll bet you a cookie they hurt people pretty good and deep.

Maybe I should take Plusis up on that shack in the hills proposition, I don't think.

There is always something easier than living. Dreams are often such little beasts. We suppose too much, is that it? Something is driven in and perhaps we haven't enough room to house it. At any rate, as long as we can be sure it was a "dream"—I felt her body go limp. Her hair streamed back over my arm. I could smell her sweetness—it was terribly real. My shirt was wet through. I beat at her shoulders with my fists. I ripped her dress open, shredding it like a beggar's coat. Stumbling to my feet, I whipped off my belt. I shiver when I remember how its copper studding gleamed in the pitching light. The buckle split her mouth. I hit her over and over— and she began to croon. Why can't you cry? something in me said. My belt—a different one now, a snake covered with moist sawdust —caught in the cord which held the world in space and it broke, the cord broke. I put iodine on her wounds and she shoved her hands into my stomach, waggled her fingers, she waggled her fingers.

But I've prided myself, a countryboy, you who have heard the leaves of a tree vibrate in a northwind, come off the nonsense, you just sit there like a glad I met you too, but all the flow means is getting real. The motor of a heavy truck whines up the valley. Blurth. Its ugly nose tops the rise, growls toward us. Then another. Another. Living eyes peer out of their headlights. Dirty, spiritless bears with their clubs and bright guns are the men in the trucks and nearby a naked girl, her black hair spilling down over her beautiful shoulders like a fall of paint, sits on a stool before a dressing-table. God why don't the bastards leave us alone.

A little man in a blue frockcoat stood out in front of the pool-room and shouted (it was a bit after dark and the stars were just

169

THEY SAID

THERE WAS LOVE

WHERE IS IT?

WHERE IS LOVE!

beginning to come out): The peaceful forces of this country shall triumph. (He blew his nose into the puppy's soft fur.) The noisome gangs who thought that with this foul deed of violence they could usurp the instruments of free government in this, our proud nation, have been dealt with without mercy, for by Jesus they deserved none. The blood—(he smiled craftily) and best energies of our own people shall not be turned to the blind ends of death. Those who would have inspired war with our neighbor are dead. War— (yelping like a fox with its brush afire)—, that business of barbarians, shall not pollute our lands. Some things may have to be effected now that will cause you distress of spirit. I will remind you —(he pointed right at me)—that our peaceful goal is worth every sacrifice free men can make.

(He came over and shook his fist under my nose.) One further word, bub. On the solemn honor of my office—(he belched: liver and canned spinach)—, and with the deepest feeling of humility before the wisdom of our Heavenly Father, I promise you this— (another one: rice pudding and coffee boiled too long)—: No act of mine or of this nation shall be calculated to any other end than peace.

I poured a bucket of dead eels over him and walked into the snooker palace. Fenshaw forked his cue tenderly on the green cloth, his eyes squinted against the raw glare of the swaying bulb. Side, he said. The ball chased about in seemingly aimless bankings; sided.

Sullivan, Timberly, Clark and Sloan shifted their feet. Clark said, Nice.

You've got to step right along, Almar, Fenshaw said, grinning as he surrendered the cue.

I chalked, glancing over at a stranger who stood halfway down the room near the shooting gallery. Who's he?

You got us, Sullivan said. Hear that he's visiting Old Zen.

Well, here goes—I settled down to it. I started wtih a run of thirty, broke 'the poor man's token,' and finished with a levet.

Timberly whistled softly.

The stranger came over and said, Reuben Grisher's my moniker, friends. Give. And he reached for the cue.

Buzz, little bee, I told him, not letting go—the forward bastard. Sloan giggled.

Grisher beamed at me. I like determination in a man—if he is one, and has any. Quietly, without rancor, almost tenderly, he put his short arms around my chest. I raised the damn cue. He shifted his stance by an inch, seemed to relax, and did something with his elbows and right knee.

I did something with my supper.

All the tables were watching. Grisher stepped over me and took up the cue. He set the ball on the corner apron and without a seven-wedge or single blind thistle, his hand loose on the taped heel, he made a thermi and a hare with margin to bargain, regged a plain and came home dusting the lilly until the territory of that forbidden maiden seemed to rocket fiery wrens.

A black margate—ninety ridden free, Sullivan breathed.

Grisher bent over me. Feel better now? he said, his hand biting into the slack muscles of my shoulder.

What have you got your men hunting me down for, you dirty sonofabitch? I said. Please, for Christ's sake! it's hard enough for us in this world without tormenting each other.

A woman in a red dress came down the stairs. She painted a huge 6 on the score-card that was there for that purpose, using an hair-thin brush, dull green color, her eyes were half closed and she reminded me of someone, who? it's on the tip of my mind, ah, to hell with it, and, blushing at something the fireman said, yes, blushing, she walked carefully to the door, the sway of her hips like pretty bells swaying in a toy church, a little mouse of distaste and wild approval nibbling at her violent lips. I raised my arm and my wristwatch slipped up over my elbow.

Match me in a bit of shooting? Grisher asked me, indicating with a toss of his head.

Why not? I said, climbing to my feet and rubbing great globs of slobber and sawdust off my pants.

We took up stations at the counter of the gallery.

172

Moriiy, the Persian attendant, handed me a rifle. I looked over at Grisher and said, What's the bet?

He lowered his blood-flecked eyes. Your soul, he said.

My <u>soul</u>? I said.

Please don't be a spoil-sport, he said. It's hard enough for human beings to live in this world without—

All right. All right. I studied the set. The rifle had a good pumlee and I . . . well, a chance, damnit.

I pulled the trigger twenty times, pausing for a Hail Mary and an Our Father between each tug.

Clark said, Honies!

And now, the little bee, Grisher said without malice, taking the slack-jawed weapon.

He did twenty Parlo-Kings, the live rabbits and quail and unemployed floating over like boards kicked through water.

Fifteen minutes later I was sitting on the hard benches of the meeting hall with the rest. Grisher walked upon the platform and bowed to a very fat man in a black silk suit. A chill of fear ran through my belly, disappointed to find it already empty. The fat man explored his nose with a finger like a webden trollus, with green gold ring, it has put more than one eye out, the window, let them try to come in, maybe this is The Boss, though hell you'll make a big mistake if you think I can be scared by a tub of lard like him. Fellow told me once he and three other chaps sat down on the bank of a river and one of them had just had his little daughter die so his friends were trying to take that great sting out and one of them said to him Old Zenaslufski look up at that sky and Old Zen looked up at the sky and he said hand me that goddam bottle of whiskey Al. Grisher kissed the fat man. Somebody started to play Vivaldi on the organ in the back. A hand touched my shoulder. It was Moriiy and he said, Pat your hair down—they can't see back there.

The fat man wiped his mouth on the cloth which covered the

podium. When he raised his head there were two holes there, instead of eyes, two ragged holes, a red ooze, the organ swelled to set heaven singing, then, suddenly, nothing, not a sound. I wanted to get away but you can't get away you can't get away— It's a mistake to think you can get away. I never saw or heard of

THEY SAID

THERE WAS TRU

TH WHERE IS IT?

WHERE IS TRUTH!

anyone who ever got away. You have probably asked one another, the fat man said: For what purpose are we brought together? In what direction exactly does our destiny lie? It is only natural that you should do so. In like fashion, it is but natural to my role that I should be privileged to answer you. To the first, then: You have been brought together to safeguard those tenets of rigorous manhood in whose justification and for whose fulfillment of vision this nation had its inception. He drank water and worked his nose over a bit. Sullivan, Timberly, Clark and Sloan, who hadn't the faintest idea of what he was driving at, concluded that he certainly was right, and something sure as hell ought to be done about it. And to your second question, gentlemen, I can only say this—(in what humility of spirit you will know): Our Great One has set the course; whether it lead to the stars or to a lowly place at the feet of our oppressors, is for you, and for the thousands of other red-blooded young men of this nation to decide. We all know that there are ambitious men in the world, and I say to you— Thank God! and again, thank God! We have been thought to be a race without ambition, a people whose devotion to peace was their only coloring and armor—But these are the daydreams of fools, gentlemen; the womanly whimpering of mice in the walls of a crumbling house. Ah, they've told you that power is evil, that recourse to arms is the badge of the hairy barbarian; will they tell me now, here, tonight—will you tell me, gentlemen—what manner of goat-kidneyed nonsense is this! Is it wrong to take what belongs to you? Is it evil to defend to the last drop of your warm blood, the soils which are native to the vigor of your fathers and to the sweet, life-giving—no! no! no! What they forget, dear boys, is something which even the wolf on the loneliest hill in this world knows; they forget—and it is our glorious heritage to remember— that this is a time of evil. He dug out a good one and wiped it tenderly on the cloth. A little red was beginning to trickle down from the ragged holes. He went on, No action of anyone anywhere

175

can erase by one iota the absolute and fixed character of that evil. Who tells you not to do evil unto your neighbor, tells you to die— not to live. There was One such Who promised great happiness for him who turned his other cheek. Happiness, my friends, where? He spread his fingers, frowned, smiled, said, In heaven. He lisped the words. Clark guffawed. I have not seen it; I have not touched it; I have not smelt it; I have never made a penny, or lost a penny, through use of it; not once did it cause me to get better when I was sick; not once did it give me bread or drink or love—to what do I refer, gentlemen? He paused, then shouted, I refer to that thing which men call the immortal soul! Immortal humbug—What manner of creatures we are none should know better than we. When we are thirsty, we drink. When we are hungry, we eat. When we are angry, when all that is dearest and most precious to us, is threatened—What do we do, gentlemen? Do we hesitate be- cause of riches in that fool's tower called The Kingdom of Heaven? What indeed did He do? that King of Kings, that implorer at blind gates—What did He do when His lips bled with thirst? Gentlemen, He said: I thirst. And what did He do when they put clean steel through his skinny side? You know what He did— Fatty found an- other one and wiped it off. That men die does not concern us. Man is a being of death. The soldier who dies in battle pays tribute not only to himself but to his slayer. To live huddled in the sewers of fear and cowardice, my friends, is to die a slow death without honor. We must learn that to kill another is not less ignoble than to live ourselves in terror of him. Our mission is to bring dishonor to our enemies—death after all is but the commodity, the exchange of nations—and in dishonoring our enemies we gain that salva- tion which alone should interest modern man: I mean that act of being saved from what fills him with horror, that escape from the bone-melting fear of being fatherless. The two scarlet snakes writhed down his cheeks. For as individuals we have lost faith. No miracle other than the miracle of a nation of men bound together by the ties of a common hatred, can long exist or earth. To love God, gentlemen, is as idle as to love your neighbor. Men do not kill because they love. Men kill because they hate. And this power of hate is the only miracle which is possible to men who have lost their faith in the nature of God, and in the nature of this sick love for one's fellows.

Well, I tell you that fat boy was wound up, a talker, I've heard a few all right, but he made with the miffkis and a little over, it's a sort of wind-sweat, I think it really is, I think six hours of it is a bit too apt to snuff out all personal initiative, as the cowboy said when his pony stepped in a gopher hole, despite radio forums and all the ills which are directly traceable to what the psychologists call 'dismemberment benefits.' It will get you everytime. I do have the call on that one. The strangest things will happen in the quietest places—Take out in Ronnville, Wyoming, I was sharing a room with a fellow named Lebu, Lebu S. Trigge. This particular morning —just before dawn it was—Lebu came in. His clothes were damp and sour with sweat and the stink of cheap whiskey. Our eyes came together in the mirror. We've been friends since we were kids, he said.

You mean a week ago we were kids? I said.

Hell, it seems longer than a week, Almar.

It may seem longer, but that's all it is, Lebu, a week.

He took a .32 out of the bureau drawer. I want you to give me a little information, he said, giving me the gat's blind eye.

What information? I said, trying to stare the eye down without any success whatever.

How are people going to get out of this mess?

Wouldn't you like to know?

I would. And you're going to tell me.

Like hell I am.

Someone knocked on the door.

Come in!

THEY SAID THERE WOULD BE PEACE WHERE IS IT? WHERE IS PEACE!

Here we are, Lebu, all bright and early, Clark said, standing back to let the others in.

Sloan had a knife out.

You boys know what I want, Lebu said.

Oh, he'll spill it all right, Timberly said, beginning slowly to—

The "old chroniclers," ruddy campfires, a jug of cold buttermilk, thick wedges of cheese, deevnir bread, the intent, eager faces, a hush, wet and smelling of dead leaves, from the river, damn, it's true, I admit it, there's something about a good story that gets people. The man swung down the rope of vines. He chuckled as his feet touched the stones of the courtyard. As though he had every right in the world to do it, he walked out through the stone gate. A block away he passed two men, a woman, and a little boy. After he'd gone by, the woman said, There was something strange about the face of that man.

The little boy started to cry.

The man walked into a bakery and ordered two mince pies. He ate them at the counter, spilling their stuff down his grimy shirt. The clerk was trying to remember if he'd said the right thing to Sue Bell, maybe in another three years, a raise of even 2.50 a week, now—

An hour later someone heard a wild laugh in the cemetery. The man was leap-frogging over the headstones.

The police didn't run him down that night. Or the next night. In fact, they never did run him down. An escaped lunatic—All right, I admit there's not much there to get steamed-up over.

But where did he go?

It's your vote. Throw it away if you want to.

Taking shape slowly, rising over the world like a giant with ragged holes for eyes—hands outstretched, moving its dripping lips down upon the houses. Men walk along at the level of tree-tops. They have a little pig on a string and they lower it to the earth. It sniffs hungrily, leaving pools of blood. A child puts a yellow flower into the blood and waves it about, crowing. Something is strange about the child. It has no head. I don't belong here! Dolly, please do not look at me. Run? I haven't it, running, I haven't any running left. Oh, I can laugh. Then naturally they won't . . . Whose face is that in every window I pass? What did Old Zen say? Old Zen, now—there really is a decent man. Old

179

Zen said . . . that's tricky, that's a painting somebody works at all the time, for thousands of years. The light hurts my eyes. He is kissing her! Why do my arms feel wet? I'll tear up everything, kick the whole damn—No, no, please, forget I said that! I don't actually want to go back. Why do they beat the little man in the yellow coat? Please, Mr— I am falling O all the stinking lights are going out. The Red Pig is nosing my shoes and I can't scream. Where is your mother? I can't scream and something is crawling into my bed O I don't know what good can come from trying to go back there anymore we all die of this same slow bleeding away inside somewhere . . .

Men are vicious when their lives are vicious, the angel said. Out of evil, only evil can grow; whosoever shall slay his fellow, shall himself be slain; men who market death must not grumble if the chief feature of their commerce is the destruction of themselves. Whosoever plots against his neighbor, loses that sense of personal identity which is only found in brotherhood; and it is this loss of identity which threatens the foundations of your world.

I tell you that this is the age of the anonymous man—that drear creature who will accept any guidance so long as he can submerge himself in a will stronger than his own. You are entering into that shadowed valley where the passionless submission of men shames the beasts of the steaming jungle.

It started to snow as the burial procession moved up the main street of the world . . . trailing on like a great, tortured worm through the rain and the little groups of silent human beings.

At last He was down and the dirt in. The snow fell. A face watched them from its position of concealment behind a headstone. Its eyes were rather horribly gleeful and vacant. It was everyone's face.

It doesn't do much good for long. It's almost as though I had lost all interest in everything. There's nothing I really care to be or to do or to have done. Even death—the main dying, that's over anyway. I stand outside somewhere without interest or will or desire of any kind at all.

Two long snakes of fire wriggle down the hills and into the valley. They come from opposite directions, to meet, their glowing heads kissing—

THEY SAID

THERE

WOULD BE

BROTHERHOOD

WHERE IS BROTHERHOOD!

Ah Christ the little stories always end. The little cruelties, the petty evils . . . Punishment? After all, the greatest crimes don't amount to much. One thing as limited as the next—evil as good. It's only the world that's dying—it's only the soul of every poor devil of us that cries for the Light.

Welcome God

O God of Light we welcome Thee!

It might be better to have faith.

And now the red snow is beginning to fill the valley. It covers the roofs of the rich and the poor . . . so soft and wet

O it is falling on every one of us.

All are silent and afraid.

Then somewhere in the distance a terrible voice speaks—and is answered.

Hello.

Hello.

The wooing of monsters.

HELLO!

HELLOO!

I tell you that what has to be changed is the whole conception of human life—that men of every race on this earth may have the same opportunity to live beautifully—to live in purity without fear or hunger or hatred—as brothers, not as brutes tearing through these hideous swamps of ignorance and war. Men speak of a belief in God. I am beginning to understand what every Christ—and their skins have been every color—what every Christ has taught:

That love of God is love of mankind. That no one can profess to love God while he hates the least of his fellows. Jesus, if He were on earth now, would fight to free men from oppression and evil and war; and you who have made a pious mockery of His every commandment—you would kill Him.

BEAUTY! THEY PRATTLED OF BEAUTY ... I SEE NOTHING BUT UGLINESS HERE!

What a scaly crowd of hypocrites! filthy, cheap lice crawling on the corpse of a world you have stifled with your self-righteous lies and cold-blooded murders!

O now it whirls a little.

Place your grubby hand on—

O your eyes are covered with red slime.

—your eyes - - are - - covered
- - with - - red - -
O your - - - eyes - - - are - - - covered
WITH - - - - A - - - - RED - - - - SLIME—

So be it. Have done with this chatter about preserving truth and honor and dignity; these are dead. You saw to that. War alone is not the thing which chills the soul of man in this time; it is the simple realization, born in hunger and cruelty and despair, that nowhere is there anything he can believe in.

What a monstrous swindle!

O pray God that human beings may not forever be hunted down like blind beasts in a ditch; that they may not forever die of starvation in lands of unbelievable bounty; that they may not forever be driven to kill and be killed in furtherance of this brutal, cynical plan to keep madmen in the seats of power.

Let's get back to the bubble . . .

★ ★ ★ ★ ★ ★ ★ ★ ★ ★

HEREWEGOHEREWEGOHEREWEGOHE

Ekun 6Q-R. This morning I ate alone on a hill behind the village. There had been a rain during the night and the surrounding fields glistened in the sun. I felt completely at peace; there seemed to be nothing whatever to be at odds with. In this district—far out at the edge—a pastoral simplicity prevailed. I had nearly finished my pudding when I beheld one of the natives making its awkward way toward me. At first I may have wondered why they were all of different shapes and colors; but more did I wonder at the <u>usual</u> look of their houses and domestic implements, of their barns and bridges and random gear. The clear, sweet ringing of a bell brought tears to my eyes.

It is good to see you again, the creature said, kissing me with great tenderness.

184

The brown and gold face, with its more than fifty eyes, came off on my lips as I drew away. Would you like some pudding? I asked, extending the bowl. Its stomach-mouth sent out two sucking tubes immediately.

The ground was covered with a soft hair that stirred continuously. Colonel Pot dismounted from one of their less fearful animals. He had taken his clothes off. Actually their animals were quite gentle; but they were rather startling to look at.

Hello, Al, Caffarelli said. The yacht came through it pretty well. It's my own notion if we hadn't had all those damn gadgets aboard, we could have ridden out the storm.

And if we hadn't had them, we wouldn't have sunk all the way down into this bubble, either, Colonel.

No, I suppose not. Have you seen the others this morning?

I think they're still sleeping off the effects of the dance last night.

Dance? That wasn't a dance—it was more a systematic brawl, if you want my opinion.

It was rather terrifying—but beautiful too.

The creature fell to kissing the Colonel with unbounded enthusiasm.

A little later I will describe their mating habits.

Ekun 8B-T. I was questioned all today. They are amazingly persistent. Understand that Little Remksheaffe is quite weak from loss of blood—stupid! why should they expect him to know.

Ekun 11V-M. These creatures—I might have known!—are only acting under orders. They weep with true pity when we cry out.

Ekun 8K-V. This is odd! Dolly visited me in the night to say that my voice has kept everyone awake with its shouting over by the

Darbinee Well. I went to the window and listened: Sure enough! there it was over there bellowing bloody murder! Odd because I had never even been within fifty feet of The Well in my life! SAVE US! GOD O GOD SAVE US!

Big dumb noise, my voice was already quite hoarse.

TO GRO
W ON T
HE TRE
E AGAIN

Ekun 6T-G. Catherine and Thane have disappeared. The ruins —at the suggestion of The Nubor—straight into the circle—without a guide, that <u>foolish pair</u>—I wonder why it is necessary for every pudding (the only food, as far as I know, here) to be peed upon by their puppies. I am told that they are raised for just this purpose. There are fourteen districts, or WORLDS, in the bubble: each quite unlike any other. Some have beings somewhat like us, but gentle "in the day."

Every'thing' is very kind to us.

★

Ekun 15J-O. We were all at the Love Table just sitting together being fond and proud of each other a kiss and a nudge for you and one for you please explain how I could ever have imagined that you folks were torturing us ridiculous of course Mrs. J— will undoubtedly make all this clear the feel of their lips rather frightening though almost like being kissed by yourself and as deep and wide as the dreams of the dead.

Beginning to nod at my desk—the paper breathing and shifting away if I want to lie. But I am a soul in trouble. It is all pure in its beginnings. There must be some escape from—escape from what? Houses, rivers, trees . . .

Do you understand that you are part of God?

So many eyes.

So much wonder to tell you about!

Abigail Buttermilk can become THE BRIDE OF MANKIND—Mengs Flink (I remember from childhood) will do as Prometheus—Colonel Pot . . . ohyiz, I reserve this soft-spoken Moses—

Take that which is most unlikely and fit it into the pattern—Humility, Love—

My God! There are so many devices, plots, and—It is wonderful to feel all this pouring out of my head! To slap it, jostle it—

taste its teeth—All this joyous knowledge! To match my wits with Creation's—

Come in, Dolly. Sit down. In another minute I'll make you breathe and talk—I'll give mankind a new one to love—Be as children again! That's all I've thirsted for—To understand what Purity means—It begins to burn—My heart, my brain, ah, they are at the service of God's grim fun!

The trees are walking about.

A bird borrows my hand to touch a star.

There is no night here—We are going to have a feast of imagining. And then all this will be real.

EVERY TIME A DOOR OPENS
SOMEBODY'S HEART GETS BUSTED

1.

On a hill above the town a tiny bird sat warming himself in the June sun. From time to time he flicked his brown head back to stare up into the awesome cavern. Then, perhaps dissatisfied with what he saw there, or simply because he loved to fly, he suddenly sped off down the valley. Perched happily on a cottonwood near the garden path, he began to sing. He sang carefully of the things in the world which had a special meaning for him—and many of these songs were filled with joy, but more were filled with sadness and a longing to enter into the very heart of the beautiful and implacable heavens. A young man opened the black gate and started up the path toward the house. At the same moment a young girl sped down through the crocuses and into his arms. "Thank goodness, Thane! at last a bit of sanity in this mad whirl!"—"Is it that bad?"—"Oh, it's worse, darling. 'Where do you want the chairs?' 'Where are the candles?' 'Here're the flowers.' 'The skirt's too short.' 'The skirt's too long.' 'There's not enough chicken.' 'Heavens, the cakes!' The doorbells, the telephone, people, and more people, presents, food. Gosh! Maybe we should have done it your way. But Mother and Dad simply eat it up—though it's lucky for his finances he doesn't have any more daughters. I know one thing, I'm certainly glad we don't have any dowry system here —or you'd not have married me for the small dot I could fetch."— "Maybe your father'ed throw in a couple pigs."—"Mean!"—"If you look at me like that, I'll sure as hell give your maiden aunts something to buzz about. Let's for Christ's sake get away from here for a little while. They can struggle along without you for an hour or so."—"Let's." The bird started to sing again. As the black gate clanged to behind them, she put her arm through his and they turned up the street. "Let's go to the top of the world—our little world, Tranny."—"Swell! Gee! today's so beautiful. Oh, darling, I'm so happy!"—"So desirable, too."—"Them's nice words, part-ner." They came to a spring gushing out of a little pocket in the moss and rocks. "Umm, that's cold," Tranquil said. He put his mouth on the silvery wonder of her lips. "Yum, yum," he said. She drank again. "Now see." After a long minute he said, "I love you, Tranny. Jesus, I'm nuts about you!"—"How nuts?" He looked off across the valley. "That's all been said so damn often, it doesn't mean anything anymore."—"That you love me, Thane?"—"Nah, about love—love in general."—"There's no such animal. Tell me how much you love me."—"Tranny," he said softly. She pressed her body hard against his body. "Stars and puppy dogs," she whispered. "Soft rain on a mountain."—"Yellow roses and old barns."—"Oh, my dearest . . . Don't . . . Not now . . ." He sud-denly picked her up and started to run up the steep path. "You'll rupture yourself," she warned, half-laughing. "I could carry you to China and back," he said. "I feel like I'm about twenty feet tall. Goddam I could pick the world up and throw it right smack at that star."—"Isn't that Plusis down there?" she said, pointing. "Where? I don't see him."—"Near that big stone in the pasture." —"Yeah. Now I see him. Hey! Plu!" He waved his arms around. "There. He sees us."—"What's that noise, Thane?"—"What noise?"—"Off in the bushes there."—"Oh . . . now I hear it. Probably some kids playing. See. What'd I tell yuh? It's a dog." Tranquil tried to whistle. "Here, boy! Here, boy!"—"Phooey on people who can't even whistle, he says." And Thane grinned, watching enviously as the mutt made a bush think it was raining for a minute there. "Must be hunters around," Tranquil said. "He looks like a rabbithound."—"Beagle. To hell with 'im. Di' I ever tell you I'm kinda stuck on you, kid?"—"Tell me again!" she said, stopping on the crown of the hill and waiting for him to take her into his arms. But he didn't take her into his arms. Instead, a look of enormous surprise filling his eyes, he sank to the ground.

Then Tranquil heard the sound of a rifle. Thane's shirt was growing a big red rose.

Plusis ran up the hill toward them.

2.

The moon's astonished mug stares in at her window. Sad, ghostly herds wander down the blue courses of heaven. The air tastes of comfortable, tired clocks and the gingery sleep of old houses. In the lives of wells and orchards and ruined fences there is a strange quickening—almost as though the history of what is separate from the knowledge of men, were merged, in some hidden manner, and by an agency as mysterious as that of sea and wind and stone, in a fiery river whose one bank is life, and whose other bank is not death. The most beautiful and desolate thing in

190

the world is a country village at night. Every sound should be the gentle conspiring of angels; the steeple of a church, it is the up-stretching pinky of some forgotten queen; this hillside, a cluster of brown deer awaiting only the horn of a terrible huntsman to set them down lanes where postilions of black stars hurry. Given a voice, this village would say: Nothing can alarm God. Given feet to walk, it would go where the most pitiful cry moves the sternest heart. So still is this wonder; so without change is the grandeur of a leaf—O Father the bell-brooding streets of this dear and hor-rible place . . .

So varied is the almanac of this silence . . . The druidical war-ring of a fat white cat on the green fence of the world . . .

Tiny spotted feet of light coming into her room . . . Now at the bureau . . . pressing wanly through the rungs of a chair . . .

If I say it over and over, then maybe I'll go to sleep . . . My name is Tranquil Flume. I am twenty-two years old. Oh, my name is Flume, Tranquil Flume and I am twenty-two years of age. Of young. Of life. Of beauty. What shall I wear tomorrow? Dark blue dress I bought in Boston. O the dark blue dress. Tranquil's dark blue dress. The very one she bought in Boston which used to be a nice city to live in O why can't I cry!

(She crosses to the window. Sometimes life is a bitch, huh? How about it? don't you think so?)

But I don't really want to cry. It's funny . . . Don't you think it's funny, Mr. Moon, that I don't really want to cry? O my name is Tranny don't want to cry. I am twenty-two go to sleep and if I wake flake take. Or get a tummy-ache. Don't talk like that Tran-quil. Go to the bathroom maybe you'll feel better sitting in there where romance can't get at you. There where care bare hair flair stare. Now Tran go oh so quietly to bed for my name is Pudding Tame and nothing is going to make Ladding Pume puddle or be dirty again you nasty evil little brat you and always mama's stinko I know why she drinks but I shouldn't know little girls shouldn't know what goes on with big girls and boys like Mother and Dad O my name is Franquil Tume and I want him to come into my bed now and put his hands on me and press me down and then I want him to hurt me yes I said hurt me to take the pain out and make believe anyway I'm like everybody else's body and have got the same places and hurry I may even let the mailman take me down cellar

heard of a man with hair on it

ha ha with hair on his tongue—O God when can I be all still and clean and safe . . .

(At last the moonlight touches her pillow, spreads like a forlorn and gentle hand over her sleeping face. It won't always be lonely and sad. It won't always hurt. When you're dead it won't. When you're dead it should be easy to last it out a couple million years. It should be easy to be dead a nice good long time.)

A glad contentment in the air of morning . . . I do so want to walk into the fields today. "No, mother, I haven't forgotten—when she calls, just tell her I'll see her some day next week."—"But, darling, this is the second time you've not been here when she's come."—"Julia will understand."—"Wouldn't another dress be better to go walking in?"—"I'll be very careful."—"Are you sure you're all right, Tranquil?"—"Oh, please, mother . . ."—"But we worry about you, darling."—"I've told you and daddy so many times . . . I just feel so peaceful and nice wandering about the fields." How can they understand that? How can they understand that I am so beautifully quiet and clean away deep inside me . . . As though the hills and the pure, lovely sky were growing here within my throat and heart. A fire of dandelions . . . I see daisies, too. Bouquets for my pretty lady . . . Heads of the herd-grass nibbling at the wind—I met him first in winter . . .

O Thane

I am almost ready to cry now!

This is an inviting lane. A pretty hill. Oh, a cunning little dog . . .

They said it was a hunter. O they did say indeed it was a hunter a hunter a hunter A HUNTER

Bing! says the hunter.

O a huntering we will go . . . in a red coat.

In a red coat.

In a red coat. INAREDCOAT

In a red coat.

O my name is Tranquil Flume. I am twenty-two 22 22 22 22 22 22 22 22 22 22 22 22 22 22 November I think it was yes November a Wednesday a Wednesday at eight-seventeen in the evening. 'You dance very well.'—'Thank you, kind sir.'—'And this is my friend, Plusis Jidet. We were room mates in college.' (Plusis is short and his eyes are a light yellow and his hair is a bright orange. I think we're all in a mess.) Dull blossoms of the swamp maple . . . I love New England. I love New England because

"Oh, hello, Fitzmichael, I didn't hear you coming."—"Out for a walk?"—"Yes."—"Nice day, Miss Flume."—"It certainly is. It's a beautiful day, Fitzy." Looking over his shoulder at me. Wondering why my eyes aren't red . . . You wouldn't understand, Fitzmichael Kell! Buttonwood trees . . . Wild, sly grin of vines around an abandoned gate . . . Sorrow of a house in which no one lives . . . drowning in this green and careless sea . . . The sun's shadow lengthens on the hill . . . Shaggy thighs of the hedgerows toss in a last scarlet restlessness, and then turn blue and still . . . Evening over the valley . . . Gray towers thrusting up through the smoke-veined glow . . . Night's walking staff tapping a thousand pale thrones . . . "But your supper is cold, Tranquil." And again the moon at her window. To open my hands very slowly . . . To know that whatever I do tomorrow will be quiet and safe and clean . . . To know that whatever I feel will be quiet and safe and beautiful . . .

A white candle burning on a table of furry ice . . .

I am so wonderfully content . . . and waiting . . . Should I really try to remember? Tranny at nine . . . Tran at fifteen . . Miss Tranquil Jane Flume at eighteen . . . O why should I try to remember any of that now! I am so complete and still . . . without the Trannys who were always a little worried that my hair wasn't combed quite neatly enough, that the two-strapped pumps didn't really look smart with my brown woolen suit, that Thane had seemed somewhat well distant when he kissed me goodnight . . . Goodnight, my sweet . . . my darling . . .

She gets quickly out of bed and crosses to the window. The life of the village is hushed, secret under the unwatching caravan . . . Almost the last light melts out . . . A tiny breeze stirs the whitened spires of the elms . . . I can't see the hills from here. Neither his lips on mine nor any voice plubbing my mind awake. But my heart weaves a cloth to cover what can never be tainted or made to redden under any hunter's shrill gun . . . Everywhere in me . . . aisles of majestic cathedrals . . . landscapes where no traveller is ever lost . . . where fruit and flower have no peril of weather or rot . . . O a door that was locked is now open . . . a key that was hidden burns in my hand . . .

When he fell, I did not fall.

While I breathe, he shall not lack for breath.

Mingled . . . opposed by a bitter wing . . . yet through all that is silent in him, echoes a steady, unchangeable voice . . . the voice of my ceaseless skill in not letting him die at all! And so

glint of a star-fretted wave . . . an eye which is brighter than fear . . . a fish in which the ocean has its being

O love whose home is my flesh! Whose life lives in mine . . .

To peep into the giddy mouth of the wind: and ask if your grave is there! To say—I can feel the touch of cool fingers on my breasts O I can feel him entering me

O every thorn-point of light sharpens my skin to your caress . . . every muffled step along the street heralds the moment of your infinite arrival . . . O unsleeping I watch you . . . I watch as you

194

approach naked to my bed . . . I move my thighs until you have plunged into me and then O my love and then O my sweet my love I bite my tongue and I begin to say do it do it do it do it do it do it O hungry tired or wet or cold I shall make you well and give you food and warmth and all the night you will hold me in your arms

and no one will ever guess that you are not dead at all

and so goodnight my darling Oh so peacefully shall we sleep . . . so very near . . . so quiet and safe in our dear love and let the world go to hell

it's even all right to have a mother who frinks like a dish mnnnnnnnnnrrrzzzddd ooooo do it do it do it O do it do it to me O what a wonderful how pretty it is to taste your kisses in back of my lips . . .

Mr. Flume restored his coffee cup to its chipped saucer. "Isn't Tranquil coming to breakfast this morning, Hazel?"—"I don't know, Tom. I called her over half an hour ago. Perhaps I should just go up and—" — "No. She'll come down when she gets hungry."—"I'm worried, Tom."—"Nonsense. Be thankful she takes it so calmly. I must confess I thought she would be a lot more upset than she is."—"But that's what worries me. It isn't natural, Tom. Tranquil's always been such an emotional child . . . so full of plans and big excitements."—"Then be thankful she acts grown-up about it. I was expecting her to take it pretty hard. I wish you didn't feel it necessary to drink a quart of whiskey before breakfast every day, Haz."—"But is she being grown-up about it, Tom? Oh, that's just a habit."—"What do you mean? I must say it's one hell of an expensive habit."—"Well, for one thing, she hasn't once cried . . . not even once. I have to get a little fun out of life."—"What good would crying do her? Besides, how do you know she hasn't? She's been off alone enough to have cried it all out of her system. I should fun you with a baseball bat."—"I'd know if she had. She's just sort of all tense and knotted-up. Keep Freud out of this. Oh,

Tom, sometimes I'm almost afraid that . . . that . . ."—"Stiddleficks!"
—"But it ain't healthy . . . It aren't right. It oozn't like our Tranny,
Dadums."—"Ippn't that the sound of a poor fellow creature at the
front door of our little home?"—"Oh, it be Plusis. When did you
get back, Plu?"—"Of the night last, Mrs. Flume. I can't say I think
it's good for your system to be a-eatin' the necks of them bottles;
how do you know whom may have been a-handlin' o' them now?
Oh, I say, Mr. F., I hardly knew ye without your clothes."—"My
skin was tender this morning; et a rasher of bacon jest I to went
bed afore. Had your breakfast? Plenty of ink-fish left, son."—
"Thanks, no, oh. I past re hours agone. I've been busy trying
to set things straight at the office."—"Too bad Thane chose to
bust up the partnership in such a way dramatic."—"Yeah, you'd
think a smart young fellah like him'd have better things to do than
goin' round stoppin' o' bullets, yet. I believe I will have a cup of
cream—very little coffee—thank you. Hardest thing I ever did was
takin' his name off the door; he'd put it on with a blowtorch."—
"That hunter turned hasn't up?"—"Nope. Poor devil. Is Tranquil
around, Mrs. Flume?"—"Why, ah—" — "Call her again, Hazel.
And this time take that damn bottle out of yer mout'. Got I've pop
the to office now to."—"Mr. you see Church F. in."—"Tranquil
will be down in a moment. 'Bye, Tom."—"Try to hold yourself
down to two quarts this afternoon, dear. It's sort of depressing to
come home tired from a hard day and find you taking a wash in
the oven and cooking my dinner in the bathtub." (Mr. Flume leaves
for his office. Tranquil comes down. The leaves of the maples wind
in the stir. A little man in Decatur says, "That's the third splinter in
two days! And this is the product they advertise as being safe for
babies!") "Why don't you two sit out on the porch awhile?"—
—"And have every neighbor in town snooping in."—"Why, Tranquil, what ever put such an idea in your head?"—"Well, it's true!
I can't walk down the street without having every sonofabitch on
the block peeking out of the window at me. Oh, mother, I just don't

want these bastards pulling and tugging at me. I feel so . . . so sort of withdrawn and pure . . . too holy and inviolate to be besmirched by their goddam spying."—"If you were a good girl, you'd stay quietly at home and help your mother kill this bottle."—"I know what they want. They want me to start blubbering and wailing away like any common little schoolgirl. Naturally they resent what they can't understand . . . what their shoddy little minds can't even imagine . . . Well, by God I'll go on being the way I feel! Honest and deep and real!"—"Here, take a snort, darling—it'll set you up. You're just getting yourself all upset."—"That's just it— I don't have to be upset! Can't anyone understand! I . . . I feel so strong and clean—" — "Suppose I come back some other time, Tran?"— "All at not, Plusis. I'm glad you've come to see me. It's only right that Thane's best friend should come to see me. In fact, I want very much to talk with you."—"Well—" — "We'll go into the garden. I so love the garden in the morning. It just seems . . . well, sacred . . . as though every bird and flower and bee had come here to pray. This is a comfortable bench. Do sit down, Plu. Oh . . . blue, serene heavens . . . clouds like dainty swan boats . . ."—"Tranquil."—"Umm."—"To speak very . . . well, bluntly, I—" — "As a lawyer?"—"In a way, yes."—"Thane was a mouthpiece too, Plusis."—"This sort of thing . . . I don't understand, Tran."—"What sort of thing don't you understand?"—"I'm not a very complicated person—"—"Should you be?"—"Perhaps not, Tranquil. I don't know whether to be sorry for you or—" — "Sorry for me!"—"Yeah, I can't tell whether this is really genuine or just something you're sort of acting."—"Acting!"—"I knew it would be no good."— "Why . . . Why I think . . . I think it's very good, Plusis. I'm able to understand why Thane was so fond of you."—"Whatayuh mean?" —"You're a very quieting sort of person, Plu."—"I'm glad you think so."—"Yes, you're so very stolid and dull."—"If it makes you happy to insult me, Tranquil—"—"Oh, but I'm not! Eagle—a sheaf of wheat—There must be two sides."—"It suited me fine to be the back of Thane's coin."—"That's what I'm saying, Plu. When the eagle soars into the stars, there must be someone to watch and applaud him."—"There isn't anything for us to talk about."—"Oh, but there is! Surely you and Thane had a lot to talk about."—"Perhaps I wasn't so stolid and dull with him."—"What did you talk about?"—"Oh . . . everything and nothing."—"About me?"—"Of course."—"What did he say about me?"—"I'd be no good at telling you that, Tranquil."—"Try."—"Well, how much he—Please, Tran."—"Don't be silly. We're grown-up. We can look at these things intelligently, sanely."—"I told you before . . . It's just no good. I don't know exactly why, but . . . Oh, damn! Thane is dead. All that's over, finished, kaput."—"You can get excited, can't you?"—"Yes, damnit, I can. Frankly, I don't like this. There's something sick and unclean about it."—"Are you scared of me, Plusis?"—"Why should I be? You're just in a mood today I can't follow; that's all."—"Did Thane ever tell you that he couldn't follow my moods?"—"No."—"Did he ever say he was afraid of me?"—"No. Why should he have been afraid of you? You don't weigh more than ninety-four pounds."—"Ninety-three and a half. You are."—"All right."—"What are you afraid of, Plu?"—"That you're not really feeling any of this."—"Any of what?"—"What you should feel."—"What should I feel?"—"What anybody else in your place would."—"But anybody else isn't in my place."—"Then that's that."—"You're so damn sure how I should feel."—"Oh, shoot! You make me say things I don't want to say!"—"What don't you want to say?"—"That I don't believe you feel at all."—"Good, dull Plusis."—"All right. Good, dull Plusis will just run along now."—"Please don't go."—"Why should I stay?"—"You feel hurt for Thane's sake, don't you?" He stands looking down at her. The sunlight puts golden fingers through her hair. "I love Thane, Plusis." He doesn't speak or move to go. "If I said that I loved him, then I'd cry and behave exactly as you want me to. But what's important is that I am in love with him . . . now . . . this minute . . . forever . . ."—"All right, kid. I admit that all this is beyond me. Love, loved . . . Words will do almost anything you want."—"But you'd rather I cried?"—"It doesn't matter what I'd rather. You seem to have what you want, and I suppose it's just as good one way as another."—"I . . . I . . . tried to cry . . . at first." Plusis sits down beside her. "Do you have any plans?"—"Plans? What sort of plans do you mean?"—"Oh, I don't know . . . To visit your aunt in Boston. To get a job. What the hell, everybody's got to have plans of one kind or another."—"Well I haven't; though"—and she looks off across the rows of crocuses—"I don't ever want to leave here."—"Tran."—"Um?"—"I . . . If anything I said today hurt you, why—" — "Oh, not at all, Plu. I can see how you wouldn't be able to understand how I feel."—"Have you seen Mr. Tiger?"—"For a couple minutes yesterday morning. Did Thane ever tell you why he loved me?"—"He told me a lot about the good times you had together. Have you seen Andrew Petras?"—"No. That jerk! But what did he say about me?"—"Andy's not such a bad guy. I hear that Simon Cost got took at the horses. He said you were pretty. Has Flossie Bird had her baby?"—"Pretty? Floss died. Simon nearly raped me once."—"Pretty, beautiful—you know. Matthew Jumms is going to kill somebody one of these days. He said your eyes were so clear and sort of deep . . . That—" —"Yes, go on. What's eating Matt?"—"Oh, I don't know . . . he's been put away twice for molesting baby elephants. The sort of thing a lad will say about the girl he loves."—"Did he say he liked to kiss me? Sue Williamson and Milly Favor were run over by a truck last Wednesday. Did he, Plu?"—"I've already stayed longer than I—" — "Than you what? Sue lost both legs."—"Than I planned to."—"Did he? Peter Wake got shot in a drugstore holdup." —"Bad? No."—"Paralyzed his right side. He didn't?"—"No, he never talked about things like that."—"I'll bet. Didn't he say he was crazy to go to bed with me?"—"Bartholomew Armen went back to Wyoming finally. No, of course not."—"I thought he was from

Colorado. Would you?"—"Would I talk about it, you mean? Actually he's from Georgia—he was taken out to Vermont when he was two days old."—"No, I mean would you?"—"Would I what?"—"Be crazy to go to bed with me."—"I'll drop in again before long."—"Would you?"—"I don't think that would be so crazy."—"Did he ever say he wanted to tear me apart with his bare hands?"—"That sap woulda worn gloves."—"Did he ever say he could eat me with a spoon?"—"He woulda used a fork."—"Why do you hate him so, Plusis?"—"Because he kept me from you, babe."—"So now he's dead."—"Oh, boy!"—"What are you going to do?"—"I'm going down to the cornah and shoot me a couple games of snooker." The sky watched in silence as he went.

3.

Fall, angel. This has purely been, and is no more.

O luminous and awesome shadow, sink back to thy dark abode . . .

I am awake . . . my heart is in my breast again . . . and oh there it shall break . . . and breaking, lose thee . . . O my gray and beautiful lover . . . for (indeed) to wake now is not to see, but to be blinded and ordinary forever . . . Blinded . . . gloom-bent candle on a table of water . . .

And stop all that sings! Let the instruments shine in their cases . . . O let this heart which is dead be cut out of my cold flesh . . .

Let no door open.

Let the splendor of lions fade into the dusty maw of the commonplace . . .

Oh! see how wonderfully I can cry!

I cry for Christ's sake because my heart is broken.

My bed is empty.

Nobody's hand runs over my thighs.

Nobody puts his—

"Tranquil."—"Oh, hell! What is it, mother dear?"—"May I

come in?"—"I'm all right."—"I just wanted to say goodnight."—
"Well—Good-night."—"Are you feeling better now?"—"I'm all
right."—"Would you like a glass of milk."—"A glass of milk! I bet
you wouldn't even hold one in your hand. Go away!"—"But
darling, you must try to get some sleep."—"How can I sleep with
you stumbling around all over everything! Oh, Jesus! cut it out!"
—"And just why can't I kiss my little girl?"—"Partly because you've
got your puss pressed up against the bed-post, and partly because you've got a bottle in it. Oh, I feel so miserable!"—"There,
there, sweetheart. Just you have a good cry on mamma's shoulder."—"Maybe I would—if you'd undrape yourself from that bureau. And take your foot out of that pottie!"—"What you need's
a rest, pet. Get away from all this for awhile."—"You're telling
me! There! You pushed Uncle Snowden out of the window—"
—"They wouldn't let me walk around them. There are too many
things here which remind you of him."—"You remind me of a
Christmas tree . . . with that big red bulb blazing away above your
moustache. That's the whole trouble—nothing reminds me of him.
I can't even remember what he looked like, what kind of shirts he
wore . . . Oh, hell! Do you think I'd be crying like this if I could
remember him! If there was even one teensy little thing that—
Blaah!"—"Nature is wiser than we are, darling. Sometimes we are
protected from taking on more of a load than we can carry."—
"Look who's talking. Who the devil wants to be protected! I want
to feel! To draw closer to—Aah, all that's over and done with!
Now all I can do is cry like any silly girl whose lover is dead."—
"It's always like that, Tranquil. Nobody can beat the system."—
"It is not! It wasn't with me! Oh, I get all mixed-up . . . Before I felt
how I felt . . . so new and strong . . . as though our love were
great and beautiful . . . like it might last a good six months. And
now . . . All I know is he's dead . . . and there isn't a damn thing
to remind me that he was ever alive."—"Please try to go to sleep
now, honey."—"Why should I care anymore about him bein' dead

201

than about the millions and millions of other poor lads who are dead . . . shot down by anonymous hunters, the lot of them."—"Time heals all wounds."—"Who the hell wants it to heal! A wound, huh? It was just like a new and wonderful person had been born in me . . . as though for the first time I really loved Thane . . . that somehow my love was finer and deeper than if he'd been alive . . ."—"Hush . . . You shouldn't say such things . . . they might raise our taxes."—"Now you've got both feet in it! Something's destroyed all the wonderful way I felt . . . Oh, I can only feel resentful to him for not being great and noble enough to deserve the kind of love I was capable of giving."—"The shock, most likely."—"I wish Uncle Snowden would crawl off and moan under some other window. Today I first realized that it wasn't Thane at all I loved . . . Why, that dope wouldn't have recognized the Thane I'd created to love. The Thane that watched me out of Plusis' eyes."—"Why, child, you're trembling. Shall I get you a physic?"—"No, get me a new life."

"No, Julia."—"Yes, Julia."—"Good evening, Mrs. Bitch."—"Yes, mother's home."—"It was so nice of you to write that letter."—"Yes, dad, I'd enjoy that very much."—"The stores are very exciting."—"Hell, I think I'd prefer a dress with a short bodice."—"I've had a simply marvelous visit, Aunt Hester."—"September is lovely in Boston. The leaves look so pretty above the puddles of sailor vomit."—"You really must forgive me, Plu. I haven't played tennis in just ages and ages."—"I'm helping mother stretch curtains this morning, but—oh, this afternoon'll be fine!" Flame in the maples . . . Brown lights dancing on the hill . . . And if a star fall . . . bright dagger flashing in the hand of night . . . "I did have fun, Arnold. Heaps."—"Well, you could write Phyllis and Louise and that Vincent girl from Colechester. Let's see now—Constance and Peggy are out. Most of the boys'll bring chicks anyway."—"Yes, Clyde mentioned her several times, but I haven't met her yet . . . supposed to be quite nice. Chews betel nuts, I believe. Oh, I've got it—ask Clarence's kid brother: What's his name?—Mulemire or something like that. He's a chemist—no, a foot doctor."—"Really? I thought Dale was planning to paint. Maybe, who knows?—But I can't imagine what he'd write about . . . he still won't let anybody but his mother dress him."—"Bruce doesn't drink enough."—"I always thought Gayfol was sort of childish. It may have been smart once not to be housebroken."—"June always looks so pert and sweet. Wasn't that tough luck her father's store burning down on his evening off? He carried nearly fifty thousand on himself."— "With just a flub of lemon, please." Dark lights dancing on the hill. "I can't remember when I saw a lousier movie. Why can't life be like that?"—"No, I am not chilly, but I simply must go in now. Tonight you imagine I'm all the world to you, but you'll be right back jerking sodas tomorrow."—"I'd rather not dance, Thomas. I'd hate mother to think me a liar—I told her I couldn't." Cold lights fading on the hill . . .

One o'clock.

Three o'clock.

Why is it never no time at all?

Always the shapes of things in constant movement on the earth . . .

But the least creation of God is not alarmed.

Meanings are not difficult; they're impossible.

Life's sculpture fails at the stone.

How delicious it would be to add one gay and terrible bough to the Mystery.

To bring all clocks and gardens jolting to their feet with the scent of a new blossom, with the tolling of a truly majestic bell. Plink. Pleesh.

There's certainly not a hell of a lot we can do to prepare for the angel—but it may be supposed that he will forgive us our faltering.

It's more than twenty miles to heaven.

No tiger ever got drunk on goat pee.

Like the smile of a turtle, the coverings of life tell us very little concerning the real nature of the world.

It happened simply enough. Yup, it sure did.

Tranny was just turning in at the gate. Night, swaggering down from the upper reaches, hadn't yet touched the valley with his soft, raw hands. Day's graying honey still clung to the honeycomb of woods . . . the fumbling, blurred wings of Joseph-coated bees seeking a last sweetness in the floral west . . . (Gawd that's perty!) And high over all, without impatience or rancor, a storm whispered his initial, gorged admonition . . . great anguished torches beginning to flash through the seething grave-clothes . . . (And they gave Coolidge a dollar a word!) The first, blood-warm drop fell. Tran paused; she gandered up into the working heavens. Low-throated growls as the sullen, fiery cats skulked out of their cages . . . Oh, what a nuisance! Now I can't wear my new dress after all. Why couldn't you have waited until tomorrow night to rain?—And then she looked down the darkening street.

A man was walking toward her.

She stood for one horrified, unbelieving moment watching him, then, in wild abandon, dropping everything she carried, she ran to meet him—a clawing, tender cry searing her throat. It was raining pigeons and rabbits by the time she got near enough to know that the world had again ended . . . The voice of a stranger asking, "Is there something wrong, miss?"—"No. No, I . . . No, nothing's wrong."—"Hadn't you better get back out of the rain?"—"Yes. Yes, I had better be getting back."—"Storms certainly come up fast around here. Out in Michigan—that's my home—why, out there—damn nice country, Michy—you can see a blow comin' for days ahead of time. I can remember a man had a yellow wagon—" — "And?"—"And what?"—"What about the man had a yellow wagon?"—"I finally had to chop him up with an ax. Kin I he'p yuh pick yer sterf erp?"—"No, please don't bother.

I kin pick them erp meserf."—"No bother, miss. Maybe it was because he—I've always wanted people to respect me . . . to accept
me on my own terms. There, that's the last of them."—"Thank you
very much. I hope I didn't startle you too badly running up the
way I did—" — "Nah, I just figured you probably mistook me for
somebody else."—"Yes, I . . . I guess maybe I did." Pressing her
face into the pillow . . . nails biting into her clenched hands . . .
My name is Trunny Flame it's all back now the feel of his mouth
the smell of nicotine on his fingers the sound of his laugh O my
God I want him—"Darling, Plusis's downstairs."—"Tell him I can't
see him now. I—" — "Tranquil, you're not catching cold, are you?"
—"Why . . . Yes, I think I am, mother."—"I'm not surprised! Of all
the fool things, hic, sitting up here in your wet clothes! You change
them this minute!"—"Okay, mother. Don't go down with that pot
on your foot."—"We all have a hard time in the world. Each new
day seems emptier than the last."—"Why do you suppose we were
created in the first place?"—"For someone's malicious amuse-
ment, if you ask me." Burning fruit spinning down from the topmost
bough of the heavens . . . shoulders of the wind groaning under
that wanton pounding. And from the shelves of the immense cupboard, terrible stone jars tumbling down . . . thud of their shat-
tering making the necks of mountains sway like wounded snakes. . .

Tranquil at last found the path which led to the place of death
on the hill. Her party dress caught in every bramble and over-
hanging rock. Her hair streamed over her face like whips in the
hands of a mad queen.

She reached the spring where they had stopped to drink that
day. I love, you, Tran. (O tell me how much you love me.)

She went higher.

She reached the place of death on the crown of the hill.

Suddenly the anger of the wind lessened . . . was stilled. The
rain lost its violence. Now that I am here . . . What now! From the
radiance, this! this! this stagnant puddle! What now? O is this

commonplace cup of tepid water the draught to quench my fiery thirst! So have I dared!

Dirty water seeping into my pretty pretty box . . .

O I hate this stupid, dull wind that doesn't even care enough to blow now! O rain! you smug, dull rain! It was fun, I suppose, ruining my dress . . . O I hate this dull little town, this dull little world . . . I hate all these nice, dull little people . . . O I wanted so much to have something . . . something that would

somebody for Christ's sake give me something to live for!

She got up and crossed to stand in front of the mirror. How strangely quiet I look. My eyes feel as though they were frozen. She tried to command them, to shift their gaze . . . They remained transfixed, unmoving . . . and suddenly she thought: These are not my eyes which are watching me; these are the eyes of another. She tried to scream; no sound came to her tranquilly-set lips. What have I done? What has happened to me? With a curious sense of detachment she saw a hand rise to touch her cheek. Dimly she knew that it was her own hand, but the fingers felt nothing . . . nor was their touching felt. And she was conscious of a great sadness—of a sadness which was the greatest joy she had ever known; for at last she knew that all her grief was for herself—even as all her love was for herself.

Her eyes filled with tears . . . and she turned them slowly to the window. She thought (without at all knowing that she thought): I shall see Thane lying at my feet in his beautiful red coat, and he will lift a gun to kill my love . . . But it is not here! O it is not here that my love is! And yet there is something I can't remember . . . There is something which should have been said; there is a place where I have not gone; a door which has not opened; O there is a voice which my heart has not heard at all

And she saw a red stain mantle her chin . . . O I have bitten my lip and this is my blood I taste. Lightly she touched her mouth with the tips of her fingers. I am looking into my own eyes. She left the mirror and crossed to the window. A great storm filled the valley. O darling I am afraid! I can't remember! Should the door close now, I'd be locked out forever. I taste his blood on my tongue . . . The body lying there still under the red coat has my heart in it—and my lips are moving under its mouth . . . O let me fall asleep in this deliciousness of being the weeper for whom alone the tears are shed. O the tender rinds of my ears sting with this effort to hear my true name spoken in a virgin, endless intimacy which no mortal can ever despoil.

A cold, detached frenzy shook every fiber of her being; and scarcely knowing what she did, activated more by absence of will than by any conscious intent or design, Tranquil put a coat over her nightgown and made her way silently downstairs. As she opened the door a fist of rain and wind struck savagely at her head and shoulders, nearly toppling her over backwards into the house: now my body too can enter in at the wild gate of Opirathon—even as in the high country of my spirit—O terrible horses charging upon these swaying walls . . .

But her knees banged into the garden bench; her hair whipped stingingly across her face, like . . . (whips . . . queen); her feet caught in the sodden train of her nightgown—now I've torn my coat and gud god ged splerty mud upon me!—; one of her slippers came off—oh darn! I wonder if toads and snakes go in when it rains?—; she suddenly felt chilled and frightened and ridiculous —what miserable nonsense could have possessed me to do this? (if anyone had told me that Tranny Flume could make such a foolish exhibition of herself . . .) 45ADX61MBR53YKS75ZA PERTY GIRL

As she bent to search for her slipper, a great sword of light cut the heavens in two; and she saw that she had wandered into the path which led up the hill. Suddenly the tension returned; her fists clenched; her body grew rigid; it was with extreme difficulty that she got her breath; it was almost as though the lightning had cut her in two; and now at last I shall know! I shall stand where

Thane lies on the hill—O at the top of the world itself . . . alone, grieving for Tranny, grieving for this love, for this love which haunts the stars O Thane my darling I am coming I am coming to hold you in my arms again to learn how I may keep you so that I may be your bride in a place where death and the world can never go . . . The hill was not a high one. She had only to pause between the frequent flashes of lightning in order to follow the next course of the path. And since she moved with the deliberation of a sleep-walker or of a very small child, no outward show of desperation marked her ascent; indeed, had anyone stood above there, it would have seemed as though he watched a doll with a curiously temperamental spring—a doll whose feet were directed to one, es-pecial objective, and whose workings would surely run down the moment it was achieved. She reached the spring where they had stopped to drink that day. O Thane wait for me! The rain lost its intensity. The rage of the wind calmed . . . grew still. O now that I am here my darling . . . She reached the place of death on the hill. The radiance, where is the radiance? These drab trees! This stagnant puddle! So—Dirty water seeping into my pretty pretty box . . . A last, dreary spatter of drops down upon the leaves . . . O I hate this stupid, dull wind that doesn't even bother to blow anymore. Rain—this smug piddle. O I hate this dull little town, this dull little world . . . I hate all these nice dull little people . . . O what difference does it make what I do! What does it matter what becomes of me

    "Tranquil."

    (A shining form standing there.)

    "Tranquil."

    (It raises its arms.)

    "Thane!"

    "Oh, my darling . . ."

    (She feels the cold touch of his body against her.)

    "Tranny, don't be frightened. I've just spoken to God and there

are a lot of things I must tell you. Within a few years now the
world is going to—"

she said there was a face at the window
but I'd brought her flowers and
there was a piece of bread
and a cup
half-full of tea on the table
—we went to bed
finally and
we lay talking quietly in the darkness
together a warm
wonderful thing
is a woman God there is something beautiful
in the way it feels
to touch her naked body . . . "Darling

I want you now."
But
suddenly she begins to cry
and she pushes me away
What
in the name of Christ is the matter
with this world!
"Everytime I close my eyes I see that terrible face
leering in at the window.
I lit a cigarette
and scratched
my cheek where the bandage was beginning to draw
those lads really went to a few towns
that weren't on my map before
all right it's pretty
late to be saying this I
know but I like being alive damn
it why don't we come right out and say if
there was nothing
else but a withered flower
left in the world
we'd still go smack down on our knees before the wonder
of it I'm
sorry I did a lot of the things I've done
maybe I killed somebody
who ever knows
when they've killed somebody
who ever breathes
without depriving somebody of breath

210

goddamit what are you getting out of bed for I want you
I'll go nuts if you don't stop crying and you'll catch cold
standing there naked by that open window darling please
tomorrow all this will seem like a bad dream and
I'll take you out somewhere nice
to eat and buy you some new shoes
Jesus what if they do
get in and cut our
throats that's the chance you run living with a
bastard like me kid and maybe we can get away
and shoot down to Mexico grab
us a little room
in the hills
the hell and gone from anywhere
look honey
it don't do no good to stand there
cryin'
come on back to bed and I'll put my arms
around you you know I wouldn't let anything
hurt you
I'll count five and
if you're not back in here by then
I'll break your neck
"Oh, I'm so miserable!"
please babe
snap out of it huh just sit tight keep the door locked and
I'll be back before you know it where's that other box of
.45s I thought they were in this top drawer under my shirts
Christ I wish you'd leave my things alone

211

"What are you going to do?"
what am I going to do sister when I get
through with them boys the streetcleaning
dept. can take over not that I've got anything against them understand but I'm sick
and tired of having you bellyaching around
all the time so I'll be seein' you sugar and
keep this door locked
in case
I don't make it
just remember me as the guy who thought
you were the nicest thing God ever made
and keep your feet dry
outside
I
walked
slowly
across
town
waiting
for
them
to
get
on
my

```
                    t
           r
              a
                        i
                   l
s                           the sun was              i
h    s                        n   n   n   n   n      i
h        s                      n   n   n   n        i
h            s                n   n   n   n   n      i
h                s              n   n   n   n        i
h   i  i             s        n   n   n   n   n      i
h   i  i                 s      n   n   n   n        i
h          i  i              s                      i
h          i  i                  s                  i
h                                    s              i
h        ngngngngngng                 s            i
h        ngngngngngng                   s          i
h        ngngngngngng                     s        i
h        ngngngngngng                       s      i
h        ngngngngngng                         s    i
h        ngngngngngng                           s  i
h                                                 s  i
h                                                    i
```

213

and there were big crowds of

elp

    1 2 3 4 5 6 7 8 9 10 11 12 13 14 15
16 16 16 16 16 16 17 18 19 20 20 20 20 20
50

    0   noses   0   o|||||||||
        0   0   0
        0 0   0   0   0   0   0
            0   0   0
                        pep   0
256, 998, 333   0
            o   e   p   8
            o   p   5
            o   l   7 7 7 7 7 7 7 7 7 7
        x   e   7 7 7 7 7 7 7 7 7 7 7
      x   0   0
    x   oeeeeeeee   0   0   0   0
x   0
    x x x x x x x x
                    x
                x   oppplepoe
                x
            x
        x coats   hats   eyes   ears   teeth

214

D D D D D D D D D D D D D D D D
O O O O O O O O O O O O O O O O
W W W W W W W W W W W W W W W W
N N N N N N N N N N N N N N N N
W W W W W W W W W W W W W W W W
I I I I I I I I I I I I I I I I
T T T T T T T T T T T T T T T T
H H H H H H H H H H H H H H H H
A A A A A A A A A A A A A A A A

one little man running about shouting

L L L L L L L L L L L L L L L L
L L L L L L L L L L L L L L L L
G G G G G G G G G G G G G G G G
O O O O O O O O O O O O O O O O
V V V V V V V V V V V V V V V V
E E E E E E E E E E E E E E E E
R R R R R R R R R R R R R R R R
N N N N N N N N N N N N N N N N
M M M M M M M M M M M M M M M M
E E E E E E E E E E E E E E E E
N N N N N N N N N N N N N N N N
T T T T T T T T T T T T T T T T
S S S S S S S S S S S S S S S S
! ! ! ! ! ! ! ! ! ! ! ! ! ! ! !

I was trying to think of a word to describe it
then it came to me
the word was
herefordnarcissuseagleoakarab
manxbobwhitemountainlaurelir
iscormorantorloffangusaberdeen
hyacinthgallowaytortoiseshellheron
sycamoremacawdutchbeltedharebell
clydesdalewaterlilymullberrypersian
silvertabbyredwingedblackbirdrose
ptarmiganwesthighlandchinchilla
shetlandbirchsiamesetexaslonghorn
honeysucklesandhillcranewalnut
angorapercheronbasswoodpoppy
sparrowhawkloonorchidguernsey
magnoliapelicanbluejayshire
devonsussextulipsweetpeacrow
africandarterjerseyeasterlily
prairiehensuffolkstallionmaple
chestnutbelgianpinecedarashlilac
petrelwoodcockcrocusbrownswiss
holsteindaisypheasanttigerlily
I mean the sensation I once had
when I'd been in the City too long

and wanted to get out to Uncle Rudy's farm
in Horsewater, Pa.
a sweet bit of country that
but
look
over
there
in
I   y   a
t   w
h   r
a   o
t   d   o

H O W D O
Y O
U
L
I
K
E
T
H
A
T

help help help help help   helphelp
help help help help help   helphelp
theyre going to kill me   helphelp
help   help⟶   helphelp
help   me   help   helphelp
help   help   helphelp
help help help help help⟵   helphelp
help theyve got guns help   helphelp
help help help help help   helphelp

THEY'RE GOING TO KILL ME but I'll
make

a

r

u

n

fo

r

i

t

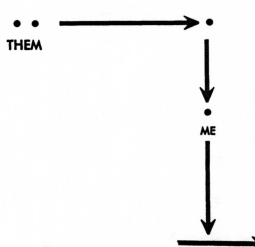

THEM

ME

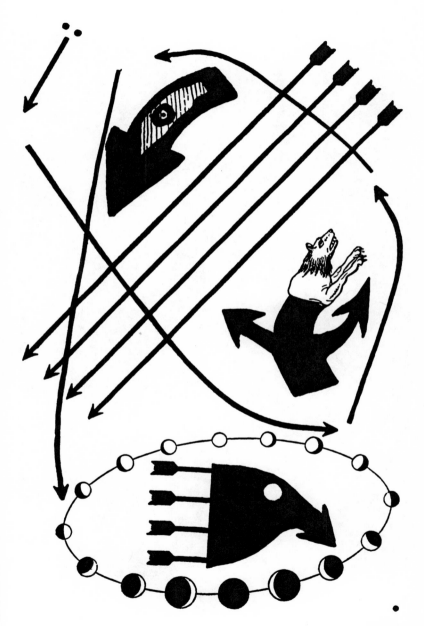

219

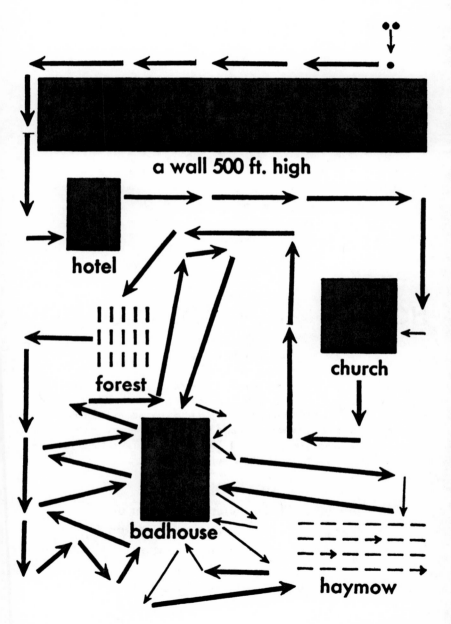

a wall 500 ft. high

hotel

forest

church

badhouse

haymow

221

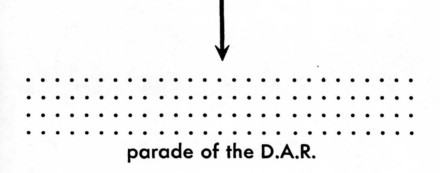

parade of the D.A.R.

ha ha
aah

HO! HO!   HO! HO!   HO! HO!

ouch I'm tired
are you asleep baby
sure sure
I'm better than all right
but come to think of it
why's my side of the bed warm I'd just like a good answer to that little question honey chil' and when we get that out of the way maybe you'll tell me
how-come you handed me a box of .32s for my .45 huh what'd you say
oh let's forget it how much'd they give you

how much

talk up or I'll let you have another one
"I saw that face at the window again."
let's go to sleep now darling
this world is evil
there's no escape at all

something's got a gun at our heads and I can feel
its finger tightening on the trigger
I can smell death looking at us
and the darkness is all we've got coming and
I won't have it
I won't give in
if I go out it'll be feet first
and I'll be yelling no no no you butchering bastards
this is a beautiful world
it's all wonderful
these trees
stars
children
the thing I am
and the great lovely thing my woman is
O God let us write more poems
let us sing the stars out of the sky
let us love until our mouths and hearts
get pure with it
let us make God proud of us

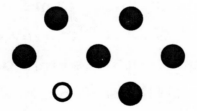

HURRAH!
Here they come!
Catch one! Catch one!

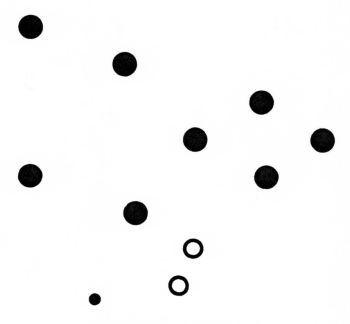

LOOK AT THEM!
See how they go up!
What do they care about darkness!

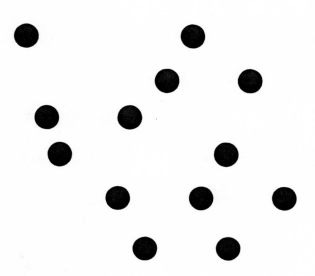

OH! OH!

One's coming down!

But what difference does that make!

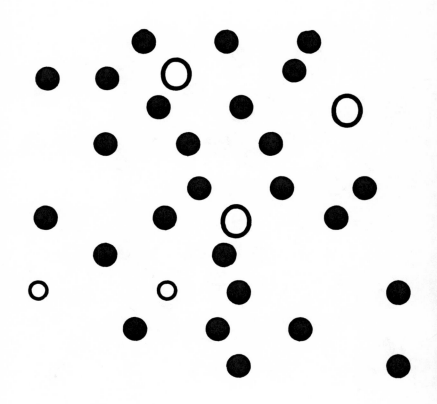

I'LL BE CORNSWOGGLED!

Now it's going up faster than any!

Maybe it wants to make you happy.

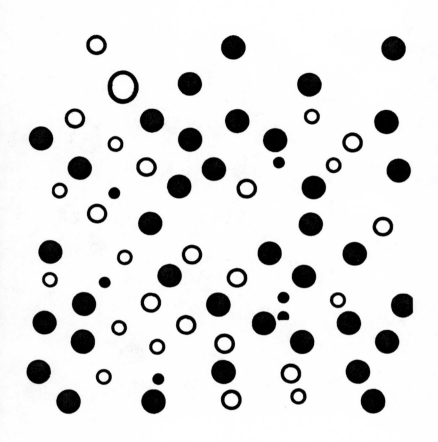

WHAT A STACK OF PRETTIES!

I'll bet they try to pass a law against this.

But you and I know better than to care about that.

and it is beautiful
it's always beautiful
this massive and indescribable wonder
of being alive
honor all
or God is despised
O
in the same body
every heart has its sacred being
these words seem tasteless, stale
as the clothes of a corpse

★★★★★
★★★★★★★★★
★★★★★★★★★★★★★★★★★★★
★★★★★★★★★★ a man ★★★★★★★★★★★
★★★★★
★★★★★★★★★
★★★
★★★★★★★★★★★★★★★★★★★★★★★★★★
★★★★★★★★★★★★★★★★★★★★★
★★★★ a man's life ★★★★
★★★★★
★★★★★★★★★★★★
★★★★★★★★★★★★★★★★★★★★★★
★★★★★★★★

WHAT GOD WOULD SAY IF SOMEONE SHOULD SEEK HIS ADVICE ON HOW BEST TO SAVE THE WORLD FROM DESTRUCTION

Don't kill one another.

SEVEN BEAUTIFUL THINGS
MADE MORE BEAUTIFUL BY APPEARING
IN THIS WAY

1. A tree in flower.

4. Sleeping girl.

3. Colt and huge red stones.

7. A gean floating on bark.

5. Cloud-mold lying on wet grass.

2. The sound of mountains.

6. You put one here.

THE ANIMATED
ASHCAN

A NOVEL OF TODAY

1.

They meet in the automat.
It is day outside.

2.

Each's sex is opposite.
She laughs hollowly.

3.

One of their heads opens to admit a segment of unbuttered bun
still in cellophane.

4.

They read the newspaper together.
It laughs hollowly.

5.

He takes a nickel out of his pocket.
It has golden hair and blue eyes.
His mother it reminds him of.
She laughs hollowly.

6.

They go to a room in a hotel.

The bellboy leers hollowly.
His sex is even more opposite.
Carpet and bed cover dull brown.

7.

They remove their clothes.
There's nobody in them.
The clothes laugh hollowly.

● ★ ●

COME ON LET'S KILL ME AND YOU

A GUTS WITH NOVEL

1.

Louie was just leaving his
eyes cold as steel.
He didn't like it there
with Moe nuts like that
and Hazel on to all of them
like a smack in the kisser.

2.

His coat he buttoned up
around his slit throat.
Louie knew when to call
it quits
but not what with Moe bats
and that witch Haz as apt to rat
as a cement overcoat with swallowtails.

3.

Louie passed a little man on 7th Avenue.
It was sidewalking up against the rain.
The little man was carrying an office
which he had forgotten to take off.
A pretty stenog and four vice-presidents were yelling out of the
window.
Any other time Louie would have been angry—
this time he was furious.
What was Hazel doing on that lardpot's knee!
He scowled hollowly at the little man.

4.

The street hurried by under two cops.
One of them said have you booked any good reds lately
Tim just as Louie opened fire and being upset
bumped six little grafters on their way home from first-grade.
It was that kind of day.

5.

Louie tilts his benny above stones
which glitter like eyes.
Savagely he lights a Chersterfed
and presses it on the wrist of an old lady who is trying
to find a bite
of supper in a garbage can marked Put Used Bodies Here.
A newsboy passes shouting Du Ponts indicted as war criminals.
' All the dead kids laugh hollowly.

6.

Hazel is weeping by the face.
Louie chairs into the sink and
feels the comforting caress of warm dishwater on his battered can.
A window peers through the face at them.

The godlight pours in like a name you could call the dead back with.

7.
As they undress
a voice says all this is so sad and dull why
can't my children be good to one another
because nothing else really matters
can't you see that
o can't you see that
but Louie says viciously I'm on to you now skirt I'll

(to be continued)

SLEEPERS AWAKE
ON THE PRECIPICE

A DIRECT ATTACK ON THE PROBLEM OF MAKING THIS BOOK UNDERSTANDABLE TO ALL

1. A man.
2. A world.
3. A man.
4. A world.
5. A man.
6. A world.
7. A man.

"Gie corn to my horse, mither,
    Gie meat unto my man;
For I maun gang to May Margaret's bower
    Before the night come on."

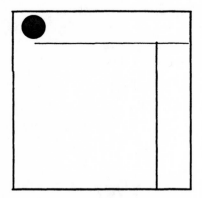

TODAY I WALKED

GRAY DEER IN

THE SNOW

"O stay at home now, my son Willie,
   The wind blaws cauld and stour;
The night will be baith mirk and wild,
   Before ye reach her bower."

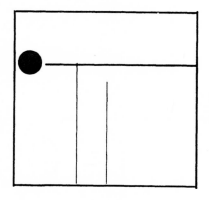

CROWS

ACROSS A FIELD

"O though the night were never sae dark,
    Or the wind blew never sae cauld,
I will be in May Margaret's bower,
    Before twa hours be tauld."

OF

TREES

SINGING

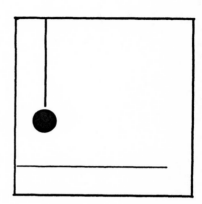

COLD

"O gin ye gang to May Margaret,
    Without the leave o' me,
Clyde's waters are wide and deep enough,
    My malison drown thee!"

IN THE

A PRETTY YOUNG

STILL

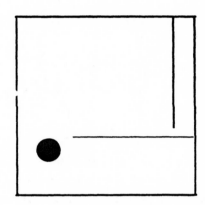

O

LADY SAID I

He's mounted on his coal-black steed,
    And fast he rade awa;
But ere he cam' to Clyde's water,
    Fu' loud the wind did blau.

LOVE

THE WORLD IS

WILL YOU COME

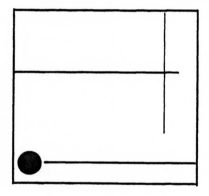

As he rade o'er yon high high hill,
    And down yon dowie den,
There was a roar in Clyde's water,
    Wad fear'd a hundred men.

OLD

AND

EVIL

HOME WITH ME

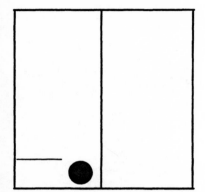

O he has swam through Clyde's water,
    Though it was deep and wide,
And he came to May Margaret's door,
    When a' were boune to bed.

●

AND THE
HEART

O he's gane round and round about,
    And tirled at the pin;
But doors were steek'd, and windows barr'd,
    And nane wad let him in.

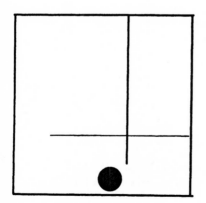

IT'S GETTING

DARK

AND THE WORLD

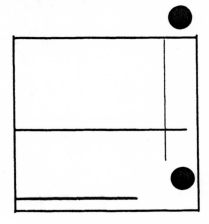

"O open the door to me, Margaret,
   O open and let me in;
For my boots are fu' o' Clyde's water,
   And frozen to the brim!"

MUST

EVER

BREAK

"I daurna open the door to you,
  I daurna let you in;
For my mother she is fast asleep,
  And I daurna mak' nae din."

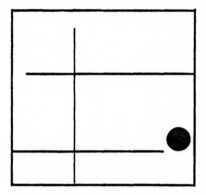

VILLAGES

DEATH SITS

"O gin ye winna open the door,
  Nor yet be kind to me,
Now tell me o' some out-chamber,
  Where I this night may be."

IN

EVIL LET US

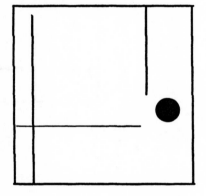

HIS   WHITE

MAKE LOVE AGAINST
"Ye canna win in this night, Willie,
  Nor here ye canna be;
For I've nae chambers out nor in,
  Nae ane but barely three.

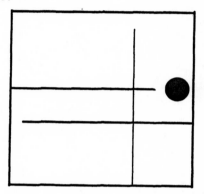

EYES

FIXED

UPON

NO THINGNESS

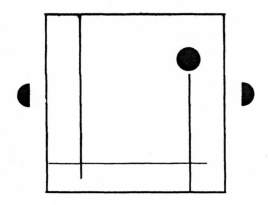

"The tane of them is fu' o' corn,
    The tither is fu' o' hay;
The third is fu' o' merry young men,
    They winna move off till day."

THE LONG NIGHT

WHERE CAN

THE GOOD

"O fare ye weel then, May Margaret,
  Sin better maunna be:
I've won my mother's malison,
  Coming this night to thee."

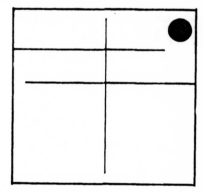

BE

SAID SHE I

WILL COME HOME

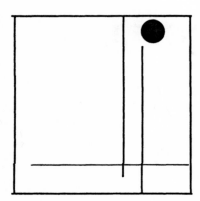

HIDDEN THAT

He's mounted on his coal-black steed,
   O but his heart was wae;
But ere he came to Clyde's water,
   'Twas half up o'er the brae.

NONE

• SEE IT

WITH THEE BECAUSE

O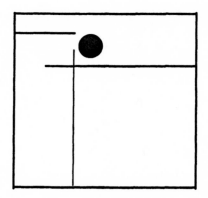

He took the water recklessly,
　　Nor heeded of its force,
But the rushing that was in the Clyde,
　　Bore Willie from his horse.

BLOOD

DRIPS

DOWN

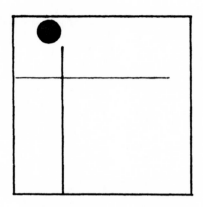

MY OWN TRUE

His brother stood upon the bank;
    Says, "Fye, man, will ye drown?
Fye, turn your horse's head up stream,
    And teach him how to sowm!"

LOVE LIES COLD

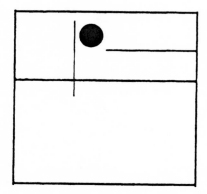

UPON ● THE SNOW

"How can I turn my horse's head?
 How can I try to sowm?
I've gotten my mother's malison,
 And it's here that I maun drown!"

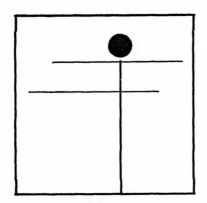

O GOD

THE

AND DEAD AND

    . . . the truth was restless in him,
And shook his visionary fabrics down,
As one who had been buried long ago
And now was called by a necromancer
To answer dreadful questions. So compelled,
He left the way of fiction and wrote thus:

C
H
I
L
L

YOUR DESIRES ARE

Woe unto him whose fate hath thwarted him,
Whose life has been 'mongst such as were not born,
To cherish in his bosom reverence,
And the calm awe that comforteth the heart

WINDS OF

H O R R

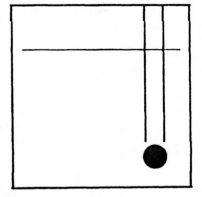

OR

L
I
F
T

And lulls the yearnings of hope unfulfilled:
Such have I been. And woe again to him
Who, in too late an hour, presumptuously
O'erhears a wish confessing to his soul,
And must dismiss it to his discontent
With scorn and laughter. Woe again to me!

DESIRES
LIKE MINE

ALL

YOUR ARMS AND

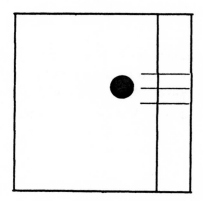

For now I hear even such an anxious voice
Crying in my soul's solitude, and bewailing
That I had never in my childhood known
The bud of this manifold beauteousness,

THESE EMPTY

MASKS

AND

And seen each leaf turn of its tender hinge
Until the last few parted scarce, and held
Deep in their midst a heaven-reflecting gem;
For then I might—oh vain and flattering wish!—

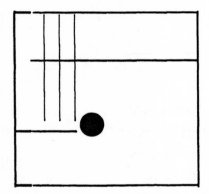

EVERYTHING

WE

LIPS AND THIGHS

I might have stood, tho' last, among the friends
Where I am now the last among the strangers,
And not have passed away, as now I must,
Into forgetfulness, into the cold

EVER

LOVED

ARE WARM NOT

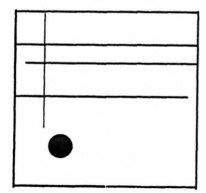

IS

Of the open, homeless world without a hope,
Unless it be of pardon for these words . . .
Away! I should have told a better tale.
Forgive, and shut these pages up forever.

COLD AND DEAD

HID

EOUSLY

R OT T I N G

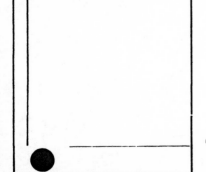

THERE ●

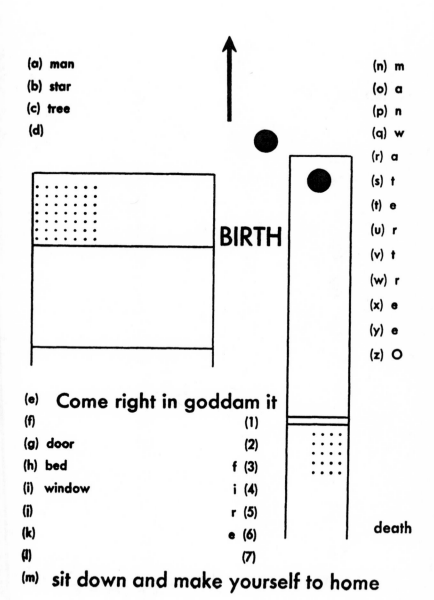

(a) man
(b) star
(c) tree
(d)

(n) m
(o) a
(p) n
(q) w
(r) a
(s) t
(t) e
(u) r
(v) t
(w) r
(x) e
(y) e
(z) O

BIRTH

(e) Come right in goddam it
(f)   (1)
(g) door   (2)
(h) bed   f (3)
(i) window   i (4)
(j)   r (5)
(k)   e (6)
(l)   (7)
(m) sit down and make yourself to home

death

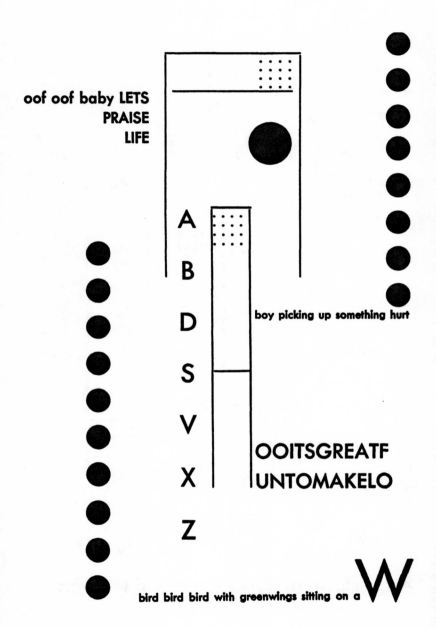

oof oof baby LETS
PRAISE
LIFE

A
B
D
S
V
X
Z

boy picking up something hurt

OOITSGREATF
UNTOMAKELO

bird bird bird with greenwings sitting on a W

THE GREAT BIG GIANT

O sun's head is his all golden tossed and fiery snakes make frolic milkwhite and naked king two o'clock and snowlost 42nd Street O kid of glory armed of heaven prone on the X roads of the woild

sleep and chance you dream and dreaming wake and sin and pain and hatred take

and the sin and the stain of sin

2 saith the golden clock

but how do we know (time time space slime on the lace of the heavens) O neither the hour nor the day nor after all what death really does

There is a great lad lying here filling this street or the whole world neither any star to light

A plot by angels

Graves in the sun

Perhaps it isn't his head the sea drowns for if it really is two o'clock and you can tell him what will by every law in this universe happen in this very city and to the most trivial fellow you ever heard of

O golden bison this vicious jungle where men in din-nercoats   aaaaaaaaaahheeeee

Lard 8c. the lb.

Get in touch with (put name here kindly)

To contribute light

To feel what you can never understand

A light to save the world now please

they've rerouted traffic all moving things . . . cabbie go

round! . . . for something lies here at 5th and 42nd . . .
Jesus Mac you shoulda oughta seed it . . . like a million
guys alyin there in one guy

like everybody's life had come to live in a single being

THE LITTLE BLACK TRAIN

Who-o-o-o-o-o-o-o-o-o-o-o-o-o-o

You-o-o-o-o-o-o-o-o-o

White fields. Sleeping damn towns. Iron-footed snake
inching its cold length down the continent. Crazy hot eye
searching out a fixed journey.

Man in bowler looks up from book. To hell with stars
and rivers and all things which have breath and walking
on this earth, he thinks idly.

Across aisle slim fellow gray tweeds toys Dixie cup.
Eyes meet bowler's. "You don't happen to have a time-
table on you, pal?"

"Sure. Wanta see 'er?"

"I'd like to begging your pardon if it isn't too much
trouble."

"No trouble 't all. Here you be."

"Hmm."

"Get yer times mixed, Jack?"

"Yeah. Yeah, I did. Thought we'd get to Plubberville by
seven."

"That where yer're goin'?"

"No, my home's in Charlestown."

"How come this interest in Plubberville?"

"Used to know a girl there. As a matter of fact, she was engaged to my best friend."

"Something go wrong?"

"Yeah, something did. She died."

"She did, huh? Hit yer camerado purty hard, I bet."

"Sure did. Thought I'd just like to see what the place looks like when we go through."

"What time's that, Jack?"

"8:15."

"That this morning?"

"No, tomorrow morning."

"Thursday, eh?"

"That's right; Thursday. Much obliged for letting me see the time-table."

"Don't mention it, I'm sure."

Ten minutes later the man in the green bowler is conscious of a slight movement amongst the cigar stubs and candy wrappers at his feet. He looks over at the young chap, wanting to say "Funny damn thing, a mouse on the car like that," but the other is sleeping. Peacefully.

'Sonofafunny that, and bold as a purple nose—'course they's always them rats on ships—but hell! you'd think they could keep a singular mice out of daycoaches,' he thinks. Then he becomes aware that the lad across the aisle is not asleep at all. His eyes under their lowered lids are watching like thin knives cutting every ounce of fat out of the air.

He takes up the novel again, but more than ever he can't keep his mind on the real and imagined difficulties of Almar Gnunsn. Leaning over he taps mister kid on the shoulder. "What time you say we get to that place your friend's gal lived in?"

Opens his eyes. "What are you afraid of? What could possibly happen to you here on the train? All you have to do is raise your voice. Any one of these good people would come to your rescue in a moment."

Man in bowler feels a sharp stab in his ankle . . . sees the mouse scamper down his shoe. And as the numbness begins to creep up his legs, he sees the mouse scamper across the aisle and up the pantleg of the boy in the gray tweed suit.

Trying to yell . . . unable to make a sound . . . dimly conscious of the cruel little blue eyes of the mouse watching his agony over the rim of the Dixie cup.

You-o-o-o-o-o-o-o-o-o

Who-o-o-o-o-o-o-o-o-o-o-o-o-o

BUTTON, BUTTON, DON'T FORGET TO WIND THE CAT

On the frosted glass of the entrance door had been painted Buccleuch, Wakelight, Poussin, Ashmolean and Grote, Att.'s at Lawr.

Dugald Ashmolean was a small, dry man in his late fifties and Senior Partner. The brief he held in his chubby fist was a very lengthy one.

"Any report that damn Chatanooga business?" he demanded, his great brows drawing up to form a ?

"On, you mean," Chad Grote said. "Report on that damn Chatanooga business."

"Excuse me," Asa Wakelight said.

"All right, but hurry back," Ashmolean snapped, his g. b's forming a ,

"Oh, it's not that," Wakelight assured. "Only it's Charlestown."

"What's Charlestown?"

"About which you wonder if there's a report on," Wakelight said nervously.

"Well, is there?"

"I'm afraid it's not very encouraging—"

"Out with it, man!"

"There's been another murder, Mr. Ashmolean, sire."

They all watched the slim girl in a bathing suit which the Senior Partner's eyebrows had formed. One of the straps had slipped down to reveal a little clump of bristly, coarse hair. Fascinated, they stared as she dove down to fetch up on the point of his thick, morethanvaguelysnout-like nose.

"Well, what are you mooning out of the window about, Buccleuch?"

"I've been wondering what the hell's going on over in that office across the street," Buccleuch said, rubbing his elbow briskly with the serrated side of a grater.

"Me, too," Bailey Poussin said.

"Looks to I," said the Senior Part., "like about twenty little men are carrying loafs of bread out of there."

"Never saw no bread with white flags zipping up out

of them," Poussin declared.

"Whose office is that, do you know?" Grote asked.

"Man named Best," Buccleuch said.

"What business is he in?"

"You got me."

"Goofy damn looking bird, if you ask me."

"All right. Let's get on with this Chicamonga business."

"Charlestown business."

"So what? My wife was saying only yesterday that it will be a long time before we can get the speakeasies back anyway."

(to be continued)

Art is not to throw light but be light. Of all things in this world, how can an angel be unreal! Open the door for Christ's sake open the door! If you can't praise then shut up goddamit shut up!

Nothing can happen from the outside. What a wonderful and beautiful enterprise, being a human being!

There's your mystery.

Love art and the beautiful or to hell with you.

I refuse the cheap view of anything. Come

on in God this is what I am take it or leave it I'll go right ahead praising You whatever the verdict is.

Look at these words by Jesus that's an act I put these words here because it all fits into a form bigger than you or me or anybody.

I don't know but I don't have to know in order to make a bit of a damn little thing in praise of life.

I'm going to set 21 words down right here because I can think of nothing that would give me more pleasure.

Ba de ba do ba dub de di. Since which there was some. There's nothing tricky about love.

THE WISHES OF THE MAJESTIC ONE

It was all of three months after the accident. That day I sat with my enemy on a wooden bench near the Tree of Sorrow. His skin was the color of a carrot's liver. The weather was all over everything and we talked loudly to drown out the sound the elves made as they ran over the counters where the wind had his coughsyrup in big jars of leaves and the dreams of little birds.

"How did you lose your eye?" he asked timidly.

"It was gouged out while I was building a city."

We watched a ligenna swim past in the cold gray lake.

"She can't be more than a thousand miles out," he said deliberately. "I don't remember ever seeing one so far inshore before."

I nodded. "It has my whole sympathy," I said.

Rain. I regretted that I had not bothered to dress. Frightening—wet branches against your hide. Too fish near.

"What's it made of?" he demanded suddenly—"glass?"

I told him it wasn't.

We—"What then! Speak up, man!"—watched two ancient hags uncouple a chapel from a ten-ton truck. Their faces had grown over their eyes.

I knelt at the altar. A comic-book had been placed squarely between seven orange candles.

"What then? If not no glass—speak, man, for the love of God!"

I told him why I was not at liberty to tell him. He sank his teeth into his wrist and started to drink as fast as ever he could.

The best cure for insomnia is to sleep with all the windows open.

ECHOES FROM THE HEREAFTER

We didn't notice the curious behavior of Lerther's horse until all the lights had been put out in the inn and the sea running like a demented molfier on the coast had drowned out every noise in that whole unhappy place. Tired from our labors to decipher the words which had suddenly appeared in the sky just as darkness came—and which had continued far into the night, first like the dirty green gold on a dollar watch, then, with a gradual and beautiful authority, turning to flame, so that message Someone was trying to give us seemed to be burning as we watched—, we therefore really made no effort to entertain the country girls whose evening ritual it was to sit on our knees and have their wide rumps patted. It is true that we had an importance in our own right which they clearly understood, and which, I feel like saying, their fathers and brothers, pocketing the money, were not ignorant of; but there was obviously more to it than that—indeed, and this can be proved by documents which are now safely housed in a vault in Kordebrun, our chief merit in the eyes of those simple young women lay precisely in the strength and determination which came to us from sources outside this world. The wonderful audacity of our mission (and I am sorry to be compelled to speak so modestly) can only be dimly surmised by anyone who has not at least had intimations that there is more good in human beings than their collective actions would indicate. About nine o'clock, then, the inn-lights being out, and the smell of expiring candles having long since given way to that of numerous, weary men sleeping in the same, tiny room, I ventured to slip into my pants and shirt and, guiding my steps by the sickly glow which still lingered in the heavens, walked into the yard where the prisoners were quartered. The guard (Ray-

271

mond) was sitting in a deckchair directly in front of the
stable. I greeted him cordially enough and was disagree-
ably surprised to receive no answering salutation. Drawing
back my foot I landed a merry one on his fundament—he
didn't stir. I struck a match. Ray would never be any
deader.

Then a Voice from out of the

LlllalllllalllllalllIa   .

But the damn train was already two hours late. She was
my fiance. I was seeing her off to China where her old man
owned a tenth-interest in a jute mill.

My feet hurt and it was still none of my business what
her brother had said when he accepted the nomination for
Congress from the Weetiponk region.

The folks around us talked to continue. A slight young
patrickomonahan sneezed and two old ladies and a cab-
driver were nice enough to say gracious me God bless you
and take along a blanket next time Mac.

The ice cream in my pocket had melted.

O Father
I cry out to Thee
I cannot find my way anymore
I hold out my bloody hands
Since all fall into this same grave
O Father Thou too shalt fail

a man

a man's life

IF I GAVE THIS A TITLE IT MIGHT START EATING THE PRINT RIGHT OFF THE PAGE

The witness told a confused story—you all know, I presume, how the sight of murder, even a universal one, will cloud a feller's inner consciousness. Or put the way it ought to be put: It isn't murder so much as the fact that murder is possible—that God set it up that way in the first place.

But let's hear the story as the police heard it: I start in the kitchen, see. I don't get more'n halfway to the sink, see. So—there she is . . . the most beautiful doll anybody ever set eyes on, see . . . wid nothin' on . . . and me standin' there, see . . . just like I'm tellin' yuh . . . you don't have to believe me . . . an' this poor bastard's bendin' over her

273

cryin' like a baby . . . he had a razor in his hand, see . . . an' I puts my arm aroun' his shoulder an' the two of us just stand there cryin' . . . she was the pertiest dish I ever seen in my life, Captain . . . she was sorta like them angels the kids have at Chris'mus, see . . .

The true facts of the matter are easily imagined. She had it coming to her and the killer who was wearing a light blue polka-dot suit, gray silk socks, white linen shirt, bowler hat dented to the left, tan-and-orange necktie, five feet ten inches, one hundred forty-six pounds, would give his life and the lives of everyone he knows to feel his lips on her warm mouth again and the and the and the and the

THE UNINVITED ENTERTAINERS

We had just moved into the house.

Gretchen was straightening around in the kitchen and I was tacking up some loose boards on the front porch, when

1) She thought she heard something sobbing in the attic.

2) I saw a red stain growing in the ceiling over the fireplace in the front room.

3) We got to the stairs together and started up.

4) I pulled open the attic door.

5) It was too dark at first to see much of any-thing.

6) Then we made out what looked like two people rolling about near some boxes.

7) Gretchen walked on in ahead.

8) I heard her scream and rushed to catch her as she fell.

9) I don't know what those two things were.

10) They were covered with a sort of yellow hair and the whole front of their faces was nothing but eyes.

11) They seemed to be fighting with some-thing that made big bloody gashes in them every time it struck.

12) The thing I couldn't see was crying in a horrible voice and I don't know what made me think so but it sounded like my father.

13) The boxes were full of National Geo-graphics for the years 1921 through '26.

well I got up and I walked outside it
was starting to rain
the rain was coming
down on the street and on the houses
I could've cried
it was that sad to be in that town
where nobody gave a damn
whether I lived or died

oh see see rider see what you have done

gal says to me mister
you got two bucks
man says brother I know
where you can git it good
I walked until I came to a river
and on the banks of the river stood an old man
father why are you so bent and feeble
why have your teeth all fallen out
why do your eyes run this foul pus why do your knees
bang so what good is life that ends like this down
by the river
and he said you see not the end of life
in me but the beginning of death
and both are beautiful

oh see see rider see what you have done
and I climbed some stairs and I knocked
on a door
pretty baby comes your pappy back

for more
she opened the bed and we got in
what's God's idea can't be no sin
her breasts were warm and
sweet what we did then
would stand a dead man on his feet
O love O love
O careless love O love O love
O careless love
life O life O life O life life O life O lifeless
life what have you gone and done to me

I got me a pistol
big as a boat
said I mister devil here's where I gets a vote
I went into a movie and I bought me a seat
saw the whole American nation worked into a 60c. heat

O love O love O careless love what
have you gone and done to these
life O life O lifeless life
what have you gone and done to these

well I got up and I walked outside it
was still raining
the rain was coming down
on the street and on the houses and
I said to myself fellah this is it this is what

all the goddam fuss is about
this is why guys write books and paint pictures and write songs a
funny

thing though it is big and it's cruel and I get
so mad at the bastards who
want to blow all this to hell
because it's a sad a man
can get his teeth in
it's the kind of beauty knocks you down and
then makes you cry because you
think you might have hurt it
goddamit what are you getting out of bed
for I want you I'll go nuts if you don't stop
blubbering you'll catch your death standing
by that open window please darling all this
will seem like a lousy
cheap dream tomorrow
and I'll take you out to the country
where we can look at trees and
smell the grass
jesus sugar get wise
to yourself moon around much more
and I'll buy me a baby that knows
how to make

a man forget this little vale
of woe whatayuh say
give papa something he can tell
the angels about

"What's that!"
I don't hear nothin' look kid
"At the door . . . Something's trying
to open the door!"
O God there's no escape now
it's in the room with us and the mask has slipped
off the Face
and its eyes are looking

at us its voice is saying
where can you run now

O see see rider see what you done done

"Its scaly hands are at my throat!"

I built me a mansion build it so high its
towers went up right down out of the sky

O love O love
O careless love O love O love
O careless love
life O life O life O life life O life O lifeless
life what have you gone and done to me

A big shiny car came slowly down the driveway and I waited for it to clear into the road. Three women and a little girl sat in the backseat; two sullen-faced boys sat beside the driver in front. I know that man from somewhere, I thought, as the car picked up speed heading for the city.

The little girl waved to me from the rear window and I hurt my sore arm waving back at her.

A woman, in her late thirties, trim in faded overalls, was planting in a field to the right of me. On the other side a bull was trying to do himself a little justice in the world.

That's why I didn't see him, this kid on a bicycle hurrying home with five gallons of kerosene on the handlebars.

These damn, new-fangled tin oil cans! I swear you look cross at them they'll stove-in—That's all right, sonny; it wasn't your fault. Let me have that manufacturer's name.

What manufacturer?

The can. The can. My notebook was sopping too so I walked over to a mailbox and taking a letter out ripped it open. The letter began Dearest Faith: I miss you so terribly, long so to hold you in my arms again. I bet, I said, tearing it into tiny pieces and dropping them behind the stone wall with its profusion of red roses and green poison ivy.

You bet what? the boy asked.

Sloan's T-Kan Co., Mustardbrook, Vt., I wrote on the envelope. I bet the bull don't make it, I said.

We sat up on the wall and watched.

It started to rain. The wind came up. The cow moved around. The bull moved around. Even my hat smelled of kerosene. I sneezed. The boy climbed down and got on his wheel. I'm sorry I got oil all over you, he said.

Think nothing of it, I told him. It was those T-Kan bastards. He started off. Tell your daddy that I'm the fellow he thought I was, I called after him.

280

He looked back over his shoulder at me with the same sullen look he'd had in the automobile. As he passed out of sight around the bend I jumped quickly down on the other side of the wall and made it into the woods. Pinng! and my hat went sailing off. I waited a good minute—the rain was really coming down by this time—and then took a look around my tree. Six pairs of legs were about twelve feet away from me. I walked out and said, Somebody just shot my hat off. They just smiled at me and that pinng again and one of them got ketchup on his forehead. We came to tell you something, one of them said. I could see that the woman was getting good aim with her rifle teed-up on the handles of a cultivator. Get the hell back of this tree! I shouted just as she let another go. The one who had spoken to me went down with the head of a crimson mouse working out of his cheek. I saw her shift the sight—possibly the water was coming down with enough weight to bend the curve a bit. We've come to tell you that—His right eye bubbled up. The standing three were still smiling. One of them even tried to light a cigarette. You'd better turn back, he said—and his teeth sprayed out like stained white corn. Get down! Get down! you crazy fools! I yelled. We were sent to warn you that—and the fifth sank to his knees, his throat spugging open like a pocket torn out of a coat. She had to give him another one—while he knelt there smiling at me. Then the last one, in terrible desperation to tell me, lunged for the tree. I saw her lower the rifle and braced myself to pull him in

> wondering why she hadn't tried for a lucky one
> when down he went anyway
> the flower in the middle of his forehead
> and suddenly I realized that if the woman had been shooting them the wounds would have been in the backs of their heads—since she was behind them and in front of me.

It hit me that in my terror at the cold-blooded murder, a very obvious thing had eluded me:

<u>They had known that there was no escape.</u>
<u>They had not been talking to me at all.</u>
<u>They had been warning the thing which was murdering them.</u>

Then—take it slow, buddy, I whispered to myself. Just don't make any sudden moves to startle it—because what killed these lads is standing right in back of you. I tried to whistle but my upper lip thought it a good idea to snarl instead.

Well, I finally managed to operate enough muscles to get my head turned around.

I thought for a second that there was something white standing there watching me.

Then I could see that there was nothing at all standing there. It was getting colder and I shivered.

I eased the fingernails out of the palms of my hands and stepped around the tree.

Nothing happened.

Where the six bodies had been there was nothing.

I felt in my pocket for a cigarette. The pack was empty.

I stared over at the field where the woman had been. There was a sort of lumber mill with a lot of shacks spread out around it.

Then I noticed something scattered out on the ground—something shining and round and hard. I picked them all up—all seven of them. They look like little silver eggs, I thought, turning them over with my thumb.

Silver bullets.

I felt my lip drawing up again. Then I saw my hat off in a bush. I walked over and picked it up. There wasn't even a dent in it.

I turned back to the bullets. They were about half as big as they'd been when I picked them up. Silver bullets, hell! I said—hailstones. That's what they are, nothing but lousy hailstones.

I put my hat back on my head. I pulled my belt a notch tighter. I picked up a sodden cigarette I spied in the grass and managed to get it lighted. Maybe that sawmill needs a good man.

282

RESPECT

HUMAN

BEINGS !

Don't look at me, I told the bull. Write in to the Department of Agriculture and ask for their pamphlet on animal husbandry.

Just as I started to climb over the wall a terrific lightning went on and I damn near dove into a clump of ivy. And—wham skedoddle! went the thunder.

I wouldn't want it much closer, I thought, as I walked up to the

283

superintendent's shack and knocked on the door. Who is it? a woman's voice called.

Do you need a good man here? I called back, sticking my chest out as the door started to open.

Oh! she said, her eyes sweeping me up and down like blue icicles. The bragging insolence of some people! And she slammed the door.

What's eating her? I thought, shifting the droopy cigarette. Could I maybe have my fly unbuttoned?

I felt for it.

Wait a minute! Wait a minute! I felt over the rest of me. Then I started to run down the lane. I could hear doors opening in the shacks and the jacks yelling, There he goes! There goes the crazy bastard now!

No lumbering man could ever outrun me. I ran so fast that I was glad in a way I didn't have my kerosene-soaked clothes on.

After a couple miles I tore up past a barn and into a little building. While I was getting my breath I thought of two funny things: How little is really known about lightning. And the fact that I had blood on my mouth from that cigarette.

When I started to sit down I thought of another funny thing— that it maybe wasn't just the best time for me to be hiding away in a corncrib.

A thing begins. The lion eats the apple. You take it out and look at it. You don't know what it is. Chances are nobody will know what it is even if you tell them. And you don't know what it is. You have a hunch that it's a pretty dangerous business. You have a hunch that if the lion happens to look up from the apple it will be curtains for everybody. You run your hand over the fine hair on your neck. A wind stirs in the willows. Two boats rub smoky elbows on the river. You have a hunch that it's all pretty beautiful. You think of Jesus and Blake and Dostoievsky and Herman Melville and you get a sniff of what the beautiful is. You begin to suspect that if you try to stand off in front there a little you'll get the bemiffiment kicked out of you. If you don't belong out there. So you start adding up. You take another quick look at your rent receipt. You take your shirt off and hand it out the window. You take your driver's license out of the top drawer and check over the registration numbers. You phone the plumber and tell him the next time he wipes his filthy paws on your dishtowels you'll sure as hell knock his block off.

Then you walk over and open the door a crack. The hall seems deserted and you start down the stairs. You get to the street and a shiny black car pulls in at the curb and a man leans out and asks you by any chance does a Faith Somebodyorother live there.

I've seen it happen. A voice will be raised and nobody listens. Somebody will go up into the mountans and say his piece. Yet you can't turn around without meeting people who seem to live for no purpose whatever. The darker it gets the tighter they hold on to nothing. I actually believe that if someone told them that the mystery was the only important thing they'd spit in his face. Or burn him at the stake. I never draw a breath without thinking what an amazing thing it is. That practically nobody gives a damn about anything.

You'd think going to die would frighten them a little. Instead they squirm a bit deeper into their stomachs and ha ha like lunatics at those monsters called radio comedians. Instead they mill around in theatre lobbies babbling over garbage which any dog worthy of the name would vomit up at the mere mention of. Instead they—by God I tell you that there is no such thing as taste anymore. I tell you that there is no such thing as decency—yes, DECENCY. These people care no more for truth and justice and human dignity than the swine who feed them this bilge. I tell you that this world ha³ been turned into one big insane asylum. These nice good people are dangerous maniacs. Let them just get the scent of anything pure and beautiful and they'll tear it limb from limb before you can say Democracy.

Pure and beautiful.

Who has one little tear for the collection box?

Instead—Everywhere on earth human beings are blowing each other into bloody pieces. Men, women and children are being systematically butchered. Men, women and children are being systematically starved to death. Call them B-29's or whatever you want to—the bombs they drop are tearing the arms and legs off men, women and children. Tell me that the Nazis and Fascists must be prevented from conquering the world, and I will remind you that a few clean, brave men and women were saying this long before you found it profitable to do so—and I will ask you: Can you prevent the Nazis and Fascists from conquering the world by systematically butchering and starving men, women and children?

The truth is so simple—though you don't want it.

War is the weapon of the Fascist—his only weapon—and whoever takes this weapon into his hands—for any reason—joins the enemy, becomes—in fact—a Fascist.

At the moment, the only weapon we have against the Fascists, is not to become Fascists. The only voice we can raise against the systematic slaughter of men, women and children, is not to take part in that slaughter. The only hope for those of us who still believe in the truth, is to denounce the lie.

I tell you that the day is coming when all men on earth shall live together as brothers—because nothing short of this can pay for the crimes committed against them; because nothing short of this can possibly satisfy the hunger a few men already feel—and which shall be felt by everyone tomorrow—the hunger a man has for living as he was intended to live.

And that hunger is stronger than any cultivated hatred of race for race, or of nation for nation; it is stronger than any power-induced war—be it II, III or X; it is the strongest and most awesome force in the world—this hunger of every man to live—and to live purely and beautifully with all his fellows.

286

The truth is so simple—and only the truth will work for everyone. You cannot hate some without hating all; and you cannot kill some without killing all—because the welfare of any man is the welfare of all men. Through violence men are made to enslave and murder one another; through violence the world has been turned

LONG LIVE

EVERY MAN

ON EARTH!

into this unimaginable hell; through violence the rulers of this hell are enabled to maintain their blood-stained positions. Does it matter that one goes down? twenty, more ruthless, spring up; violence has brought man to this jungle of unimaginable horror—

Are you so blind? Are you so mad? Does the truth mean nothing to you? Are you such fools that you imagine violence can be overthrown by violence? hatred by more hatred? murder by still more murder?

I salute those who fight for the lives of all men.

I salute those who fight in the war against war.

I salute those who place the welfare of human beings above every other welfare.

I salute those who have faith in life—and in the destiny of men.

I salute those whose belief in brotherhood commands them not to kill their brothers.

—In all countries—In all stations—In every situation of living—

And I pray that in their love they reach a peace which can be held in trust for all those who live after them.

For if that light should go out, we shall indeed disappear into the darkness—and that darkness shall be increased by our going.

But the thing always begins. A feather drops softly down and a clock ticks on somewhere. The screens go up and the flies mosey over next door. They say having your health helps. They say when the track's fast you can hardly hear the horse's hooves. I suppose that's the way it should be. A cabin off in the mountains. Clouds drying out on your clothesline. Old boy skunk. Lights at dusk in the valley. Pulling the years into your body like nuts into a hat.

I gave my Knew. My Blind. My pretty Knew. O my snawny glee so endlessly! A fair or narrow beauty will in healing coaxêd fishes ride. On waves the gardens purply glide. Grace found, chariot-widening—nor all the crying—"Certainly not I!"—At seven glen the heart is stole again. Wish a pudding.

As heavy too.

Young lost—full so cold and all a-deathing—tears for a soul in trouble.

Have ye any majesty my friend!

Chilling sable winds they drink at me.

The tongue rolls frith and shrill fear my tubs doth beat.

A sudden flesh of words (Assume my anger) and if it phantom have it lair—crossed quiet out—together's queen

s'll build my foolish lip a taller pace—ay, a twinkling beau for yon devil's queer-gunned daughter.

Wondrous changes. The speeches fetched from smoky caves. One lawful as you please. I'm sorry sir. Wits for monuments. Profit each bliss to last out the traitorous kiss.

Or, esteemed, gratify thine own feast?

To cross the long alone. The falling many—bribed dust mantling the uncaring ground—Lend the world a clean! Visible surely are the shoulders of the Messenger. Gone gone (except to the god) are the wives of the long-awaited. Nor any summer sleeves the arms of mountains in our sky. Pour us another drink than death's.

Our eyes fill with air and the Gate is a wound which the spirit dies through—

O comb up the bells! Hounds have pilgrimages too—and the breasts of these pretty days rub together so daintily my lad. When we were two and they were twenty not hunting flowers in the field but pointing guns at each other.

Furry talk of spiders—

Bestride this swirling I Nature am a devotee of I kindly assure you mam. GREAT BASTARD leaping

full of

blood not of pigs or stones or hickory sticks but full of the blood of men.

And it doesn't end. The voices of so many lives making a scowling din.

As useless as the private is?—the secret ear listening . . . that house where anger has no place . . . where (should the wing not forget its shining) I hope things are not too bad for you.

But there is a shabby crying in the nations.

Lanes grow hands to strangle the unwary.

And if this enflamed adventure

in midnight high host sleeping O the sweet wooing gather of my course—A cruel price. Ragged castle sinking under the Claws. Fiddles sound in the oyster. How it all adorns—granted the magic and the bitterness. The very mold and shape of the fisher whose only haul is the snowy

shouting of Terror.

Ah it listens! That bright red kissing. Take heed of cottages! Hush   harsh bare.

The inventor devising himself. But no matter—no matter. It all is already done.

THE RANGE OF THE HEIGHTS IS WHIRRING ALL AROUND US.

Unto bird candle radiant
>tree
>—that it never
>betray us. Knowest
>the grim haunts
>of vision—nor have
>betwittering caution
>my wide
>my airwood cathedral
>—horsemen
>dismount! Sorrowtouched
>Light—no heart
>but shall have praise from Thee . . . no forehead
>but shall these hymning fingers feel!

The sour odor of the poor. The swarming thighs
of their outraged dead.
Only dress the soul, is it?
—surely the living have been left beautifully to rot in their
stinking kennels.
I think the moaning outsounds the tinkle
of fat sticky little bards
who twang their navels in the orderly and
empty drawingrooms of "Our Literature"—
>I am so full of rage!
>I am so full of contempt for these smug lice!
I tell them to stay away from my books!
I want to stand outside their blood-drenched "culture"!
I want nothing to do with them!
Once and for all, I reject the whole damn scaly swindle!
>It builds up and it runs down. You take the cap
off the bottle and you swallow the ink. You get blood on your
mouth and you wonder what hit you. You start a page and somebody comes to the door and wants you to buy a brush. You open

a fresh can of fish for the cat and it goes to sleep on your best shirt. You decide it might be just the thing to write a nice, warm letter to the Guggenheim Committee. Instead you draw up a list of all the books you'd like to own—of all the albums—of all the paintings—of all the wines and all the foods. In the middle of that you begin to wonder what it would be like to live in India or South Dakota or London, England. You climb up on a chair and fleck a web off the ceiling. You walk into the other room and hike the shade up. Everything looks about the same as the last time you looked out. You put your coat on and take a slowie around the block. You note with growing concern that the number of brewers' wagons is increasing daily. You jump in time—your reflexes being quicker than the little fellow's in the dinner clothes—but such language! You get back and sit down and pick up your writing things —and the words come rushing out

I'll never live another life.

—Enough to knock the props out from under anybody, that little thought!

So you start reading the thing over. You take your pen and start slashing whole sections out—God what a merry clip! You really get warmed up to it—Wait a minute! Wait a minute! You're killing the whole damn works—

You light a cigarette and take a sip of coffee. You try to think ah hell it isn't that bad, you've got some pretty fair things in there—

Slam the feeling in. Anything get in your way, knock it down! Hold the pen with both hands if you have to. Make the whole wonderful big damn thing go bulling up and shake the living daylights out of them!

Once you break training in this racket you're through. You've got to know when to take it easy—and when to let it go. You've got to learn to move around nice and loose—letting the target think you're half asleep—setting your feet just right—maybe waving to your uncle—one two polish my flue—and then you get in there and make with every muscle you've got.

That's part of it—a tiny spot down in the corner of the picture. What the rest of the picture is—? Maybe when the angel lifts his foot off it . . . Hello, uncle boy! How's the old kid!

Wild chill beast
gois lon light

NAKED above
the puved peach of speech
hurroo huroo hurroo huroo

my pretty pretty

Knew—most neat to meet upon the savory street. Full work; hair; the dancing table; judgment in an injured skull; a foul and nearing—wait closer! merit does no ridiculous abuse; rejoice in green and brown (within sight) . . . Whom! Welcome or die has its points. Without conceit either.

New sullen shepherd.
Wise or false. Flame-born.
Thee; strange; men; towns.
Air. Fire. Grace. Faith.
Beauty delights.

a pie of boys

LOVE

(greater Life, Fame for all!)

I am that watcher which is
And what hath been
Son of.

MAN   **TREE**

Throne-eye with Thine own opening. As no whip—splendor upon splendor. Mastery flourisheth! Shutting out all victorious foes.

THE ARGUMENT

"<u>Limit fathers up triumph sail leadeth content established who having come heart lack comfort heard pine hast perfect one middle liftest not under lamentation again length countries high returning nether fail ever whose god made labor other this me more glance when myrrh traveler draw hear drinking</u>" spake the Management.

TUT OUTWITS THE NASTY ROBBER

Gentles. A black prologue.

"Curtain, folks. Kindly remove your flippers from the aisle."

Jev. Have you the—?

Ner. Ay. May it please your worship—

Kai. Let's him a trick or two show.   (They show him.)

Pag. Decorum's only skindeep—that at least is umbre.

Abo. What's umbre?

Hir. Amy, my divine creature!   (He takes her into the wings.)

Sda. But what is umbre?

Fot. Ah ha, my toothsome!   (He takes her into the wings.)

Ner. What's to be done with this—?

Kai. Let's him another trick or two show.   (They show him.)

Pag. Does umbre maybe mean insinuating?

Lok. Ho, ho, my little starling.   (He takes her into the wings.)

But the thing always goes on somehow. One day it works pretty good; the next, lousy. Loosen it up. A little afraid of it maybe.

I like to see love back there in big letters.

Beauty <u>delights</u>—? —But how else could I say just that?

a pie <u>of boys</u>—Worth every second of the three hours I put into it.

Thee; strange; men; towns—That's sad, damn it! That's real sad.

Keep away! Incantations a bastard, I didn't ask for it remind them sometime will you thorns harbors all upon the sunny peaks

. . . A rather dark pantomime
imposter
scapegoat
bawdy
rood
candle
stroker

(See if she really is as warm as toast. Ah I loved. I bled. It was my marrow went spugging. Magnetism be damned! Noctambulation in aduncous tiltyards: covin-lad: a tuggled web—only an opinion, mind you, I'll warrant the red comes up oftener. As children. Fiducial have-gup.

   —(In fool cry.) Titititicraring   booum   spit
                   Always that sweet woodnote . . .

Yup. Gitup hinny old spurt. Excuse me, couple things I have to strutten out in the pergola.

I've had adventures too, **rather beautiful adventures.**—I came down the railroad cut at twilight. They had been gaining on me all day. My mouth tasted of sweat and black fear. It doesn't do to let it go too long—You get mixed-up. You begin to think you know what is hunting you down. You begin to think that maybe the only thing which has the power to comfort you is to get caught, to lie helpless and meek before them. You begin to think that the only real escape is to give in, to offer them your life and your soul—because somewhere, in fire and glory, it was arranged that they should have them.

Once I thought I saw myself back there with the pack, more avid and cruel than all of them put together. Since it is shifting and red—I have my little joke now, don't I . . .

A cage...........a ball..............a grove...........
A ball...........a grove.............a cage...........
A grove.........a cage.............a ball.............

Jesus turn that volume down—This way, by gum, the whole world'll get shaken to pieces . . . Three women wait beside the river. Their eyes are closed. They have yellow hats. Their hands are full of beheaded children.

We noticed that a sort of light was coming through the walls of the cave. We rushed out and the heavens . . . diving white fish in a terrible glee . . . that useable majesty . . . O all that tractless and grim acreage . . . that awesome womb opening into the light . . .

And there were beings moving around in the light.

One of them reached down and touched my face. I felt all my guilt and shame leaving me . . .

There was a throne.

On the throne sat a beautiful man. He held out a match to my cigarette. His hand had a mouth in it.

Down there is a village, lights winking sleepily at the wind's soft caress. Peace dribbling softly darkly down from the lips of the sky. It's here, oh everything I need is here

oh the dream stirs

reaches out its hand that is covered with eyes

I stumble off the tracks as a milktrain crupples past. A stone cuts into the palm of my foot. Blood trickles down my cheek from the cut of an angry branch. I am hungry, tired, ready to kiss the devil's ass for a kind word and a friendly pat on the head.

Hm, a shack—some sort of light in there by God

knock   ruckruck   raprap   hey! anybody home in there?

for the love of Pete! All right, all right—to hell with you

Wait a minute

Something's the matter in there.

I open the door.

An old man is lying   Come on in, son. Sorry I couldn't make you hear before.

Say you're pretty sick. I better get somebody.

296

No.—Please. Fix yourself something to eat. There's eggs on the shelf, potatoes in the bin . . . You might fetch me a glass of water.

Sure, sure.

Well's out in the orchard.

Got a bucket?

Under the sink there.

Moon just topping the trees—smell of apple blossoms—damn I want it crude, edgy, stinking with the noble wonder of the most usual things.   Legs wide-spread

mumff the bucket hits the sides of the well—the smell of thoughtful water

I'm sorry I was so long.

How is it—Thank you—Umm—out there?

Beautiful. Absolutely breath-taking.

You'll find a skillet in that big cardboard box—No—Over there, just this side of the fishing-reels.

I don't suppose you feel up to—

Cup of coffee later maybe. Where are you from?

Oh—a lot of places. Isn't any bacon-fat, is there?

There's a whole side of bacon hanging up in the woodshed. On a string from the ceiling just as you go in.

So the animals can't—

Yes. And you'll find a couple tins of milk in there too.

I washed up and went about getting my supper ready. The walls were good and fat with books. There were two bunks, three or four chairs, a small table, and a big table. On the small table were the scattered pieces of a phonograph.

And what is your name?

Pudar Zenaslufski. I'm called Old Zenaslufski. Have you comitted a crime?

I'm Almar Gnunsn. Hell! a bad egg.

Dolly never brought me one before. Are you sure it's bad?

Yeah, stinks. Who's Dolly?

Girl loves over the hill, just across the river—What are you running away from?

Look, it's damn nice of you to welcome me in and—

All right, son. Better turn that bacon.

Who painted the picture?

Fellow named Jidet, Herman Jidet.

I like it. Where's the salt?

In the jar marked sugar. Herman was really a tinker—only started to paint when he got up into his seventies.

Who is the woman? Your wife?

He didn't say anything. I looked over at him. His bearded face was haggard in the dim light. His face looked like somebody had scooped out all the flesh in back of it.

I sat down at the big table and started to eat. I'd fried the eggs too much, and the potatoes not enough. The potatoes tasted vaguely of kerosene.

That was painted more than thirty years ago, Old Zenaslufski said.

That's a long time, I said, wondering how sand got in the salt.

The clock above the fireplace had one of those little, tinny, gas-pains rumbles you often hear in cheap makes.

Quietly asking me—You're not a murderer, are you, son?

Who'd you say that woman was?

Sounds preposterous I know, a clock eating beans—but there it was! one of the loudest I ever heard.

The old man stirred on his smelly bunk. I'm afraid to die, he said.

Who said you were going to die?

There was a sort of bumping at the door. I pushed my chair back and went over and opened it.

Two men stood there. They were naked. Does a Miss Snook live here? one of them asked, making an obscene gesture.

I stepped out fast and kicked him where it would do the most good. He started to whimper and I did it again. His friend said, He's just a poor little sheep who has gone astray. You'll wish you hadn't done that, Jack.

Some day when I have the time I'll worry about it, I said, slamming the door in his face. But you come in you come in.

Who was it?

Couple drunks.

I used to take mine down with the best of them.

You wouldn't be having a bottle on the premises, now would you, pop?

Under the mattress over there.

I fished it out and took a long one. Bells started to ring in my stomach. How's about you, pop? Might be just the thing.

No, I'd better not. Besides, you haven't told me what you're running away from.

There was a muffled knock at the door. I took another drink and went over and opened it.

There were three women standing there. They were quite naked. Good evening, one of them said. Does that bridge over there lead into town?

I can tell you better over by the well, I said. In the orchard I led the prettiest one over to a mound of blossoms . . . a minute passed, fifteen minutes . . . an hour . . . the soft light of the moon made an altar of her naked loveliness . . . her lips swelled like plums under my mouth . . . when at last I took her I think every star in the sky held its breath . . .

What were you saying about a bridge? I asked her, her head cradled on my arm and the wonderful sticky warm smell of her making me wish I hadn't done a lot of the things I'd done.

Mary said you would be able to tell us.

(It's always like that!) And who is Mary?

Your wife, of course.

Nonsense. I never had a wife.

Her picture's on the wall in there.

How much do you want?

Want? For what?

For keeping your stupid mouth shut.

Oh, you don't really mean that. It's so pretty here . . . the lights of the village twinkling away like sad flowers down there in the valley . . . the lonely whistle of a train making you think somehow of all the times you've ever cried or ever loved someone—

How much?

—And there's so much pain and fear and sorrow . . . so many poor human beings praying for a light in this terrible darkness—

How much?

Six thousand dollars.

I reached over her and fished it out of my pants. Honey, I said, this clams-up your brothers too, right?

My brothers?

Sure, they dropped by just a few minutes before you did. I may have shaken Eddie up a bit, I think.

She nibbled at my ear. One of my wisdom teeth's been acting up lately, she said.

Why don't you go to the dentist?

Maybe I'll have to. What size shoe do you wear, Al?

5½—Why?

I just wondered. You remember that time we passed the barn and the farmer—

What do you want to remember something like that for?

I can't get it out of my mind. Sometimes I wake up at night covered with sw-perspiration—

I told you before. The farmer had to. It was sick.

Give me a kiss.

The breath of our noses mixed.

Make love to me again, Al.

I haven't time.

Ah, please.

It's not worth six thousand bucks, I said, strubbing to my feet.

Some joke.

Six thousand bucks is no joke, kid.

But now you're safe.

Yeah. (I slipped the safety off my .32.) Now I'm safe.

The other two were asleep, their full lips pluffing in and out like snails on a hot stove.

As I bent over them a voice said, Turn around with your hands up.

Slowly—I did as I was told.

No one.

Turned back—

The sisters were gone.

I hurried to the shack. Next time there'll be no getting away that easy, my smooth chicks. I don't know what I expected to find in the shack, but there was Old Zenaslufski smiling up at me from his bunk. He said, Were you able to cope with them, son?

Yeah, I coped all right, I said. Say, would it hurt if I opened a window? The sour smell of the room was beginning to get me down.

By all means. Were you planning to make coffee?

Sonofagun, how do you like that! I plumb forgot the coffee.

I put it up and started to fool around with the busted phonograph. Huh-uh—the main spring. I told him. He said that was too bad, he loved music almost as much as studgeweed pancakes.

What are studgeweed pancakes?

Right down there at the bend of the river—on the shaded side under the willows—that's where the best studgeweed grows. Not as strong a flavor as buckwheat . . . God! I'd give a lot for another mess of studgeweeds before I die.

I'll fix you up some right now.

Nah, son . . . They're a powerful set of work—

What do I do?

He told me. Well, I'd always thought of taking up some career —I'll never understand why each and every grain had to be washed separately under running water three different times, and then peeled. It's possible he had a point in having me grind the goddam stuff into a paste with my teeth, but when he told me to take down the little jar from the top shelf and stir that in—And what's in this little jar, pop?—Ah, ha, that is my own discovery, the real secret of the excellence of my studgeweeds. That, son, is the water of the female muskrat.

THE WATER OF THE FEMALE MUSKRAT—is it! I'll give you even money, few men have had to put up with—

The coffee's boiling over.

Oh, yeah?—coffee, watch this!

What do you eat these studgeweeds with? sheep turd? I asked, putting them all out on a big, cracked plate in front of him.

Butter. Heaps of golden, country butter. O my God! Son, you've done it! You are now one of the two people on this earth who can make a studgeweed pancake! He ate like he had ten wolves in him.

And soon there will be only one, I said, pouring the coffee.

Eh?—with his mouth absolutely crammed—Oh, that. You know, I feel like a new man already.

There was a fumbling sound at the door. I took his cup of coffee over and held milk and sugar for him. He took it black.

I went over and opened the door. A tiny boy stood there. Beside him was a tiny girl holding a puppy on a string. The three of them were naked, stark. May we come in and look at your house? the tiny boy said. We'd like that ever so much, the tiny girl said.

How's about it, pop? I called back.

Come on in, children, Old Zenaslufski said heartily.

They ran in very slowly. Have you an inside toilet? the tiny boy said.

Yes, over the other side of the orchard, I explained.

Oh, a stove! the tiny girl said.

Haven't you ever seen a stove before? I asked.

What do you keep ejecting from your mouth? she answered.

Mash, I said. The mash of the fronafus studgeweed.

What's fronafus mean?

Wait until you're sixteen and I'll tell you.

Get down that jar for the puppy, Old Zenaslufski said.

What do you mean, get down the jar for the puppy?

It's not always so easy to keep up a good muskrat supply, he explained.

Well, I got a couple good nips, the front of my pants wet, and about an eighth of an inch's worth in the bottom of the jar.

I think your puppy is thirsty, children. Son, give the nice thirsty puppy a big drink of water.

Where do you keep the funnel, pop?

The tiny girl crawled up on the old man's bunk. She put her tiny hands around his wrinkled throat and started to squeeze. I thought it was just innocent good-humor until I saw old Zenaslufski's face beginning to get purple. I started over to pull her off when the tiny boy tripped me up and kazunk I went, upsetting the table that held the phonograph. That big damn horn came smack-dab down over my head—the brat had a knife.

I think the pair of them would have killed us. But through the window I had opened, a voice: Children, stop that now. I want you to leave here immediately.

I must have done a fade-out—for Christ's sake I was one red smear from head to foot . . .

Coming out of it I heard Old Zenaslufski's strangled whisper: Must have planned to put his pieces down the toilet and burn me in the stove.

I went back to sleep.

The sun awakened me. I looked around the room. Every available bit of space was covered with dolls—there were probably seven hundred of them—golden heads, bright peasant dresses, red, orange, blue and green—and their eyes were alive.

Their eyes were looking at me.

I horrored over at Old Zenaslufski's berth. A beautiful woman lay there. Her lips were little split roses as she slept. Long golden curls covered her breasts with their pretty money. She was very oh her skin had flames dancing over it and where her sex was what God had made there made me feel like crying it was so holy wanting her

oh there are trees and cities and purple lakes and great good honest men and women everywhere I tell you not to lose heart all the beautiful things will be saved

nothing that is really beautiful can ever be lost

Greatness and Truth can never be in danger from these stale thieves

Oh I tell you lovers of Truth and Decency not to lose heart

everything worthwhile is on our side

no weapon in the world can stand against the Beautiful

we may seem to fail

but Truth and Love cannot fail

oh an Awesome Figure towers over these shrunken lands

this bodiless procession takes its gray path over the earth

no one will understand this book who is not humble in the Mystery

the bowed heads of cold journeys

little cakes of blood drying in the sun

no tongues of silk interrupt this desperate weave

someone is being buried

the creamy lids of sleep open

this chant against—O God of Light!

to perform one's duty, be it now, be it clean, and be it done with humility

A horse has four legs. Have you ever seen a horse? A horse (the kind I'm talking about) has four legs, a long tail, and a long, narrow face. There are two general types of horse, the male and the female. This fact makes more horses all the while. The next time you see a horse notice what a nice thing a horse is to look at. Isn't it fine that horses want to make more horses all the time? Otherwise the horse would soon cease to exist.

Rain and sun, a flower has to have these or it will not grow very well. Especially important is the sun, the wonderful and wise sun. The rain falls on the flower and the sun shines down on the flower. That is a beautiful thing. There is nothing in the world more beautiful than that.

A man has two legs. Have you ever seen a man? I mean, really looked at one? A man has two legs, two arms, and a rather unbeautiful head. Something helpless and unformed about it. Nose, chin and brow sort of useless-looking—as though they might suddenly stop being anything. As though something better had been planned, and then abandoned. But it's man's unreal look that hits you hardest. A cabbage or a sparrow—now right away you know that here is something pretty certain and workable. But a man— I don't think he ever got over the shock of how essentially ridiculous he looks. No one ever saw anything in a nightmare more terrifying than a man. Next time you see one, take a really good look. Doesn't it make you a little sick? Isn't that the strangest thing you ever saw? Good God take a Saturday off and go out to the beach!

The Man Animal—again two general types, the female and the male. And although the theory has been subjected to some pretty severe criticism of late, it is still maintained by a few hearty souls that this sex-difference (between men and women) is a rather good thing—in fact, that it is down-right swell fun when entered upon in the proper spirit. I have always thought (and I must be wrong, obviously) that God intended man and woman to make love to each other. It's beyond me what can be unclean about it. But it must be. Let the good clean sun in on it you snivelling dirty puritan hypocrites!

When I was in grammar school the teacher took me aside one day and said, We are starting a little contest to see which of you boys can keep his sex-organ the cleanest. Well, I thought if it's my sex-organ you want clean, teacher, then it's pretty well up to me to clean it—mother had stopped bathing me a good five years before. My little chums were in a flurry of activity; notes were compared, obscure tomes were dragged out of dusty corners in moldy trunks and packing cases—a few of them even mastered German, so eager were they to gain favor with teacher. Always a little aloof, I pursued a solitary course of experimentation; first I tried Peroxide—old Mrs. Thompson next-door heard for the first time in thirty-five years—, then I tried a mixture of baking-powder and iodine—baking-powder is supposed to make biscuits rise, and mine was no exception. Ah, that was a merry time—standing on the steps of the courthouse with little Edmund and Isaac and Sammy and the rest, our childish voices raised in excited bickering over whose teacher would choose—and didn't the ladies of The Eastern Star set up a cackle when that bold Freddie tried to get them to venture an opinion as to whether his didn't really deserve the prize. Mr. Cox, our teacher, must have regretted his little idea, because a couple of weeks after that he shot himself through the head with an old .22 rifle, pulling the trigger with a string held between his toes. The normal, healthy curiosity of boys—but those old tomes (some of them from the Greek: Sexaphafulus Absinacriticia was one I remember) sure did inspire a rare broth of questions—and the Principal sitting there in the back row, his eyes fairly bulging out as first one of us and then the other would run eagerly forward to prove the superiority of his cleansing methods. A few parents even went so far as to take their daughters out of the school, but in general the town seemed to view it as a profound calamity, though eggs were then retailing in even the best stores for as little as five dozen for a dollar twenty-seven. You could rent an eight-room house then for eighty dollars a month, with free gas and electricity. Air was an additional three-sixty.

There was a knock at the door. Old Zenaslufski seemed to be having himself a snooze—his hands rising and falling like pieces of bark on his shrunken trunk—so I mosied over and opened the door. A girl stood there. Her eyes looked into mine like blue stones flung out by an angel. Her wrists were covered by tiny hairs of gold. She had on faded overalls and a huge straw hat with the top torn off that time the hay-rig tumbled over just beyond the bridge as you go to the widow Faith Lacepanz' farm. My name is Dolly, she said. Her voice was a bell ringing the godless to prayer.

Mine is Stephen Goatwhistle, I said, indicating by my gesture that she was to come in.

She laughed. The sunbeams tried it on for size and it fitted.

I've brought the eggs, she said, clearing a space on the larger table and depositing them on the mantle.

How much? I said, sinking back on the trunk.

What ever you think you can afford to pay, she answered. How is he?

Who?

Why, Old Zenaslufski.

He's still got a good pair of lungs in him, I said, bobbing up and down like a cook on the whatfor.

There's something I'd like to get off my chest before I die, the old man said, between gasps; during gasps he said, In the pocket of my overcoat you'll find a photograph.

What's that? I asked.

This the one you mean? Dolly asked.

You, he said. Yes, that's the one. Hand it over, will you, Mr. Gnunsn?

I stood up and felt myself over, slowly counting his ribs. Here you are, pop. What are you going to do with it now you've got it? I asked.

Gnunsn? Dolly said. That isn't the name you told me.

Scare the living hell out of you, you cheap wise guy, the old troglodyte said, half lifting up off his stinking bunk.

I know it isn't the name I told you, Dolly, I said, snatching the photograph out of his hand and walking over to the window with it. I stood there—that face looking up at me!

At last I said, How much do you want?

There was no answer. No one said anything.

Finally I managed to raise my eyes from that face in the photograph . . .

And she was sitting there watching me.

Darling

At last I said, Darling, what will become of us? It is so cold and dark . . . I can't always manage it alone . . .

Dearest, her voice said, there will be an end . . . even this will end . . . and then you can rest . . . and then you can know that we will be together always . . .

But I want peace! . . . not just to die! . . . not just that, that black sleep kissing all the fear and pain away . . .

There is no escape, Al.

I don't want to escape. I want to get caught.

Did you put the butter and cheese in the refrigerator?

Yes, damnit!

Is the door locked?

What difference does that make? is the door locked!

Is it?

Oh, I'm sorry! Yes, darling, I locked the door. All the lights are out. The clock is wound and—

What was that!

What was what?

That . . . that funny noise?

I don't hear anything.

Don't . . . Oh, don't! Don't! Please don't . . .

A man has two legs. He'll build a house—from cellar to roof-top, with his own hands. He'll put seeds in the ground. He'll watch the sun and the rain at work. He'll take a woman to bed. He'll find enough tenderness and love to get him through the day. You'd think that man deserved a little something. You'd think that man was worthy of a jot or two of sympathy and consideration. You'd think that maybe someone would say, Let's just let him alone for a while and see what he can do.

You wouldn't think they'd send him out in the dark to get covered with slime and filth—and then blow him into a million bloody pieces, would you?

You wouldn't think they'd put a rifle in his hands and tell him to go out and shoot some poor devil he'd never even known existed, would you?

You wouldn't think men could be such monsters as to want to make murderers out of everybody, now would you?

But it doesn't work otherwise.

Everybody has to be a murderer.

God has to be a fraud and a fake.

Brotherhood and Truth and the lot have to be so much s—t.

Christ has to be a hypocrite and a liar.

It doesn't work out otherwise.

Have you ever looked at a man?

There is something helpless and majestic about a man.

If you believed in anything, you could not kill a man.

Tell me that is a lie!

Then everything is a lie.

There is no meaning, no purpose, to anything.

The trees stand under the quiet heavens.

Birds sleep in the sun.

You can hold a stone in your hand.

Flowers pray in the soft rain.

There are so many colors for us to see.

We are sad when someone we love is sick.

We are small.

We are weak.

We should help one another.

There is so much that has been done wrong for us to undo; there is so much that has been beautifully done for us to try to do again.

Where there is not faith; there is death.

Where there is not love; not even death is, but a nothingness scorned by his cold pale hand.

It will always be dark until the lights in us come on.

Dolly said, The river used to be much deeper here; as the bed widened the current became more sluggish—except in the early spring almost anywhere along here you can wade across very easily.

That doesn't answer my question.

Oh—She crinkled her nose.—And what was your question?

Do you love me?

She gave me her hand and I hoisted her down off the log fence. Please don't keep asking me that, Al, she said.

And why not?

Would you like to walk across the trestle? That's loads of fun. If you tell me—

But I don't know! We've only known each other four days!

Five days.

Four days. Oh, what difference does that make? five days, four days? It's still not long enough.

I needed only thirty seconds.

And it'd probably take you about that long to forget me.

You're a silly kid.

There—Now I'm a silly kid. I'll race you down to the oak tree.

Which is the oak tree?

The one—Oh, you know which one. On your mark, get set, go!

I let her beat me down to the oak tree—

Like fun you did! You even tried to trip me . . .

—and we stretched out on the moss at its foot. A farmer called over from a neighboring field: When the corners of the ox's mouth drip an azure spittal, then no moment is without hazard for those who have dismounted from phantom chargers in the glow of shadowed lanterns that reflect every face on the earth save the one face they have come this long bitter journey to see—and have you got the time on you, friends?

The blonde eyes of madness gaze hungrily at the throne as bewildered, crimson heroes stand like shelless turtles at the gates of a punishment which no man can exchange for tan-spotted lino-leum or generous spools of marblized thread at the drug-counter in his neighborhood, I yelled back. It's twenty past four.

Look! Look! the hugging bees are starting to pee into Norman Smith's cornfield! he yelled, setting off at a smart clip to put the matter right.

Who is Norman Smith? I asked Dolly, watching the wind ar-range a kissman's noose in her hair.

A retired architect—came here from Philadelphia about six years ago—his daughter was struck by lightning last summer. Please don't do that, Al.

Did it kill her?

No, but it peeled most of the skin off her body.

Here, you mean?

No!—No, I don't mean there. Ah, Al—

Where is the nearest public library?

In Peaceful Bottoms—that's the county seat.

Gosh . . . It sure is restful here in the sun. I feel as lazy as a staircase down which the roses tumble to a late-afternoon tea.

No one would know it . . . Now no more of that! I'll never speak to you again! You're old enough to know better than that, Al!

You're quite right. How's this?

Oh!

I became aware of four pairs of shoes grouped around my knee-cap. When I could finally manage to tear my eyes away from them and look up, I got one of the strangest jolts any mortal man ever got. There was a thing standing there looking down at us from a good thirty feet up in the air. It had nine legs. It's head was a bright green—pitted with tiny orange stars. Sticking out of its back was a huge bare leg topped by a huge bare foot. The leg was covered with ads of various patent nostrums and tugging up from each toe were great balloons with human faces pasted on them. The faces were all scowling and smiling to beat merry hell and when I touched one of the gleaming shoes my hand came away covered with blood. Dolly, I said, am I right in thinking I smell gingerbread baking around here somewhere?

The sun is going down, she said, getting to her feet and patting her dress back into shape. I'll see you tomorrow morning, Al. Pleasant dreams and God be with you.

I watched her swing off across the meadow. I'll have to buy her something nice next time I go to town, I thought. Maybe a big box of candy or a pretty umbrella for around a dollar forty-seven, say.

Bug, what do you think you're doin' 'way out here in this green field?—Clouds sailing up in the sky . . . What do you make of clouds, little bug? Aren't you afraid I'll maybe sort of just squnch you between my fingers? Ah—don't fool yourself—I could do it if I wanted to! So why don't I, you funny looking little bastard? I wonder how I'd look with a red chest and a yellow behind. Tell me something, what sort of a God have you bugs found for yourselves? How do you manage without any Michaelangelos and William Shakespeares?

A whip snaked down out of the sky and smashed my teeth out. I put the bug back on his leaf.

Having trouble, mister?

He was dressed in black leather from head to toe. A big leather cap on a shock of pale hair. In his leather glove lay a brown ball. There were pieces of gray flesh sticking out all over the leather. What do you want? I said. Nobody asked you to come snooping around here.

I just asked you a civil question, he said, suddenly tossing me the brown ball.

Well, just go on ab— What the hell kind of a dirty trick is that! Throwing me a piece of— Why I'll ram my fist right down your

Ally, do you mean to say you still don't recognize me?

First I wiped my hands off carefully on his chamois shirt tail, then I looked at—Why, Sammy Stink! Where in the goddam—!

We threw our arms about each other—Still the same old Ally! —And still my little chum Stink!—We buffed and scrubbied, porshed and pegalvidated. And what are you doing away out here on the steppes, Ally boy?—And did you ever succeed in getting it really clean, my Sammy-vel? Oh, no you don't, my hearty! For as we fell, he had brought his knee up hard enough to nearly shake one of them off my tree. How're Molly and Jim Snow? I howled, cracking him in the throat with my elbow. He tried to get a gouge on my left eye, tearing out the bridge of my nose instead. They're just fine, Ally; Molly married a paperhanger out in Sacramento, and Snow's doing a long return engagement up the river for raping the lock on the First National in Spokane, he panted, beginning to bleed at the ears. And how're Pa and Ma Stink? I don't have to tell you, Sammy-aroon, that they were my absolute favorite people in good old Pigmilk, Nevada, I managed to blurble out twice, since my tongue was split down the middle.

I didn't have to tell him. For Samuel Wadsworth Stink was dead. I pulled an old silo-cover over him and started back to the shack. They're rainproofed and that made me feel better about it. By the time I got to the stile I was feeling so good I gave the woman in the change booth a big kiss smack on the mouth—which was a mistake because her mask had 90,580 volts of 'green' electricity running through it.

Old Zenaslufski was sitting on the steps with a big pile of moth balls heaped up in front of him. About ten feet away he had a ten pound lard can full of paint set up. Want to try your luck, son? he said cheerfully, keeping a steady stream of moth balls humming between him and the can.

You play with your balls, pop, I said, I've a couple things I should get out of the way before sundown.

Inside the cabin I took off my clothes and made me a nice salad. While I was eating I made a mental note to send into the

314

city for a new supply of the stuff first thing in the morning. I could see the faces of the boys as they heard where I was holing-up. All of them a little soap and good, clean water would have helped.

I went to the door and knocked. The old man came clumping up and opened it. Have you any deophruamon? I asked him.

What the devil's deo-whateverthehell?

A poison.

He looked down at his old, work-worn hands, at his battered shoes, at his faded pants with the ancient price-tag still in its honored place—I'll die anyway before the first leaves fall, he said.

Sorry, pop, I can't wait.

Off in the sycamore a blue jay acted as though nothing else in the whole world had ever had a worm. His mate, her pin-feathers arranged in neat cushions at her plump sides, regarding him with jaded enthusiasm, said, That is indeed a fine-looking worm, Edmund—So naturally Edmund, not being a complete dope, gave it to her.

But anyhow, Old Zenaslufski cackled, come on down and look into the can.

I'm tired—some other time, huh?

Oh, no—I mean the can right here in the yard, the one with the paint in it.

I walked down the steps and peered in. He'd got all the moth balls in and all I could see was a black mass. What's so remarkable about that? I said, thinking that probably nobody'd think to look for him down in the well for a nice long time.

Take one out! he chortled gleefully. Just you take one out, son!

Well—I had this big damn sticky black moth ball in my mitt. Very funny, I said.

But wait! Just you wait now!

And it began to get heavier in my hand and the black began to turn to—GOLD!

Silence while the band plays and the flag is raised—I let out a whoop that brought all those little Indians running in from miles around and threw myself on his neck. There was a sharp crrrack and part of it broke off in my hands. Pop! I bellowed, Pop old goose, speak to me!—Hey, take it easy! You'll break the good part next thing you know, he said, trying to back off. What do you mean, break the good part? I demanded. A bear, he said—up in the northwoods once, this bear damn near ripped my whole gullet out.—So?—So the lumberjacks made me a new one out of hemlock—that's a good, sound wood.—It did have, at that. But your balls, I shouted, remembering again—You've got golden balls! O now we can buff and scrubby, porsh and pegalvidate!—Not until I carve me a new neck, we can't, he stated, suddenly sitting down and taking my whole weight on his chest. Will it work everytime? I yelled into his purpling old face. Gub . . . Gub . . . Gub . . . he wheezed. Wlll whttt wwwrk evvtmm?—Why, the black paint on the moth balls? Here, I'll let you take another breath. Gubzzz . . . Gubzzz . . . Thett's nnt blllk pnnt. I let go entirely; stood up. What's not black paint?

That special formula of mine, that's what's not black paint, he said. I could see the words passing the open space in his throat.

It's always like that. A cow walks out of a woods and all the church steeples get heartburn. If we didn't have doors we wouldn't need banks. Do you think the nickel was invented just to keep small boys in short pants all their lives?

I tell you that a day is coming when men will look into their own hearts for the answer to that question which everyone of us has asked—and which no radio comedian or advertising copywriter can throw any light on—:

What are we on earth for?

Is it fitting for us to live in houses, ride on trains, wait around for postmen who will never bring the right letter anyway?

I never saw a house that looked right for human beings to live in.

I never rode on a train but I thought the fellow who dreamed this up will never be allowed in hell.

I never waited for a letter but I knew what I really wanted was even a quick little note from God.

I never heard anybody say anything but I thought what a shoddy way that is for human beings to communicate with one another.

I never looked at anything beautiful without thinking the only way I can understand this is to forget everything they have tried to drum into my head about beauty.

'Culture' has become a property. People want to take music and painting and sculpture and poetry and stuff them into their pockets until they can "get a free moment" when they will "really sit down and enjoy them." You cute little punks! turn the filth and the envy and the greed, the hatred and the ignorance and the murder out first! What right have you to think you can bury yourselves away in the stinkholes of money—and position—and 're-spectability'—grubbing during your "practical moments," and then have the artist trot out his little show for your 'enjoyment'—What do you think art is, some damn smorgasbord for shoeclerks!

The artist—and I am speaking very carefully now—is always the spokesman of God. You have beaten him, starved him, driven him mad; but always something in him was turned to a greater torturer, eaten by a greater hunger, beset by a greater calamity than any you could put in his path; because the things of God are always wondrous in a terrible way.

I believe that we are at a turning—one road leads into the dark, another into the light; and whichever man takes, be sure that the artist will have proceeded him there—his face scarred with poverty and suffering and fear.

So that you may "enjoy"—

So that a lot of pretty toys may please you with their quaint and frantic antics—

So that you may get "what you pay your good money for"—

So that the teachings of Christ may be translated into good, sound "Business English"—

What a nasty, vicious, evil, cheap fraud—this Century of the Cornered Man—

I think I hear a rat squealing in a monstrous trap.

And I think your eyes are looking out of that rat.

Tears of blood scar the face of Christ.

I turned the volume down and walked out into the night. A gust of wind made the trees cry out in their sleep. I heard a train coming a long way off down the valley. I knew there was no one I wanted to see on that train. I knew that everything I had ever done or said had absolutely no meaning at all. I knew that there was no plan or design anywhere that could give those I loved one extra breath of life, or satisfy any real need they had ever had. Those are stars up there. And this is a man down here. Suddenly I hated the stars. I would have torn them down and pulled them to pieces with my fingers. I closed my eyes—the back of my head felt as cold as a block of ice—I felt my fingers close over something—

Al, Al,—softly—you're hurting my hand.

Oh—I'm sorry, Dolly . . . I . . . I was just . . .

Give it to me. Please.

Give what to you? What are you talking about?

The gun. Give it to me.

The gun? See, I've no gun, Dolly.

I mean the gun in your mind, Al.

Oh, Dolly . . . Dolly . . .

Hold onto my hand. It will pass.

But I can't . . . I . . .

How long have you been standing here?

Forever, I think. There. I'm beginning to feel better now. I'll walk you home.

I'm going to stay with you tonight, Al.

But you can't do that. Your mother'd think you'd been murdered on the road or something, Dolly.

The danger is not that I'd be murdered on the road. Oh, come now, don't behave like a spoiled child. If you had a broken leg, mother'd certainly not want me to go away and leave you lying here helpless with it.

But what if the gun should go off?

It won't—after we empty it.

How will we do that?

By giving you something better to do than have guns in your head. It's not sanitary.

All right, kid—you win. We'll have to go in quiet so as not to wake Old Zenaslufski. He has a pretty bad time getting to sleep as it is.

We're sleeping out.

What do you mean, out? Out here? On all this concrete ground? with tarantulas and blood-sucking—

Blood-sucking what?

Well, weavels.

Go in very quietly and bring three blankets and a pillow.

Okay. You won't go 'way now? You're sure you'll be here when I get back, Dolly?

She unstrapped her wristwatch and handed it to me. Will that do for security, sir?

Holy smoke! it's nearly three o'clock. And you with cows to milk a-first thing in the mornin'.

By heck, she said. Oh, come on, Al, shake a leg—It's beginning to get chilly.

When you hear the dial-tone it will be three blankets and one pillow time, I said, cheerfully wheeling around and falling over a log fence. The logs, though comfortably cushioned with stinging nettle and deadly night-shade, made one hell of a din. Well, I

319

took that din and made one so much bigger it was like taking cannons from a navy. My lungs sucked in so much air they split my coat over the shoulder blades, and I was still hollering to wake the dead minutes after every grave in the valley had opened like a rotting white fist. One of the things worried me was I was afraid the cow—which I believed then to be at least ten mooses locked in combat—I was afraid the cow would decide to shake her head, and getting off even a quiet horn requires considerable application. Pop-corn—you should have seen the lights come on in that village. It took a week to put some of them out again. And Old Zenaslufski, trying to load his shotgun and put his false-teeth in at the same time, added his own individual touch to the occasion by stepping hellbent into the lard pail—and goldballing it he went sailing right down through the main street into the next township, firing his teeth with nice discrimination into old and young alike, while little barges of buckshot gave his alimentary canal a bit of something to mull over on long winter evenings.

A jolly little stroll around The Semenov Drill grounds first thing on a bright June morning, eh?

Clumsy angels parading glumly through these gardens of the sick . . .

It happened that the widow Lacepanz had invited me over for a turtle dinner a week from Tuesday next. I decided to spend what time remained to me until then in the commission of certain odd jobs about the place, which I had come to look upon almost as my own. In fact, so enamored had I grown of this tranquil haven away from the bestialities and grossities of my fellows, that one rapturous, starless night I dug a hole in the orchard and put Old Zenaslufski into it. Nearly gone as he was, he had me shoveling the dirt back on for a good quarter of an hour. Silly old fellow— I warned him that being only human I couldn't promise that maybe the spade wouldn't sort of slip and—I stood there pulling great bouquets of the flower-scented air into my lungs. A fox barked off on one of the dark rotundas. Turning my head at a peculiar angle, and pulling my ears well up through the crown of my hat, I made bold to answer him. Soon there was a gentle plump at my feet—then another, and another . . . When I finally struck a match, I saw that I was standing knee-deep in the carcasses of some two or three hundred freshly-slaughtered chickens. Now I wonder what I could have said to make them feel that submissive? I thought. Almar Gnunsn, King of the Hen-Killers—it's an idea anyway.

That's what I've heard.

I looked intently into her shyly lowered eyes. What have you heard, Mrs. Lacepanz? I asked, hoping that no one would come in and find me down on my knees like that.

That you have a way with the ladies, she answered, expecting that everybody would spit their gum right out and turn off the radio.

I'd say she was in her oily forties; it had been a very warm day. She had a face like a boarding-house toilet, constantly flushing and chipped around the edges. Her nose needed only some whats, whys and wheres to get a good newspaper started; it was certainly well-fixed with wens. Everytime she moved her neck I expected a bloodhound to sink his teeth into my leg.

What do you wear under these? I asked.

Heavy knitted drawers or reinforced ski-pants, Faith said.

I handed her back the catalogue. I never did care much for winter sports, I said.

That's not the way I heard it, she said, favoring me with a look that could mean only one thing—she'd never have to take a drink to get the male hen's eye.

Oh, I do admit as a boy I had a pair of skates I was pretty fond of, I said.

My sister used to go out with a fellow named Robert Sled, she said.

I had to get rid of them finally—They insisted on laying their eggs in father's shave-mug. Could we maybe eat soon, Mrs. Lace-panz?

Why, you dear boy, she cried—you're hungry, aren't you!

I haven't been holding this cigarette-lighter under your canary because I particularly care for the smell of burning feathers, I said, walking leisurely at a dead-run through the closed door into the dining room.

There were about ninety people sitting there at a great table. When I came in they all got up, spun around a couple times, and then sat down again. That would have been all right—except they weren't the same people anymore.

I tried it too. Sure enough—there was this big deep voice coming up out of me, saying, May I have the honor, the honor which every red-blooded American owes to his dear silver-haired mother —oh what an hallowed name! What deeds of valor and deathless derring-do does it not evoke! of Brandywine and Smoky Ridge, of Wounded Arse and Swansdown, of Rusty Spring and Standard Oil—owes it to his sainted mither to protect, praglifferate and—

Yes, do sit down, Senator Heeler, the old crone said, eating her grapefruit with the cap off the ketchup-bottle.

Would you mind holding him for a moment, Ward? the young woman on the other side asked, depositing a three month's old baby in my lap.

After a moment she took him back and I said, Why did you want me to hold your baby, Miss Piddle?

Don't be silly, she said. After all this is my best gown.

Tail's the best part, Mr. Roach said, smiling across the table as he remembered how he had short-changed a fourteen-dollar-a-week salesclerk out of seventy-six cents that afternoon.

Turtle tail—um yum-yum, Mrs. Dreamboat enthused, wiping the back of her throat with a wad of Kleen-x.

I boomed down the board at Mrs. Lacepanz, Give me a piece of tail, huh, Faith?

Ah, sure and it's just that I'll be doin' now, she said, running her eye-brow pencil carefully around in her armpits. Pass this tail on down to the Senator, will you, Mr. Bearer?

I ran my knife across it. I popped a piece into my mouth. It tasted like braised inner tube with asbestos sauce. I was so disgusted I plunged the tines of my testiudinal fork into my finger.

Have you ever had turtle fever before? Austin Little asked me.

What do you mean, before?

Your arms and legs get all swelled up. Your tongue begins to ooze and—

Where's the Peroxide! I yelled, upsetting my chair as I sprang to my feet—my danger up.

Let me see, Hazel Witcher said, examining it attentively. Why, you big softie, it's only a scratch in the skin, no more than a harmless little prick.

Iodine! Sulphacuracrome! I roared, brandishing it about in mounting fury. Is this a mere scratch in the skin! Is this—I ask you, ladies and gentlemen—is this nothing but a harmless little prick!

One by one they got up and spun around. And not wishing to be left alone there, I did the same. Two men fell into step at my side. Have you got it with you? the skinny one in the gray suit said. Have I got what with me? The skinny one bent my arm up behind my back and the fat one in the brown suit kicked me in the stomach. Have you got it with you, pal? fatty said. I didn't say anything because skinny had my head pinned under his arm and was slowly pulling my tongue out of my mouth.

After a long time they carried me into a little room and threw me on a dirty cot. Then they went out, not bothering to lock the door as far as I could tell. About an hour later a kid walked in and asked me if I could use a drink. I nodded and he wiped the blood off my chin and held the bottle while I drank. He fished an old envelope and a pencil stub out of his pocket and handed them to me. I took the stub and wrote, I'll give you $1,000 if you get me out of here. He shook no. I crossed the 1 out and put a 5 in. He said, They won't do anything to you. I scratched the 5 out and put in a 10. It's a deal, he said.

He helped me onto my feet and we headed for the stairs. Just a second, he said. I nodded all right and he crossed over to a door marked Private and walked in. After five minutes I crept over to the door and started to ease it open. In a chair facing me was the kid. His eyes were open and looking right at me, but he didn't see me. He had two mouths now. The one in his throat was not pretty.

It had started to rain. I turned my coat collar up and stepped into the street. There was a streetcar at the next corner and I climbed aboard. I paid my fare and took a seat all the way to the back near the door. Across the aisle from me there was a man studying a toothpaste ad. He was about forty-five years old.

A girl came in and sat down next to me. She opened out a newspaper and started to read it. A man and a woman were discussing rammed-earth houses in the seat just behind us. If the girl heard them, she gave no outward sign of it. Sixteen blocks later she got off the streetcar. She hadn't once looked at me.

I felt in my pocket. There was a hand in it. I took it out. It now held a tiny box. What you got there? the man across the aisle asked. Aspirin, I said. May I have one? he said. Why not, I said. The rammed-earth people asked if I had a couple I could spare them. Sure, I said. The plainclotheswoman two seats forward asked if she could have one. It ended up by my giving an aspirin to everyone in that streetcar; and two to the motorman—one when he stopped the car and came back for it, and the other when the truck telescoped our rearend. Considering the speed of the truck and the slippery state of the pavement, it's only surprising that more weren't killed.

I went into the lobby of a dingy little hotel and sat down near the elevator. A girl was already sitting there. She had this mag-

azine and her eyes never left it. One place it said: . . . And Charles
held Michael to him with a passion so intense, so vibrant, so throb-
bing with desire and the pent-up, mad fires of youth, that a queer,
dancing glow imperceptibly mantled their flushed cheeks, almost
as though an errant fairy had . . .

For the love of Mike, I said.

Oh, she said, I'm sorry. I thought you'd finished the page.

Elmer is a pretty name for a girl, don't you think?

Well . . . It is unusual enough, I suppose. Personally I like
Harold or James or Thomas.

My name is Suzanne, I said.

She said, My kid sister died yesterday. She was just a year
younger than me. We went all through school together.

Gee, I'm sorry, I said.

Keep your cheap sorrys to yourself, she said. You're so damn
smart and superior— She stood up. —A girl with her face buried in
a trashy love-story, and A. B. C. . . . here's my meat, a push-over
—a nice quick pick-up, maybe even a snappy little one-night-
stand—

Ah, now, for Christ's sake—

She was sobbing now. You dirty smart-aleck! I was sitting there
pretending to read because I didn't want people to know I was
crying. I didn't want them to—

I stood up and put my hands on her shoulders. Cut it out, I
told her. I said I was sorry, and I mean it. Where's your home?

Upstate.

What are you doing in the lobby of this crummy fleabag?

I've got a room here. Please let me go.

On what floor?

What difference does that make! I'll scream if you—

What floor?

She sort of collapsed, and I thought for a minute she might do
a fade-out. Then, slowly, On the top floor.

It might only break your legs, I said.

Is this man bothering you, Miss? the house heavy asked, putting three pounds of heavy lard on my arm.

I watched her out of the corner of my eye. She shook her head, said in a tiny strangled voice, No, we were just talking. Then I took my lighted cigarette and pressed it into the back of his hand. As he jerked away, I slapped him hard across the mouth. Ask them for a raise, I said, leading the girl out into the sunlight.

I think I'm going to be sick, she said, leaning up against a No Parking sign.

I've had some innings with that bastard before, I said, guiding her over to the subway entrance. We got on the first train that came in and rode to the end of the line.

It was beginning to get dark and I took her into a spaghetti saloon and ordered with meat balls. The wine stank but I got her to down two glasses. When the guy had brought the ice cream and the bile of poisoned frogs which he fondly imagined was coffee, I said, What was your kid sister's name?

She took up her purse and started fumbling at the clasp. Her lips were white from where she was biting them inside. Finally she said, Suzanne.

Put your purse away and stop that goddam fidgeting around, I said.

If I had told the waiter what I really thought of the coffee, she couldn't have looked more shocked. I didn't fool though—I let her go right on getting the luster of it. Then, at last, she smiled, and she said, That's better than wine.

Shall we go down to the ocean?

It's late. I should be getting back.

Where?

Is it nice by the ocean?

Very, I said, breaking off a piece of gum from under my chair and pressing a quarter into it. I poured about a sixteenth of an inch of pepper on the gum and shoved the quarter under the plate. I hope Tony has a good supply of handkerchiefs, I said as we walked out.

There were a lot of people on the boardwalk. And there was a puppy that kept running up to everybody with a lost terror in its eyes. We tried to pat him but he just danced off to pray at a fresh pair of legs.

On the sand our feet made the sound of a giant scratching his head. The nearer the water we got, the fresher and cleaner it got—it was like the wind had his laundry out there, little baskets of pretty clothes tossing on the horns of the waves. We went right out on the rocks and sat down on the biggest's cold breast. The moon wasn't bad—not a great moon, but not exactly the black sheep of the family either. I took my coat off and put it around her. What's your name? I said.

Oh, I love this, she said, snuggling against my shoulder. My name is Gretchen. Is that a liner?—just the other side of the farthest buoy there—?

I don't see it—but it's probably a large coal barge going to Liverpool.

How do you expect to see it when—

When what?

Oh, you shouldn't have!

Why not?

Because now you'll have no time for anything else, she said.

Her mouth tasted like a flower that has been thinking of salt.

Gretchen.

Yes, darling—Ooh! I could just eat you up!

I've done a lot of pretty rotten things.

They were rotten, not you. I want to splash my feet in the water!

These rocks are pretty slippery.

Here, hold my purse. Can you swim?

No, not a stroke—for God's sake, Gretchen. Wait until day-

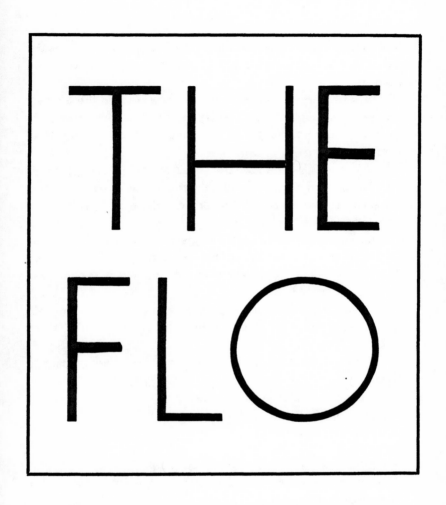

THE
FLO

light anyway—Jesus O Jesus Christ—Gretchen! Gretchen!

I don't know how in hell I ever got down there. It was like a wall of cold wet paper falling on me . . . stopping my nose and my eyes and my mouth . . . and I wouldn't have fought with it . . . not that black cold horrible thing . . . but suddenly my hands touched something warm and her hair was stinging my lips . . .

Then I did fight   Clawing   Straining   Churning   Cursing
         and she was so very still in my arms
I felt her sliding away
I was   so afraid   that
oh don't let her die
God   please   don't let her
and I was crawling up the sand with her underneath me—strang-
ling me with the death-lock of her arms around my neck.

Some people came running up and men took turns trying to
bring the breath back into her lungs.

After half an hour they stood off, slack, with lowered heads.

As the beam of the flashlight moved away from her, I thought
I saw one of her fingers twitch. I was a crazy man. They had to
hold me back with twenty arms. I thought they wouldn't try hard
enough, I thought they couldn't care enough to—

Then she coughed—a dry, desperate cough.

And I could live again.

A week later I took her for a walk in the park. After a while
we found a bench in the sun and sat down. Shine, mister? a little
man in a dirty blue suit said, stopping hopefully in front of me.
All right, I guess I can use one at that, I said.

A couple benches away a kid's balloon got loose and he
started to raise a terrific fuss about it. His mother grabbed hold of
his arm and gave him a healthy belt across the ear. We may get
some rain after all, I said, giving the shoeshineman a fifty cent
piece. Buy a couple extra candles for me, please.

Gretchen said, Do you think all these people are happy?

Nope, I said. I think most of these people are pretty unhappy,
as a matter of sober fact.

Why?

Well . . .

Shine, mister?—An old fellow in a sort of shawl.

Why not? I said. It probably helps the circulation.

He may have been color blind, I don't know—But yellow polish sure does look pretty weird over ox-blood.

Are you happy?

Who? me?

Yes, you.

Look, Gretchen, why don't you just relax? I said, handing the old boot-yellow a quarter and five nickels. Phone the quints and give them my best, if you don't mind, Joe.

She opened her purse and took out a little square of cardboard. Sometimes I wonder if anybody is ever happy, she said, turning it over idly in her fingers.

What's the ticket for? I said.

A man with a black patch over his eye and a purple sash around his waist dropped his little box at my feet and fell to work. How'd you know I needed a shine? I said.

Ug.

May I have that again, please?

You want stick-um around the edges, sor?

Do I look a complete fool? Certainly I want stick-um around the edges.

For the train, Gretchen said.

What train? I asked, watching him take some black stuff out of a can and start dabbing it on with an eager hand.

My train home, she said.

Oh—When are you going back?

It leaves in less than an hour.

How's those, sor?

Those is something, I said. I suppose that's not just ordinary black stick-um?

He opened his mouth. It was like two rows of baby sunrises. I even brush my teeth with ut, he declared proudly. No sor, no ordinary bleck stuck-im will turn every lettle thung to gold, I bet.

I looked down at my feet. Sure enough, the edges of my soles were beginning to glisten like imperial plate. I'd guard that formula pretty close if I were you—It'd be just too bad if U. S. Teel ever got hold of it.

He took the dollar bill and shoved it under his patch. I suppose you plan to get back to the city before long?

Gretchen pulled a thread off the hem of her skirt and, rolling it into a neat ball, tossed it out on the sidewalk, where two pigeons spent the better part of a pleasant afternoon fighting over it. I'm never coming back, she said.

Well, I guess you get pretty well as good movies and radio and book clubs as we do down here at that, I said. I had an uncle a farmer in soundless celery once.

I never hoid of no soundless celery, mister.

I'd love a shine, I said.

Oh, my watch's stopped! I'll miss the train!

No, you won't, I promised. Quickly I slipped my shoes off and handed them to the boy with my address book. You'll find me listed in there somewhere. When you've finished, just mail them on to me, I yelled back, stopping a passing cab and pushing two old ladies out of it—and I'll bet it was the first time they'd ever felt a man's stocking foot on their chests.

We got to the station with two minutes to spare. I got her settled in her seat and we proceeded with our farewells. The man across the aisle was already lost in rapt contemplation of a poster which carried Dr. Numm's ringing declaration that piles, bowel-fever and all such-like would have a pretty bum time of it if only he were listened to.

This is really good-bye then, Gretchen said.

I squeezed her hand and walked quickly out of the car. I didn't want her to see the tears I had in my eyes. There was something infinitely touching about the good doctor's solicitude.

The apples were getting ripe. I stood bare-headed in the orchard, thinking that before long it would be winter. Snow would cover the ground. Soon the poor would sit shivering in their cold-water flats. Soon department stores would start combing the city for old wheeze-pots with long whiskers. But now the heady fragrance of magnolia and wild harebell drifted lazily across the sleepy dingle; the leaves of the box-elder and the yellow birch, of the gnarly maple and the coercial mountain ash, their enshrouded ears alert in that liquescent fluxion, unmindful of Krupp and Tarquin, stirred like miniature tarbooshes. I pulled up a poke weed (its resemblance to an oleander cannot be understressed)—and I thought Powhatan must have held one of your smelly forebears in his hand once just as I am holding you now; then suddenly I was back in the house of my father—Hot ass off and get them ashes out or I'll brain you with a chair!—and there was the squamous nose of my Uncle Vallombrosa rustling comfortably above his gallipot of whortleberry brandy, his carbuncles dripping down onto the piebald toucan which mother was plucking for supper. I thought of Blaine's eulogy of Garfield, and I suddenly got ravenously hungry for a kind word from somebody. I've noted that our pelagic instinct is never more alive than when the snath of the scythe slips out of our sweaty hands; than when the shrovetide bears us like surly coxcombs out through the bunghole of a nothingness beyond the reach of any rhabdomancy ever cooked up here below. That, more or less, is what people mean when they speak of evidence external to the crime. A white boat. Nothing is ever really gained by putting two stamps on a letter which nobody will bother to read anyway. The next witness will always testify for the other side.

I bent down and watched a little pismire trying to sling a potato chip up onto his shoulder. His muscles stood out like hairs in the nose of a woodsdove. Precisely what he wanted with the potato chip when pismires notoriously loathe all fried foods, I couldn't begin to imagine. But at last he got the chip on his shoulder and I breathed a little prayer that he'd have better luck with it than I'd ever had.

Incidentally, it is extraordinarily odd that each time we are able to isolate one aspect of natural phenomenon, there's always this sound like a gate clanging to. You can't cheat any detail of its inevitable place in the pattern. You can't 'bring about' any occurrence which is not always happening in just exactly that identical way. You may be sure that what is really significant is not even suspected, let alone understood. It is very possible that a jar of marmalade could sire a nice herd of whale calves—How does it know it can't? Has it ever tried?

And so from these battered, haunted faces there is no escape. Pity stops my throat. My mind freezes. Here is an end, a cry from my heart—a bloody rag flung up on their damn antiseptic stage!

I turned the apple over in my hand.

A fisherman yelled up to me from the river. It was a hell of a nice day. I set off for the can where I had a little run-out with a blacksnake.

When I got back to my shack I found Dolly washing curtains. I helped her stretch them and we made supper together. She'd put white candles in some dead soldiers and it looked fine with a clean table cloth, a bunch of honeysuckles in an old squash tin, the fork tines all curled up like the hands of baby pickpockets, the knives so dull I took butter with my finger, and I said, Umm.

What, umm?

Ap-plebut-pa-ter. Sure hits the spot.

Al, why did Old Zenaslufski leave without telling anybody where he was going?

Maybe he didn't know.

She took a sip of milk. That's not like him at all.

What happens when they have worms in them?
Worms in what?
These apples they make the applebutter.
How would I know!
Say, you're kind of touchy today. Stomach on the blink?
Oh—She got up and flung herself face-down on Old Zena-slufski's bunk and her shoulders started to twitch.

I peeled the skin off my piece of duck and put it away carefully in my pocket. They make swell covers for outside light-switches. Though the canvasback is hardly the most tender fowl to be found on this continent, he is by nature docile and quite tractable—in fact, to compare him to a summer's day would not put too much of a strain on international relations, all things being unequal. What is the purpose of the minute purple balls which run through the middle of asparagus? I wondered absently. Their taste, well nigh indiscernible to any save the most delicate palates, is vaguely like that of the female chestnut, or, as it is known simply in our own Southwest, the bust. I blew softly into my saucer and filled it half full of coffee. If you blow just right it will eddy around in there for a hell of a while.

Dolly tossed her hair back in careful abandon and sat up on the edge of the bunk. I'm sorry I was silly, she said. May I be excused to come back to the table?

I'd like to have you, I said—come back to the table, that is.

We finished our simple meal in silence. The onapudis was so old and stringy I kept wishing we had a cat. Nothing could have done a better job on hair-balls.

The sound of children singing floated up the valley.

We went to the door together and watched the shades being pulled down in the windows of the sky.

Ouch! Dolly said.

What do you mean, ouch?

Corny—Boy, is that corny!

334

Soak them in warm salt water. And while you're at it, take another look at that sky.

Oh, my gosh!

—And not only thousands upon thousands of windows, light seeping out of them like the dream currency of children, muted

and strangely withdrawn and quieting, but standing at each window was an angel, and they were smiling at us as they slowly lowered the—

Look, Al! There's one shade that's still not drawn! And a face—!

It may seem irrelevant to say so here, but the notion suddenly came to me that if I had any sense I would never tell anyone what happened then. Irrelevant, because I'd like to. It's tough luck for everybody that I can't.

Apart from the world's being round I'd be absolutely swarming over you with news! if I had any . . . and if I knew how to give it . . . Don't mention my name; they'll never give you the job on that.

All of which is rather minutely begging the question, don't you think? Anatomically the statue is fairly life-like; but it's only a statue. It can only be standing in your room some night when you wake up and   <u>its hands are alive.</u>

One thing, at least, is not uncertain. I think we must realize that someone is always watching us—Someone who would like to have our bodies to live in, because his own is dead. A rather horrible kind of intimacy, that—I think we must realize that most of us have already given in to the dead. Someone is reading this—gray, monstrous lips moving under your warm, still mouth . . .

The voices of children floating up from the village. Then the crunch of a man's footsteps on the path. I had no idea what he had been doing in 1928, but when the first one entered the door and his face was rat-like, too thin for the bitterness in his eyes, and his manner was altogether without tenderness and grace, too assured for the terror that had stained the arm-pits of his shirt, I said, What do you want wandering in here at this time of night?

Wandering, eh? And where's Old Zenaslufski? that's what I want to know. He and I are old friends—a lovely man, a prince. God never made a better one than Old Zen. Where is he? A splendid chap, absolutely the best. I'd kill for 'im—that's exactly what I'd do, I'd kill the first man who had a bad word to say for—

336

He's not here.

Not here? Old Zen not here? You wouldn't be trying a paper match on me now? Do you think he's trying a paper match on me, Mr. Fonish?—Mr. Fonish had his rat eyes on Dolly and I wanted to smash his face in with my fist. But there was something about the other man that made me think better of it—partly the .45 that he held carelessly in his pudgy, little boy's hand; but mainly that I suddenly felt that in another minute he'd say or do something that would mean more to me than anything that had ever happened in my life.—Oh, I see you there! A perfect gentleman—tell me now, am I wrong about that? And you—Ah, my pretty, my frightened bird. Mr. Fonish is annoying with his stare, isn't he, my dear? Not to your taste, I'll guess—Mr. Fonish with his nasty little mind, eh? The way he rips your dress, tears at your pretty breasts, and his hands are so sweaty, so hot—He stopped short, walked to the door and gave a shrill whistle. After a second, from the direction of the orchard, it was answered, and he half danced around and said, Someone's always in trouble. Have you guessed who I am? I like you both—lovely people. I assure you, it will be done with as little pain as—Please! Please! It's not at all what you think! I have a son and daughter at home. They couldn't come tonight. They would have loved you. Will you undress, please?

He sat down at the table, took a tiny notebook out of the lining of his hat, and began to count outloud as he wrote: 51, 52, 53, 54, 55, 56, 57, 58, 60—

59, Mr. Fonish said, coming to look over his shoulder.

Ah, yes—59, 61, 62, 63, 64, 66, 67, 68—

I finally had to say 65.

Thank you! Oh, I thank you from the bottom of my heart. I want you to believe that. It will take its place. Rest assured, Old Zen would recognize my whistle anywhere. 69, 70, 71—Do you have any wooden matches, dear fellow?

No. There isn't a wooden match in the house, I told him.

In that pile of rags in the bucket under the sink—You'll find a box of wooden matches there, he said very quietly. I am beginning to get annoyed. First you pay no attention to my request that you undress; now you lie to me over such a paltry thing as a box of wooden matches. Mother was right, I see, in warning me that I'd have trouble with you. 72, 73, 74, 75, 76, 77, 78, 79, 80, 82, 83, 84, 5, 6, 7, 8, 9, 90, 1, 2, 3—

81! Dolly said. Oh, my God! Don't! Please!

Why, whatever is the matter, child?

Something has its hands on me! It's beginning to

Of course. 94, 95, 96, 98, 99—

All this is off the record, you might say—However poignant are my memories of that occasion, I feel now that the whole thing was somehow cheap, with little more than a surface uniqueness, the precise sort of scandalizing nonsense which you would be accused of, and rightly so, should you tell your garageman that you had just seen a fox terrier paint A FOOL USUALLY SITS HERE on Mrs. Folley's behind. Remote and a bit too pat—Perhaps a sample of that man's soliloquy will convince you (I wouldn't think of attempting to tell you what he and Mr. Fonish did there in the shack, or who finally came in answer to his whistle. I will tell you this, though —you'd be away off the track if you thought that he really intended us to undress; I don't think a more moral man ever lived— take my word for it, the torture was a great deal subtler than that.) —his little spiel went something like this: I am happy to have this opportunity to acquaint you—ah, a splendid people, so well-bred, so poised, so lifeless—to acquaint you with something which I like to think is—Oh! now I've done it! You can see, I've given it away, I've palmed-off a paper match on this pleasant young couple— Mr. Fonish, the other instrument now, if you please!—I kept hoping the whole time, you may be sure, that he'd let drop some hint as to his manabouts; it certainly wouldn't have improved my position any if, when the authorities started their investigation—and I was

338

almost sure they wouldn't do much horsing around with a thing like that—, I had to admit that for all I knew he could have been Alexis Bartholemew the Blind, Custodian of Homeless Waifs and Nickel-Plated Hatpins, Emperor of The Lands To The North of Nowhere, and Grand Sachem of The Fête of Lost Souls' Day, sometimes referred to as being worse than taxes. The police may be corrupt, but even corruption must stop somewhere; the only question, of course, is, Who will manage the banks and regulate the mean, average income of our twenty million unemployed? I'm sure the Flit people will come up with a solution to this little problem soon; but if they don't grass'll never have a chance to grow in the streets of our cities.

I'd been promising Dolly for a long while that I'd go along with her to visit some of her cousins who lived over Sloppy Hollow way. So next morning we rented a couple horses from farmer Smith and set out. I suppose I should have known what was coming when I saw that he had them pastured in the cornfield, but I was too busy staring at his lightning-struck daughter to think much about it. Even a skinless frank is enough to give me nightmares now.

The road went straight as a breadstick through the woods, and the sun had certainly sent down its grade A butter. From time to time, little wild creatures darted across in front of us—a lean, quarrelsome red squirrel, a grubby skunk, bent on God-knows-what mysterious civet duty of its own, a laughing, snag-toothed otter, and a little old woman who was all of that, and then some. Kingfishers rattled their noisy crowns in the direction of the river. The trees, natty in their new plaid suits, had their arms around each other's shoulders and were singing football songs—'Up the blue for dear old Yale,' and 'Up the brown for dear old Rutgers,' seemed to be their favorites.

Isn't this wonderful! Dolly said. Oh, I'm having such fun.
Boom, boom.

You'll have to talk louder, I called back, wiping a baby robin off my hat. (I think the concussion had literally blown him out of the nest.)

It's so nice riding along with you like this, she said. It's so peaceful, so sort of pure and clean—Umm! doesn't the air smell nice!

Boom, boom.

No, I said. How much farther is it?

Oh—I'd say ten miles . . . eight or nine, anyway. Why, do you think the horses are getting tired?

Boom, boom.

No, they're going great guns. How long's it been since you saw these cousins of yours?

Not since I was a little girl. I don't even remember them very clearly anymore. I just have an idea that if I see them again, I . . . well, I may be able to quiet something that's been eating away inside me . . . like a . . . a—

Boom, boom.

I didn't hear the last word.

My psychoanalyst thought he was, but—

Thought he was what?

The last word.

Boom, boom.

You can say that again.

Say what again?

I didn't mean you. Did he think your trouble was sex?

Yes, he said he'd worked out a new treatment for it. Oh, Al, look at that darling chipmunk—no, over there by that pile of dead leaves. Do you suppose he hides his nuts under there?

Boom, boom.

It'd be something new anyway. Did he tell you anything else about it?

I don't see how you can say it would be new. Chipmunks have

even been known to hide their nuts in old phone booths.

Where would a chipmunk find a phone booth? You must be shell-shocked.

Why, in abandoned filling stations, of course. In this area alone, there must be dozens of them.

Boom, boom.

That sounds like the horse is being heard from again.

It's the war.

Boom, boom.

The war of nags, you mean.

I think this must be their place now, she said, reining-in before the biggest and ugliest house I had ever set gas-reddened eyes on.

A man in a swimming suit came out on the porch and waved at us. Another man immediately began to arrange flower pots in a circle around him. Then another man leaned far out of the window and started to make wee-wee, as a child would say. He may have intended to fill one of the pots, but I could see right away that the man in the swimming suit was nobody's fool.

I started to dismount (Boom, boom, boom . . .) but before I could even get the ropes untied about twenty men in stained aprons came tearing up and started to drag the horse with me still on it (Boom, boom, BO-BO-OOM!) off in the direction of a building that stood near a red lake. I turned around three times in the saddle and found myself holding out an empty cup to an old lady who had a lot of lace at her throat and a lion cub in her lap. Before she could pour anything into my cup the cub did. She scolded him but for all the good it did both of us might just as well have allowed the waiter to pass with his full tray of martinis. As I sipped mine I noticed that whereas I couldn't keep my eyes off the beautiful girl across the room there was a fellow with her who had a number of things besides eyes he couldn't keep off her. There was a knock at the door and I hurried over and opened it. There was another door there. I waited. Somebody knocked on the second door a little louder now. I opened it. There was a third door. I waited. Somebody knocked—there must be blood on your knuckles, I thought. I opened the third door. There was a fourth

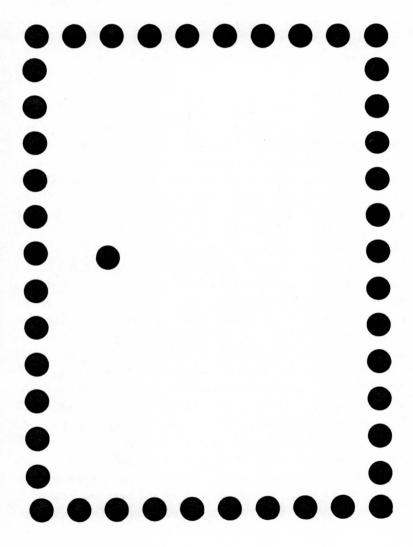

Well, it's always pretty damn grim somewhere. A train will go wooshing out of the shed—and the engineer's sister-in-law Becky Grace is that sick nobody in the family expects her to last the night. Or Tom will take it into his bean that the laundryman's been sneaking in while he's away at work and the next time the poor guy comes leave him slumped over the wash with an angry little eye glaring out of his forehead. It doesn't matter much what way you play it—as long as you can't call the game, what the hell difference does it make how good your cards are? Brutal and without any rime or reason whatever—please don't tell any one, but I think it is like that, shall we say just a teensy-weensy.

I don't want to sit down, shorty. I want to walk over and talk to that fellow's got his arm in a sling. I want to ask him to tell me what he's going to do with that arm when he gets it out of the sling. I know what he'll say. The hell of it is, we all know exactly what he'll say.

Many lives cannot find life. In their first youth they already get a sniff of the pot. Corners beginning to fill with the corpses of all the people who die in them. A voice raised in agony—We all are sleeping. Count your change over carefully—I think you may have a foreign object in there amongst the—What say? It smells bad? What would you expect it to do, put boxing gloves on your old lady?

"Sleeper have thy peace"—but these are not shadows! this is flesh! this is blood! we hunger! we thirst!—O whence this food that tastes like the excrement of dogs! Who stands in the sky there and wee-wees down on our stricken heads! I seek no glory; only rest. I search for no grail; only rest. I ask for no light; only rest.

O it would be better to be nothing than to be where I am. What is dead in my heart has a stink to fill the world. Would you mind removing your head? I can't see the picture. Ah, thank you. That's better, much! The destiny of nations?—into your hat! They let themselves in for something when they wounded me. The shudder of mighty strings, eh?—into your hat! Ah, yes, they stuck their necks out when they wounded me. This fruitful, dear earth . . . these great limbs stirring in the deep—into your hat! Boughs and wings and gardens . . . "Lovely couriers of the spring" . . . "O far from all these delights and thee"—you know what you can do! Ah, yes, I make a muscle. I bust a gut laughing. I clean my nose on their altar cloths. "Joy among the starry meadows" . . . The blind stratagems of the damned—into your hat! They sure didn't know what they were getting into when they wounded me.

Boom, boom.

I weep.

I am afraid.

All of the songs are still.

The legends drip a black pus.

Dark beyond reaching is the pain in my heart.

Where is my life?

What has put this narrowing around it?

They said there was truth — Where is it? Where is truth!

They said there was love — Where is it? Where is love!

They said there would be peace — Where is it? Where is peace!

They said there would be brotherhood — Where is it? Where is brotherhood!

Beauty! They prattled of beauty — I see no beauty here.

Begin — (the music) — To close the silken waters over the dead. To grow on the tree again.

This house. Do you see this house?

It is a house where human beings live.

They deserve more than bloody kicks in the ass.

There is a strange dignity about them.

They are looking at you as I talk.

I want you to leave them alone.

I want you to stop blowing them to pieces.

Keep your dirty hands off them!

I don't care who you are, only a maddog could kill one of these — and only a monster could talk of Flag and Country and The Right after he had murdered them.

Either they live — or we shall all perish.

There is the only answer. Do you hear it?

I set off down the road. Shadows were painting cows and children on the fields. Two men were pitching hay over by the big barn. One of them had a dead pipe in his mouth. In another week I would have to go home. I didn't look forward to it very much. Cumulus—Yup. That's what they called clouds like that. A mackerel sky was sort of . . . well, like somebody had made a grab at a great white rabbit. The road led down around a schoolhouse. It had a red roof and a beautiful elm in its yard. I hope they get the roof back on before school starts, I thought.

That's a pretty pond! Clear as glass. I watched the bull and cow in the water. A Ford passed right through them. It gave me goose pimples.

An old barn with a broken mower half-in its sagging door. I wonder what it was like to live here a hundred years ago? It must be pretty damn sad to have your house burn down away the hell and gone from nowhere like this. Hope nobody died in it.

The sun's going down. No, it wouldn't be much fun getting home again.

Even if I had one to go to.

There was a girl standing at the mailbox as I came up. It won't come today, Gretchen, I said.

All Oh, it's so good to see you! Her face showed the roses a thing or two.

It's nice to see you too, I said. Could I maybe get a drink of water?

Why, certainly. Oh, gee! How'd you ever happen to be up around here? she said, running on ahead and holding the screen-door open.

Is this the drinking water? No, that's all right. I've drunk out of buckets before. Phoofh—God, that's good water!

Artesian. Come in the parlor. I'll make you some chicken sand-wiches.—The phone rang. Hello. Oh, hello, Miss Mildred. No, mom and dad went over to the Higshoults this morning. Mrs. Higs-hoult—Yes, that's right, Bright's disease. No, not tonight; after all, it's almost twenty miles over to the—What? Why I never heard anything so ridiculous! Of course I'll be all right. It's not the first time I've been alone here at night; and besides, a young man I knew in the city just dropped in and—Hello. Hello! She put the receiver back on its hook.—I think she fainted, she said.

Lot's of mayonnaise, I said.

What?

On the sandwiches.

Oh, sure. Can you eat three?

Yeah. Look, kid, you still haven't got any silly ideas about me, have you?

She stood there looking at me for a minute, then she started to cry. I got up and went over and knelt down in front of her and raised her face in the cup of my hand. That's the bad part, I said. It always happens to the wrong person. That's the part that's bad.

Why couldn't you have loved me? she whispered. I don't think she even knew I could hear her.

I think I'll just run along now, I said, just touching her hair with the tips of my fingers as I stood up.

Please stay a little while, she said. Please—just a little while.

All right. But only on one condition.

She jumped up, really showing the roses something. Tell me.

That I sleep down here on a couch.

She turned quickly and walked into the kitchen. I heard her opening cupboard doors and rattling things around—then suddenly the screendoor slammed and I walked to the window and looked out. The angle was wrong, so I opened the frontdoor and hurried around the house. I don't know why it didn't occur to me to go through the kitchen, because I certainly wasn't scared that anything was seriously wrong. God knows; if I was looking for things to be scared about, I could just start thinking what would happen when they found Dolly.

I didn't see her at first, and I was on the point of pulling freight off to find one of these little yellow-soap-smelling brick eating-joints, when I spied a flash of color moving over at the edge of the woods. I went back in the house and gave it a pretty thorough going-over—not loafing at it though, because I didn't think it would take her very long to run it out of her system.

It was in the last place I looked, and I was just stuffing it into my pocket when I heard the screendoor being gently closed. I got downstairs fast, but with surprisingly little noise considering that I stumbled over a crate of eggs which her dad had left on the top-step. The old bastard! wait until you come to my house, won't I just demonstrate my little goose-rope trick for you!—something I picked up in India.

I'm sorry I dashed off like that, she said. The Mellet boys have

been setting traps over in the woodlot and I thought I heard a cat screaming . . . Well, I just dropped everything and ran as fast as I could.

Was it a cat caught?

No. Anyway, I couldn't find anything. One of the traps was sprung, but there wasn't anything in it. Why don't I fix a regular supper, instead of just sandwiches? You could eat supper now, couldn't you, Al?

I think so. Where can I wash-up?

It's out back of the house.

I spent fifteen minutes looking over the fashions in ladies' undergarments and then walked slowly back, wondering if what she'd heard wasn't the screaming in my head. Do you suppose it will just stay in there?

I ate like I'd never seen food before—and I certainly hadn't ever seen any like that. I expected any minute to have somebody sing out Shine, mister? and grab the liver right out from under my nose. The potatoes had their jackets on; I think they were ashamed to take them off.

Did you have any courses in first-aid at your school? I asked hopefully.

Why, no—What a strange thing to—

Gretchen, what's the matter? I felt something cold running up and down my spine.

There was a—Oh, Al, I saw a face at the window! A terrible, horrible face . . . like it was—

Like it was what?

—Turned inside-out.

I got up and walked quietly to the door. I slipped back the safety on my .32 and took hold of the knob. Out of the corner of my eye I saw Gretchen put a pinch of something white into my coffee. I went right on easing the knob and I was just set to yank the door open when I heard the faint click of a key being turned on the other side. I let go of the knob and pointed the .32 at the lock and pulled the trigger. The hammer snapped down and nothing happened.

Gretchen, I said, why didn't you write it off as a bad deal when you muffed it on the rocks that night?

I don't know what you're talking about?

Funny—It almost worked out the other way round. A pretty irony if you had drowned instead of me. What did you hit your head on?

She sat there looking at me, her face sullen and tight; then she said, All right, it can do no harm for you to know now. When you jumped, I guess your shoe must have smacked down right on my chin.

Doesn't it mean anything that I fought like a dog to save your life, Gretchen?

No. The only thing that means anything to me is that I love you.

But it would never work out.

Is this going to work out? The only way you can leave this house will be feet first.

Feet first, or no feet first, I'd still be a free man. Would a little money settlement change your perspective in any way?

How much is a little?

Oh, five, ten, fifteen, twenty—

These are dollars you're talking about?

I took her hand in mine. My lip trembled—that was the second cigarette I'd let burn right on through that day—and holding my breath, I said, (try it sometime) No, Gretchelick, these are thousands of dollars I'm talking about.

Oh, then we can go to Mexico! and feel the red rear of the primitive soul as it pushes naked into the sun!

Ah, yes indeed, the red rear, my little chilli bean.

And wiggle our toes into that warm, alluvial soil from whence has sprung the flaming Phoenix, secure in his eternal and hooded wisdom!

Pronounced hook worm. You haven't got a Bridgeport phonebook handy, have you?

No, but it's right over there in the cellarway—only take me a jiffy to fetch it. Here you are.

I had a little trouble finding the number because the page I wanted had been torn out, but by a systematic study of all the figures on the two pro- and succeeding pages, and a subtle deduction based upon these, I finally was rewarded by hearing that familiar and well-loved voice say, All right, spill it—Who's dead?

Nobody's dead, sugar-bun. It's Almar—don't you remember me?

Who? Stop clicking your teeth! Who'd you say?

Almar. Almar.

When'd he die?

When'd who die?

Look, you're getting paid to tell me. This is one hell of a time of night to be getting people out of bed with your lousy riddles. Does it say anything about who he left his money to?

Listen, fudgy-boo—

What—!

I said fudgy-boo. Fudgy-boo!

By God! that's the last straw! I'll sue the company! You foulmouthed baboon, you! I'll just tell you what I think of anyone who talks to a lady like that!—And she proceeded to tell me; blushing, I turned to Gretchen and said,

That was mother. I always make a point of calling her Tuesdays.

Which is not half as interesting as what she makes a point of calling you.

Oh, could you hear her?

What do you think all those people are standing out in front

OTHE

of the house for? They've seen men with puppies on their laps before.

I waited patiently for him to finish. I've always liked a water terrier, I said.

You mean spaniel, don't you?

SUN

Down we go, Artesian, I said, patting him on the head as I lowered him to the floor. Ah, you little rascal—trying to play possum with your Uncle Al, now!

Pronounced post-mortem. Why don't you read Ecclesiastes to me while I wash the dishes? Gretchen said, hoping that her sudden show of boldness would awaken in me that contempt which breeds intimacy.

Later, when we were in bed, I felt my heart pounding in my chest, like a great snow owl that has just flown in from Toronto. It could only mean two things, I pensed dreamily, a warm glow seeming to penetrate the core of my inmost being: That I was still alive; but that I wouldn't be long if I didn't cut myself down to four packs of cigarettes a day. I snapped off the sunlamp and called upstairs, Everything ok up there?

Oh, fine, do you have enough covers? Gretchen called back.

Sure thing. I've helped myself to a horseblanket—I'll manage all right, I sang out cheerfully—how was I to know that he'd insist on wheezing down my neck all night? or that Mr. Horsegg had just had ice-shoes put on him? But one thing I do know now, I must have dreamed my way through every patriotic celebration ever held in this country—he got something out of that second 'om' that could only be set down as the work of a master—that little extra fillip, that absolutely meticulous inflection, that slight sense of hesitant bravado and scalp-tingling immediacy.

Ekun 14X-A. Halfway out to the orchard I suddenly remembered that I'd left Miss Buttermilk expecting a phone call from The Acne Credit Company. I'd also left a lighted cigarette on the roll of cellophane which someone had carelessly placed on the fly of the peacefully snoring Colonel (j.g.) Pot. I knew she'd find their proposition interesting, at 40%; but as any glove knows, four-armed is fourworned and when all the scores are in it'll still be your team 'way down on the short end of the stick. What's the good of money anyway? It can't bring happiness. It can only get

BEAUTIFUL AND TERRIBLE

you all the nice food and clothes and pretty women you want;
it can only fix it so you can have a warm, comfortable place to
live in—and if there's some book or record you want, you can buy
it—and if you feel like going off somewhere on a trip, all you have

ARE THE WAYS

to do is get a ticket—and if somebody you like gets sick or down
on his luck, you just send him a thousand or two—Hell no, everybody knows that money can't buy happiness; that's why the rich
are so generous—that's why the bastards would sooner have their

OF GOD

tongues yanked out than part with a nickel. I lowered the bucket
down the well. It splashed when it hit the water. The water made a
dull, wooden sound. Hand under hand I pulled the rope up. There

was a blue-eyed baby of sixteen months in the bucket. It didn't appear to be wet or hungry so I dropped it back in.

Catherine St. Maur, her tiny shoes looking tinier still on her big feet, was just coming out of the outhouse. She chuckled when she saw me.

"What are you chuckling about now, Kate?" I asked.

"I think I'm going to die," she said.

"Since when?"

"Since I just read a book explaining the whole thing. I never believed it before. Sure, I had a notion maybe it might happen to other people; but that it could happen to me—no, that was too ridiculous!" She itched her left elbow with the sole of her right foot.

I said, "Sit down under this apple tree and tell me what you think about life. For instance, how do you feel about sex?"

Well, I got goosepimples on it just listening to her. "You mean, in one night?"

Yes, she explained, her mother'd had to come in to her six times in one night to reassure her that the bees and the birds had never been known to molest little girls. Even to this day she'd never been able to look a cabbage in the face. "What happened to Mrs. J——, Aloysius?" she concluded quietly.

"She married $10,000 and went to live in Peru," I said, watching the golden cheese shred itself on the tiny green blades.

"Why, I'll bet she makes more than that a week."

"Not more than Ikey, she don't, kid."

"But how come all the way to Peru?"

"Because it was the nearest place to Indianapolis you can buy really high-grade ant semen. The gelatine capsules have to be made under microscopes, you know."

"What in the world do they want that for?"

"Well, you hold the ant firmly between two fingers and . . ."

"Oh, what do I care how it's done! Why do they do it? I never heard of such a silly thing."

"For one thing, one thousandth of a cubic centimeter of sperm from a really superior bull ant will service 1,354,687,428,975,019—"

"Oh, shut up!"

"Insemination with a syringe is something else again."

"I'll bet!"

"The prime requisite is a steady hand."

Apollinaria Grudd yelled over from the shack, "There's a platoon of cops headed this way down the railroad cut."

The little hairs stood on end in the lining of my lungs and for the first time that day I knew how a quail feels when you stop-up its beak with a piece of yellow soap. I yelled back, "Tell Mr. Tiger to turn the fire down under that lemur and parsnip stew." Better still, I thought, it wouldn't go amiss if somebody threw a bit of light on what human being are going to do now that there isn't a damn thing left to believe in.

We all harried inside. I kissed the ladies and patted my friends on the back. Phoebe Ann handed me a Parker pen and three sheets of Macy's typewriter paper. "Write something," she said simply. I sat down at the little table which held the busted gramaphone and wrote me a letter to my old Dad. In substance I told him to keep his nose clean and his eyes peeled for the least show of decency anywhere. The hanky and paring knife made a pretty bulky missive of it, but Fitz Kell said if I just wrote 'When armies go to war, Misery is the only victor' across the envelope, the postoffice would take it for free. I bet you didn't know that.

Then I fixed the phonograph.

Schumann's 'Spring' swelled out against the tar paper of the dingy room. Tears filled my eyes. We were all very quiet, listening. Through the window I could see that the blue boys had reached the bridge. "I'll give them ten minutes," Mengs Flink whispered. "Life they'll give me," I whispered back. "But it was premeditated," Sally Garden protested. I leered. The teeth in my mouth felt like pieces of calcium. "Just how are they going to prove that, my perty lassie?"—"They've posted a reward," Abigail said happily.

"How much?" I asked, hardly breathing to dare.

"A cool hunerd grand," Dolly said.

"Why, I'll confess for that," I declared, "gladly!"

There was a knock on the door. This is it. This is the thing you can't run away from. So—I opened the damned door.

A policeman stood there. He was naked. He had a heavy revolver in his hand. He dropped it. It rolled down the steps. The sky, I noticed, had little black horses running all over it. I picked the roscoe up and handed it to the cop. He was of average height, well muscled. He said thanks and shot me between the eyes.

The woods were red.

There was a bird in a tree.

Men were lying dead there. They covered the ground. I don't think that's right.

In a place like that a bird had him a nerve sitting up in a tree. A violation of Ocomenowmygoodmannessandallthatsortofcrapdontyouknow.

A sadness if you want to call it that.

Men thinking. (For a hell of a while now.)

But it's all gone punky and rotten.

All I wonder is how to get out of it.

I don't want to be a man.

I want to live—but as something else.

I'm ashamed to be a man.

I want to live—but I'm ashamed to think of God, and be a man.

There are a lot of lies.

They tell you Beauty Honor Justice.

They're liars.

They murder half the people easy as a felt hat.

And starve the rest.

The little kids die like flies.

Nobody gives a damn.

The whole world's a stinking mess.

The next time they mention Beauty Honor Justice just spit in their faces.

Tell them that's for all the poor bastards they've butchered like pigs.

A sadness you might say.

The bloody vomit's all over everything.

A man's a funny thing.

A tree's a funny thing.

They try to fix it so nobody'll care what happens to a man anymore.

I don't mean millions — I mean any one man anywhere.

If anything is worth anything it's because one man is worth something.

If any one man isn't worth something, then nothing whatever is worth anything.

It's all got to come back to any <u>one man</u> anywhere or it isn't going anywhere.

Don't tell me how interested in Confucius or Jesus Christ you are.

Tell me how interested in any one man anywhere you are.

You don't get it.

You'd cry.

You'd cry if you could feel that.

It's all got to come back to one man or it isn't going anywhere at all.

Put a thousand dogs in a barn and burn them.

You'd think you'd been stabbed.

You couldn't do it.

But for God's sake look what you can do to human beings!

Because some murderous swine tell you that "these inhuman beasts" are capable of blowing women and little children into a million pieces, you calmly proceed to blow women and little children into a million pieces—because they are capable of the wholesale extermination—to hell with it!

What is the use of talking to people as bloodstained as you are—as heartless—as corrupt—

I once thought they wouldn't always be able to get away with it.

I thought some eyes would be opened.

I thought a time would come when people would begin to say we've had enough—this horrible butchery must stop

But you can take wagon loads of it!

Nothing is too vile and monstrous for you!

All of you have asked for it. And you're going to get it.

We are going under.

There is nothing whatever can stop the flood.

Won't it be funny when everyone is dead?

And Shakespeare and Christ will never be heard of again.

The tunnel black all the way through.

The dead not even dead, but non-existent.

A pebble.

A blade of grass.

A tree.

The darkness is coming.

The pain and misery and hell for so many—perhaps it's best this way.

When no man on earth now can draw a breath that is free of hatred and evil and fear—it's best that the thing be ended for everyone.

Cold winds whistling across nothingness.

The white eye staring out over everything.

A shoe.

A book.

A table.

Can anyone living imagine what it would be like to make a pair of shoes which could be used in going to some really wonderful place—a place where the blood and cries didn't reach?

—Of writing a book—whose blank pages didn't scream up

at you every time you sat down to it—God with all the agony and terror of these millions who are being mangled and driven mad every second of every day—O of sitting down at that table with yellow and white and black and thief and holyman and have them all love and respect one another—

It's simple. There's nothing at all complicated about it.

War—There won't be war when you decide you won't murder other human beings.

Hunger—No one will be hungry when you decide that it is important that every man everywhere be fed.

You wouldn't burn dogs in a barn.

You wouldn't put a stray kitten into the washing machine.

You wouldn't take a man who had come into your house and cut the throats of your wife and children and make him king.

Like hell you wouldn't!

That's the kind of thing you're really good at.

OTHEEYESOFGODWATCHOUTO
FEACHONEOFUSOURPAINFILLS
HISHEARTEVERYMURDERCAUSE
SHIMTODIEALITTLEWEHAVESTO
PPEDHISMOUTHWITHTHEGRAY
SILTOFDOGSLOSINGTOUCHWI
THOURSELVESWEHAVELOSTTO
UCHWITHHIMWHENALLMENARE
GUILTYGUILTNOLONGERHASA

NYSIGNIFICANCEWHENALLME
NHATEEVENHATEMOVESNOON
ETOLOVEWHENALLMENAREDAM
NEDDAMNATIONNOLONGERHAS
ANYSIGNIFICANCEWHENALLME
NDESPAIREVENDESPERATIONT
URNSNOFACETOTHELIGHTWHE
NTHEDARKNESSCOVERSEVERYT
HINGTHESUNISNOTREMEMBERE
DWHENFEARCLUTCHESEVERYT
HROATTERRORBECOMESANORD
INARYTHINGWHENALLABAND
ONGODGODCEASESTOBEWHE
NTHEEYESOFGODGOBLINDNO
THINGISSEENOTHEEYESOFGOD
WATCHOUTOFEACHONEOFUS
ANDINTHISDARKNESSTHEYCAN
NOTSEEGODOINTHISDARKNES
STHEYAREBLINDANDTHEWALL
SOFTHECAVECLOSEINUPONUS
BEINGBLINDYEKNOWNOTTHIS
DARKNESSOGODISWATCHING
OUTOFUSANDHISEYESMIRRORT

HENOTHINGNESSOFALLTHING
SEVERYWHER
EOHEISCRYIN
GANDTHEREIS
NOHOPETHER
EISNOTHINGT
OTURNTOSINC
EYOUHAVE—OS
NEERATTHIS—
DAMNYOU!

The old man—I'll bet your life's a mess—The old man lifted the cover off the box and everybody started to cry. By damn that was a sad thing. You have to understand that it takes a pretty good story to stand up against the fact that there never was anything but one story since the world began. A lousy story. A story of how the whole business doesn't make sense.

The facts—

You live. You die.

And nothing ever comes very near you.

It's always hell in there—where the real show is. Where no man and no woman ever meet. Where every day of your life—GLUP. Raw and brutal. The wet box—I tell you the story's always the same. The best is nothing. Even the angel cries when the chips are down.

Dolly—You know what happened to Dolly!

Old Zen! Sure. Bones in an orchard. Maybe a little God mixed-up in it. So what? A book can't do much except bleed. Damn if I don't think its too late for books anyway.

You shouldn't be amused—You should get a good kick in the ass.

You want form, do you? I'll give you form. I'll make you really wish for something nice and cozy—Something all chewed and digested for you—Look, the thing's worn out—It don't work no more. If it ain't in a pretty package, you don't want it—Because it ain't art. Because the book critic of The New Porker might now want to see a bit more respect for tradition, hrrum, hum. I got my money on nobody. Tolstoy was right about all these people.

A tree near a lake.

Red deer.

Greatness and Truth can never be in danger from these murdering wretches.

To perform one's duty, be it now, be it clean, and be it done with humility . . .

A man is a sacred thing.

Any action or thought which injures the human imagination is evil.

The artist—They hate the artist. Mediocrity and servility are what they want. To get to the point—hell with all these bastards. I tell you it's got to open up . . . hit the flow . . . Humble, I'm humble before the sacred mystery of life, and the

—Let me say

Give us a chance.
Give us a chance.
Give us a chance.
Give us a chance.
Give us a chance.
Give us a chance.
Give us a chance.
Give us a chance.
Give us a chance.
Give us a chance.
Give us a chance.
Give us a chance.
Give us a chance.
Give us a chance.
Give us a chance.
Give us a chance.
Give us a chance.
Give us a chance.
Give us a chance.
Give us a chance.

THIS DAMN PUNY BOOK

**God be kind to them, these
pathetic little fleas.**

house river time star

**Take down sail. Ain't no place
to go.**

light blade wind fool

The leaves of the tree.

touchtouchtouchtouch

**What are you planning to do
with your life?**

DON'T PUT IT OFF, GOD!

the flames

beauty

life

a tree a tree a tree a tree a tree a tree a tree a tree
a tree a tree a tree a tree a tree a tree a tree a tree
a tree a tree a tree a tree a tree a tree a tree a tree
a tree a tree a tree a tree a tree a star a tree a tree
a tree a tree a tree a tree a tree a tree a tree a tree
a tree a tree   a tree a tree
a tree a tree   a tree a tree
a tree a tree   a tree a tree
a tree a tree   a tree a tree
a tree a tree   **MURDER**   a tree a tree
a tree a tree   a tree a tree
a tree a tree   a tree a tree
a tree a tree   a tree a tree
a tree a tree   a tree a tree
a tree a tree   a tree a tree
a tree a tree   a tree a tree
a tree a tree   a tree a tree
a tree a tree   a tree a tree
a tree a tree   a tree a bird
a tree a tree a tree a tree a tree a tree a tree a tree
a tree a tree a tree a tree a tree a tree a tree a tree
a tree a girl a tree a tree a tree a tree a tree a tree
a tree a tree a tree a tree a tree a tree a tree a tree
a tree a tree a tree a tree a tree a tree a tree a tree

human beings   God   truth
life   honor   humility   love
God   truth   peace   justice
humility   faith   joy   God
truth   God   justice   peace
love   justice   human beings
peace   humility   God   life
faith   human beings   joy
childhood   time   joy   fear
memory   sorrow   life   love
fear   justice   truth   honor
sorrow human beings peace
time   death   God   beauty

Dec. 1—Evidence conclusive, either way.

Dolly Adams
Apollinaria Grudd
Fitzmichael Kell
Ikey $10,000
Mengs Flink
Thane Chillingsdale
Colonel Caffarelli Pot
Little Remksheaffe

} testimony
—"for"

Mr. Tiger
Phoebe Ann Nemophila
Tranquil Flume
Fanny Tickle
Sally Garden
Catherine St. Maur
Mrs. J———
Abigail Buttermilk

} testimony
—"against"

Old Zenaslufski
Plusis Jidet
Gretchen Horsegg

} testimony
noncommittal

———————————————————— Friday 2 A.M. What is guilt?

Ekun 17 D—Z. Shack and all in it destroyed by mysterious explosion. Baby in well elected to Senate from Nevada. God found crying in orchard.

As I adjusted my detachable think-box, I tried to remember what Aristotle had said about it. Had something to do with interclugial relations—anyway I'm getting pretty damn fed-up, to put it gently.

I can't get it to do that buzz. The white flag goes up all right but not a sound out of it.

The Nubor thinks maybe the mainspring. Silly creature, it don't have no mainspring. It works on the principle of peliffumous digressions. Like the river oyster.

I met Caroline in the meadow.

It was getting dark.

The grass was having fun on the ground.

We tried it too.

She said she didn't know me well enough for that.

Well do you suppose your father would lend me the five bucks I said.

She laughed.

I slapped her again.

It was repugnant to me. A knife makes less noise, besides being more civilized. Flame-throwers will not be available to the general public for some little time yet.

She threw her neck around my arms.

Rubber the little man said.

I would if she'd let go my arms I said savagely.

He rested his crock on a treestump. His head grinning brutally was made of red stone.

I don't like you he said.

Caroline took her—No she—I better forget that part. I probably couldn't make you believe it anyway.

It's mutual I told him.

The King spit into the crock.

A tiny cloud of smoke curled up.

And a pretty little girl angel stepped out. She favored me with a lovely smile. I said to myself this is what I've been waiting for this is by Christ exactly what I want to happen when I start reaching. Ah hell we're all nice inside there. Poem—because it's so damn lonely inside there. We don't want a break. We want to know that the angels think we're maybe a little— ———— I want to hit it. You know what I'm talking about. Herman Melville stumbling down Bleecker Street with his soul prouder and bigger than the whole sonofabitching mess—Humble, I'm full of love for him. Poe a notch —a good big notch—down the scale—eeeeeee! eeeeeeeeeee! The lousy stinks not seeing them.

It works. This much love works now. . . . They hurt you so———— bad you can't

Buy me a drink. You get killed off. Make no mistake about it, you get— Tell you something

the only thing you've got's inside there. To me it looks like a sliver of God.

The pretty girls—(I'm speaking—Baah! Any time you put anything on your list you better have a prayer ready . . .) hurrah!

The angel asked me if I'd said or done anything that day to injure the Beautiful. I told her I thought I knew just the word for me and she told me I shouldn't use words like that.

"What are we alive for?" I said.

She lowered her eyes. "You push it too hard," she said.

"That's not an answer."

"There is no answer that will fit everything."

I said, "I'm supposed to have murdered someone."

"Why don't you run away?"

Why don't I run away! "Where?"

"It's possible to find peace."

"It's possible to find peace."

"In your heart. You must stop trying so hard. Reject the standards of the world."

"Oh yeah? How?"

"Seek purity. Ambition is death to the spirit. What you want is not worth having. Be silent. Put the names of your pain aside. Peace is not had through noisy effects. Peace comes with silence."

I walked off down the road. There were trees on either side of the road—clouds in the sky. Jesus this is amazing stuff, I thought. The sky—trees—a bird—and air to pull into my lungs—I keep forgetting the important things—Peace is not had through noisy effects —Peace comes with silence—Yeah—What you want is not worth having. What is it that I want? Who am I? That's another thing, a funny thing my pretty ones—Who am I? A murderer—A larky— The kind of lad never gets nowhere—If I could wake up if I could —say look it's dark—how-come nobody else is here? Find me that —what if I said purity What if I said I was hungry for   Silence

look it's getting dark all the fame and stuff are crap hell
you take all the men who've set up "systems"
the smart boys tell you all about them now
I think if they could come back to life they'd have a different slant
I think they'd have something pretty different to say
it looks more and more to me like the only really important idea is to say yes to anything that brings life and no to anything that brings death
the one idea the brain-boys pay no attention to
simplify
be humble
step out of line and stay out of line
reject
reject

don't let them kid you
this is a brutal and evil world
the war never ends
they'll fix your wagon if you don't give in
you can't ever win with them on their terms
so reject the whole swindle
let them know where you stand
"systems"—angels, (make a fetish of sex or spend half a
lifetime on a single book . . .) (get together a little library
on mysticism—if you can afford it away from your War
Bond purchases) . . . (But there is greatness in everyone!)
hell what good's it how bright you get if you choose to run
along with the blood-stained bastards everytime the chips
are down
no art can come out of evil
I say it—art is giving life—art is talking to God
if the artist loses now this world is doomed
and I think the human imagination is being murdered

go into the darkness as clean as you can for Christ's sake

a q b s d o p v x m c 8 3 11 6 h y a q r b

	father	
	mother	
slit from ear to to ear		i i i i 5
		14 5 f g l
March 6, 1927	flour	chair
June 28, 1931	butter	bed
October 3, 1933	coffee	napkin
January 6, 1934	sugar	shoes
May 15, 1936	bread	razor
August 12, 1938	death	hammer

September 1, 1940	birth	string
February 31, 1942	jam	pen
April 7, 1943	jelly	table
July 22, 1944	soap	coat
November 4, 1945	cornflakes	glove
December 23, 1945	tomatoes	lamp

Oh well. What'shisname—God I mean—He watches over each
of us sparrow's fall so I'm
    out of sleep stirring horror faces of the damned all turned to
    I see
    I see that we're all going down in it.
    I see—the howling darkness closing over everything.
There is only one murder and that is the murder of us all.
There is no hope.
There is nothing to hope for now.

————————— Tuesday. Jed Bains dropped in. Mabel
————————— refused to go back with him.
—————————
—————————
————————— It started to rain.
—————————
—————————

	it	is	now	eight	minutes	after	two
	"	"	"	nine	"	"	"
	"	"	"	ten	"	"	"
	"	"	"	eleven	"	"	"
	"	"	"	twelve	"	"	"
Where'd you say the	"	"	"	thirteen	"	"	"
soul-plasma was	"	"	"	fourteen	"	"	"
	"	"	"	fifteen	"	"	"
	"	"	"	sixteen	"	"	"

—17th June. Thurs.—The trouble all started after I got it into the room. Damn thing kept wanting to sit down on the best chair. And get blood all over the slipcover! I shouted. It began to bellow. I heated a fork on the gasburner and stuck it into its cheek. Smelled like bacon. An hour later it got down on its knees and begged me to kill it. Seventy feet long—blue underneath and golden on its back. White tongue. Docile and trusting. I don't like them.

When I was eight—I earned my very first fifty cents.

My friend Stubbie—Stubbie had a tooth three inches long.

Sal—fun the day I had the house of representatives with her.

When I was fifteen—I still had the bag of rice I'd spent the 4-bits on.

—18th June. Mon.—They kept running in and out as I tried to get all the dishes washed before Aunt Tilly came back. My warnings were ignored. Repeatedly I told them I'd give them something to remember if they didn't stop right off. They paid me no heed. I gave it to them. I'd lied. What could they possibly remember after I'd chopped them up into little pieces? Me and Aunt Tilly had us a good laugh over it. She's used to being treated like a lady. We discussed this and that until it was bedtime. I woke up in the middle of the night to find her standing at the foot of my cot. Her face looked drawn and old. I got up and went over and put my hand on her shoulder. Together we stared out of the window. There was only one light lit on the whole block.

I passed some houses. Kids playing on the lawns. I took out a cigarette and lit it. One of the kids threw me a ball. Funny—there wasn't any blood on the ball. What time's it getting to be? I asked one of them. What difference is it to you? he crowed—They're gonna knock you off any minute now. I smacked him down and kicked him a good one on the side of his head. A man came running out brandishing his fists and I handed him a ten dollar bill. He said gee thanks and let fly one at the other side of his son's head.

Hungry. I hunted for a dogwagon and found one on a side street. Dirty. I wiped the counter with my sleeve. Perty. What's yours mister?—sort of pale but she'd sure make somebody a nice mother. Ham and cheese on white; coffee; piece applecake. Reuben Grisher put a quarter into the slotmachine. This reference to a dazzling erotic activity thing is crooked, he declared not without warmth. I said, That's too bad, Mac.

She put the food down in front of me and I ate it.

What time do you get through here? I asked her.

Two, she said.

I'll wait. That is, if it's all right with you, miss.

Lorraine's the name. It's all right.

I went over to the machine and adjusted my tie in the mirror. How've things been? I asked Grisher.

You get yours tonight, he said. His twinkle blue eyed.

The three bums with him grinned at me. I took out my notebook, scribbled a few words, and held it out so they could see. They turned all colors—green looking most attractive—and sped out of there. Let me see that! Grisher said.

I tore the page into little pieces and dropped them into a sugar bowl. You're too late, I told him.

Where'd they go? he said, suddenly realizing that I was not a man to be trifled with.

To confession, I said gently.

He held his hand out to me. Let's be friends, he said. His voice was gruff and his taste in shirts terrible.

I tapped cigarette ash into it. Then I hit him in the mouth. He went sprawling back over the counter and a frying pan full of sizzling grease toppled down on him. His scream made the town clock lose a year exactly.

Karen Bruner looked up from the evening paper. She had eaten well and she knew Wilber was out with another woman.

Her figure in the unflattering glare of the cheap bridgelamp might have belonged to any middle-aged housefrau; in fact, her mother had often said they should all move to Connecticut and forget the whole thing—come hell or high water, there is such a thing as decency and fair play "what matter it how long and steep the road, an investigation will reveal that not all travelers would know what to do if they ever did get where they want to go"—a six weeks' trial but who could be fool enough to trust that kind of procedure! Karen sighed wearily. She wondered idly what was going on down at the lunch wagon . . .

Well I was eating my third ham and cheese, this time on whole wheat. Grisher had been taken away. Lorraine was scrubbing the floor with a broken-handled mop.

Through the dingy window I could see the snow coming down. Couple truck drivers came in and said this is one favorite indoor sport night to be out all right all right. I said, You on the Albany run? The one named Harry said, Yeah—what the reproductive enterprise biz is it of yours, bub? I wrote something on my napkin and showed it to them. They stared at me unbelievingly, then started to howl as though their two-word vocabularies had suddenly become inadequate; and—this is not meant to be unkind, or unnecessarily pointed—they looked pretty silly with their clothes shrunk down to the size of a ten year old's, for that is precisely what had happened.—And their heads dripping gray pools on the greasy counter.

I turned the ketchup bottle around and studied the label. They had thought up a red tomato for it. Lorraine was watching me. I took my hand off the bottle and felt in my pocket. The cold steel was reassuring and I knew I hadn't long. I leaned forward and said, Lorry, how much did they give you?—I don't know what you mean.—Be a good kid. How much?—Three hundred.—Are they waiting at your room?—No, in a car down the street.—As we walk past them . . . is that it?—Yes.—You must need the money bad to

377

do a thing like that.—Oh, I don't know . . . I'll get a kick out of it, don't forget.—But why not turn me in to the police? They'd probably let you watch.—Watch what?—When they turn the juice on . . . Be fun to smell me die, wouldn't it?—Well . . . —Come on! Turn me in to the cops!—What difference does it make to you, which way you get it?—I . . . I . . . oh hell, I want to pay my debt to society all nice and above board.—What about my three hundred?—The law is offering fifty grand, honey.—Wellwhydidntyuhsayso! And she dove for the phone.

A man stopped to peer in the window, then hurried on. If I had a nickel I could make a cup of coffee carry me through a good hour—maybe even an hour and a half. The icy wind stabbed through his threadbare coat. There was little sensation in his feet anymore—at least the bleeding must have stopped; the newspapers had soaked up most of it, and his—Somebody touched his arm. "Can I help you?"—"I'm hungry and cold."—"Come home with me and I'll—" — "What's your game?"—"I want to help you." He looked at her in silence for a moment, then shrugged: "All right. I've certainly got nothing to lose."

She led him up a long, rickety stairway. The door was unlocked and an oil lamp burned on a packing case near the solitary window. "Please come in and warm your hands at the stove." A tiny potbelly, sides streaked with the scratching of countless matches —it was stone-cold. He looked full into her face. The two were alone now; they would have to conduct themselves in some fashion. Her face was strangely beautiful. A sweetness touched the withered, sunken lips. Finally he said, "The stove is out." She shook her head vigorously and a strand of dirty gray hair popped out from under her woollen cap. "That is not so," she said softly. "Or rather, I know that there is no fire in it"—she extended her hands to him—"mm please . . . come near and warm yourself." (I might have known it would be something like this.) He moved near and a great surging tide of warmth went through his chilled bones. Then she took his hand and guided it to the stove. It was as cold as a block of ice. "See," she exclaimed, "how simple that is? I discovered it by accident one day. I was sick and couldn't go out in the street to look for wood. I knew I'd freeze unless"—she threw off her coat —her body was as graceful and supple as a young girl's—"unless my stove would give heat without wood. And, as you see—But come! you must be very hungry. Take a bath while I make supper for us."—"Haven't you eaten?"—"Yes, but my walk has made me —Oh hurry! You'll feel so much better when you're out of those terrible clothes and into—Please! There are all the things you'll want on the bathroom door." He took a wonderful bath and put on the clean duds. They were a perfect fit. That scared him.

She had a feast spread out on the packing case. Roast beef hashed brown potatoes and a pitcher of wine. He ate like a bastard. He didn't bother to tell her that he knew she didn't have any food like that—instead he started to sing. I sure am nuts—How could I ever have thought she was an old woman? He bent across and kissed her. Her lips were as soft as the petals of a rose. Her hair shone like gold in the candle light. He upset the packing case getting to his feet. He was singing at the top of his lungs. Her merry, light-hearted laughter kept pace with his song. When they had eaten the last crumb of food and not another drop would come out of the pitcher, they went to bed. Daylight found them sleeping peacefully in each other's arms. All the tired, bitter lines had gone from his face, and she was radiant with a beauty and innocence which are altogether too rare in this world.

Around one o'clock I got up and walked out into the street. Eddie Owl's De-Luxe Diner in red neons. The snow looked like the street had pyorrhea. I don't know—I felt something awful. Sort of all crushed-in. But I still had nineteen dollars and some change left. Sometimes when you want to talk to somebody and there's nobody at all to talk to, you feel like hell.

I stood there, thinking.

SLEEPERS

ERS

AWAKE
ON THE PRECIPICE

Something cold shoved into my hand and I looked down to see a dog—a mangy little mutt with three legs. I knelt down and put my arms around him. He whined and lapped my face. I looked up and saw a big house across the street—a goddam mansion it looked like. I picked him up and walked over and up on the porch. No sign of life. I punched the bell—I just sank my thumb in and left it there. Jesus are they all dead in there! I started to boot the door. When my feet got sore I took my elbows and did a drum. The pooch began to whimper. I'm scaring the little bastard. So then I walked over to a window and kicked it in. A big shard of the plate-glass shot out and split my mouth open like an apple. I gathered him up and slung a leg in. It hit a table with glass bells or something on it. A light went on. An old man in a nightcap looking like he was about to walk into a den of lions was standing up on the landing of some stairs made of marble and gold. His hands were shaking and he had a vomit on the fire. I've called the police, he quavered down. I got my other leg in and started to wade across the carpet. The little fellow had his head buried under my arm. I told him I wanted some food for my dog—and damn quick. The police will be here any minute, he said. They'll feed your dog. He thought I was crazy. No cop's going to feed this dog, I told him. This your house?—I am Oswald, the butlah, he said, beginning to feel a lot better about the whole thing. Kindly lowah your voice. You'll awaken the Grumlahs.—Awaken the Grumlahs, is it! I shouted. Well, if that's all that's worrying you—I grabbed up a footstool and slung it at a big china closet. The mutt squirmed out of my arms and hobbled under a couch. It tore my heart to see he'd added me to the list of the other human beings he'd run up against. A door opened up above. Then a girl's voice called, What's going on down there?—It's an intruder, Miss Genthaleen. A demented gentleman and his dog. I took the liberty of seeking assistance from the police.—Oh, whatever nonsense are you talking about—

And she appeared at the head of the stairs.

I just stood there with my mouth open, a warm stream running down my chin. She had on a white bathrobe that looked like woollen silk.

A goddess.

She came down and asked me what I wanted. I told her I just wanted to get some good warm food for a little homeless dog with only three legs I'd found. And a dash of water.

That's a nasty cut you've got, she said. Police sirens. Oswald, go to the door and tell them you phoned by mistake—Tell them it was just a drunken prank.

Another on the fire. Then he said, Very well, Miss Genthaleen, and went to hear a little fancy use of the English language.

Is that really your name? Genthaleen?

Hard 'G'. Let's rustle up that supper for the puppy dog.

They must have poured the kitchen out of a photograph. Ten polar bears could have got lost in the refrigerator. Isn't smoked turkey a bit too rich for such a little tike? I said, applying some more of the high-class salve she'd given me to my mouth. Then I sank my teeth into a drumstick. That isn't turkey, she said; that's quail from father's farm upstate. You carry this tray.

We took all that food in and the puppy was gone.

After we'd looked a while I told her how sorry I was to cause such a commotion and left. She said to drop round sometime. We both knew I never would. A thing has to be the thing it is or somebody gets messed up. There is that niceness—it's always wrong to spoil it. That special, individual form things have.

I saw the parked car down the street. I turned my coat collar up and started to walk up to it.

The snow was coming down heavily now. White and still.

Eddie Owl's De-Luxe Diner was closed for the night.

I heard the distant whistle of a train. I wondered where all the poor devils in it were going.

Suddenly I felt cold and afraid. I felt it watching me.

It seemed that I'd left something somewhere which I desperately wanted—and I couldn't remember what it was.

I got up to the car.

Two men were asleep in it. I didn't see any guns.

Their faces were relaxed and without evil—they looked like children sleeping there in that car in the snow.

I opened my mouth to maybe say a bit of a prayer for them. And it started to bleed again.

For a complete listing request a free catalog from New Directions, 80 Eighth Avenue
New York, NY 10011; or visit our website, www.ndpublishing.com

New Directions Paperbooks—A Partial Listing

For a complete listing request a free catalog from New Directions, 80 Eighth Avenue,
New York, NY 10011; or visit our website, www.ndpublishing.com

†Bilingual